Highlander ʾ ⁻⁻⁻⁻ ⁻⁻⁻⁻
A Cree & Dawn Short Story

by

Donna Fletcher

Donna Fletcher

Highlander's True Love
A Cree & Dawn Short Story

Cover design
Kim Killion

Visit Donna's Web site
www.donnafletcher.com
http://www.facebook.com/donna.fletcher.author

Chapter One

Cree stood outside his bedchamber, his hand hovering over the metal latch. He did not know how much longer he would be able to keep his hands off his wife. It had been a little over a month since the twins were born and after witnessing the pain of childbirth he was hesitant to touch her. Besides, Elsa, his healer, had firmly suggested he give his wife time before resuming any intimacy with her. So he had kept his distance, though with great difficulty, especially so when he had walked in on her just after finishing a bath.

He shut his eyes, the memory so clear that it invaded his senses and turned him hard. Her breasts had been but a handful and now they were full, plump, and heavy with milk for the twins. Her waist had been narrow, her hips full, but now her curves were more defined, more sensual and her creamy skin was even softer to the touch.

Cree silently cursed his thoughts that had turned him harder and harder. And to make matters worse, Dawn had made it all too clear that while her body recovered from childbirth, she would be only too happy to ease his ache. He had been too concerned that they both would lose control, since their need for each other never seemed to abate. It only grew stronger and stronger. It was as if their intimacy sustained them, though he knew without love it would not have mattered. Dawn would be just another woman to poke and relieve his need. Now it was not about a simple poke, but about making love to his wife.

He took a deep breath to fortify himself and silently prayed that Dawn had fallen asleep.

Cree opened the door to find his wife standing by the bed in her white nightdress. One look told him that she was ready for bed, but not for sleep.

Dawn stared at her husband and she felt her stomach flutter and the ache between her legs grow stronger. She missed his strong body slipping over and into her and also the times he would hoist her up and plant her against a door or wall and make love to her with a fierce passion that sent her soul trembling.

She had known he had kept his distance from her on purpose. Elsa had told Dawn that she had advised Cree to leave his wife be for a while, and he had done just that. But she had gone too long without him. She was starving for his touch, his kiss, and to have him deep inside her.

Their abstinence would end tonight...she would make sure of it. And from the hungry look in his dark eyes and the bulge beneath his plaid, she did not think he would object.

Dawn sauntered over to him, letting her hips roll invitingly. When she reached him, she placed her hand to her chest, and then rested it on his chest.

Cree felt a jab to his gut. He always did when his wife told him that she loved him. Dawn may

4

have been born without a voice, but to him he heard her clearly through her gestures.

Her hand moved slowly down his chest while her eyes remained on him, and the fierce passion he saw stirring in them was like storm clouds gathering before a raging storm that would pound the earth with much needed nourishing rain. That she hungered for him with the same such rage was undeniable.

Dawn intended for there to be no doubt that she wanted him, nor did she intend for him to deny her. She trailed her hand all the way down the front of him, and then slipped it beneath his plaid to gently cup him in her hand, though only for a moment. Her fingers wrapped around the hard length of him and her chest heaved with a sigh of pleasure. She had missed touching him, feeling him throb and swell in her hand before she would guide him into her. She stepped closer, eager to rub herself against him.

Cree's hand shot out to grab the back of her neck. "I want you like I have never wanted you before, but what if I leave you with child tonight? I cannot bear the thought of you suffering again."

Dawn motioned with her free hand as if she ate something, then patted her stomach and shook her head.

"You are taking the potion Elsa recommended to keep from getting with child," he said with relief.

Dawn nodded, though quickly patted her stomach, then chest and pulled as if taking something from her mouth.

5

"Until you want another babe, then you take it no more?"

She nodded and stroked him.

He groaned and smiled. "You know I am going to make love to you several times tonight, do you not?"

Dawn frowned, shook her head, and extended her arms out.

"You want to make love all night?"

She grinned widely as she nodded vigorously.

"You are a greedy one."

She nodded again.

"So am I." His lips came down on hers and passion exploded.

Dawn let go of him and threw her arms around his neck, pressing her body against his as if she could not get close enough to him.

He grabbed her around the waist and hoisted her up, and she wrapped her legs around him. His hands went to her buttocks and cupped it firmly as he continued kissing her, never wanting to stop.

He walked over to the bed, eased her down on her feet, and took hold of her face. "I have missed the taste of you and I intend to taste every part of you tonight."

Dawn tapped her chest repeatedly and nodded, letting him know she felt the same.

"You are mine, Dawn, and I will love you always." He kissed her and their hands went hastily to their garments.

A pounding at the door had Cree ripping his mouth away from Dawn and yelling, "Whoever is there go away or I will ripe your heart out with my bare hands!"

Dawn sighed heavily, not that it could be heard, and rested her brow to her husband's chest. She silently pleaded that they not be robbed of this time together.

"It is urgent."

"Nothing is as urgent as what I am doing now."

Dawn lifted her head and kissed her husband's lips lightly, though she would have preferred to devour them. But it was better she let him settle this first before she kissed him senseless.

"Cree, you had better come now. It is urgent!"

"You are doomed, Sloan, if it is not," Cree called out, though knew that Sloan, his second in command, would not bother him if it was not important. He only hoped the matter could be settled hastily.

"I may not be the only one doomed," Sloan called back.

His reply sent a shiver through Dawn.

Cree took hold of her chin. "Worry not. I will settle this. Nothing will keep me from our bed this night." He kissed her quick. "Do not move from this room. I will return."

Dawn nodded and watched her husband disappear out the door, hoping his words would prove true.

Cree shut the door behind him and stood a moment, staring at Sloan.

Sloan motioned him away from the door and the two men walked down the hall to the stairs.

"What is it?" Cree asked worried that it might be something he could not settle as quickly as he wished.

"A woman demands to speak with you," Sloan said.

"Demands?" Cree said angrily. "Who is she to demand anything of me?"

Sloan hesitated a moment before saying, "She claims the lad of two years she has with her is your son."

Chapter Two

Cree entered the Great Hall with angry strides and stopped abruptly when the lone woman in the room turned away from the table, she had been bent over, to face him. Her beauty startled him for a moment, though he showed no signs of it. Dark ringlets fell around her lovely, unmarred face and neck from the mass of curls pinned atop her head and her large blue eyes glared at him as she tossed her chin up defiantly. She took a stance as if prepared for battle, though she could not keep her shoulders from slumping. She showed strength as well as exhaustion.

Cree was about to speak when she stepped aside to reveal a sleeping child on the top of the table. His light brown hair had threads of gold running through it, resembling Cree's hair coloring, but his features bore no signs of Cree. Even with smudges on his face, he was a handsome child and looked well fed, not like his mother who was far too thin.

"He is your son. I named him Aidan. He is two years now."

"So you say," Cree said, approaching her slowly.

"I speak the truth."

"Again so you say, but what reason do I have to believe you?" He stopped a few feet from her. "Why wait two years to claim him as mine?"

The woman stared at him a moment as if at a loss for words, then said, "He needs his father."

"And so you chose me?"

"Like you chose me that night," she said, forcing her shoulders back and her head up.

"And what night was that?" He folded his arms across his broad chest and settled his dark eyes that could intimidate the bravest of souls on her.

The woman took a step back. "It was a cold winter's night and you sought shelter from the unfavorable weather at my family's croft near Loch Rannoch. You asked me to warm your bed and I obliged."

He had sought shelter from farmers now and again, though he had provided them with much needed items in exchange for their generosity. There was just one problem with her story.

"Never would I have been so disrespectful as to proposition a daughter of a farmer who granted me shelter."

Her face flushed red with embarrassment. "You did not ask me to warm your bed. It was I who sought your bed."

Her response troubled him, for that had happened on rare occasions Mostly, when he had been celibate far too long from far too many battles. He would spend a whole night appeasing his hunger only to poke the woman once again before leaving the next morning. But had she been one of the very few women?

Another question begged to be asked. "How can you be so sure the lad is mine?"

"I knew no other man before you or after you," she said with great pride.

"So you say, but again it is only your word I have."

Her chin went up a notch. "It is all I have left. My da was killed by a band of mercenaries a few days after you left. I was not there at the time or I would have suffered at their hands before meeting the same fate. I went to live with my sister, but her husband took ill and she could barely feed their family on what little they had. I knew it was time for me to seek you out and ask that you be a father to your son."

"It is a good story you weave," Cree said.

Before he could say more, the woman said, "It is the truth," —she pointed to her sleeping son— "and he is proof of what I say."

"He could be anyone's son," Cree argued his thoughts turning to Dawn and how she would feel when she heard of this.

"But he is not anyone's son. He is your son." She shook her head. "I cannot believe you do not remember me. You were so kind to me that night. I shall never forget how loved you made me feel."

"I have been with many women and believe me when I say that if I bedded a woman as beautiful as you I would have remembered it."

Her eyes turned wide, but not at his words, her glance had settled on something behind him and he knew who she was looking at. His heart clenched in his chest.

Cree turned and faced his wife.

She had slipped on a blue tunic over her nightdress but her feet remained bare and her dark eyes were wide with questions. Her hands began to move much too fast.

"Slow down," Cree ordered.

"I believe Dawn is telling you to summon a servant and have a room prepared in the keep for the mother and her son," Sloan said.

Cree shot him a look that had Sloan taking several steps back.

"You heard the whole tale?" Cree asked his wife.

"It is not a tale," the woman called out.

Cree turned a scowl on the woman that had her quickly lowering her head, then he looked to his wife. This time her gestures were slow, much too slow.

He reached out, snatching her hand and yanked her to him. Keeping his voice low, he said, "Do not speak to me as if I were a child who cannot understand you. As for that woman, neither she nor her child will ever occupy this keep." He grabbed her other hand before she could gesture. "I am not finished. The woman and her son will not be turned away. I will have a cottage provided for them while I sought this out."

12

Dawn smiled and nodded pleased with his decision.

Cree knew his wife well and her smile lacked its usual enthusiasm. She was troubled and he could not blame her, though if she had obeyed him—which she was forever failing to do—she would not have heard him say that the woman was a beauty.

The thought annoyed him all the more and he said as he released her hands, "You will go to our bedchamber and stay there as I had ordered you to do, while I see to this."

Dawn's eyes narrowed.

"Do not think to disobey me on this," he warned sternly.

She gestured, pointing to him and then to her, then tapped her mouth and pointed her finger up.

"We will not discuss this matter when I join you. I will see it resolved. You are not to concern yourself with it."

Her hands went to gesture and he grabbed them. "No more. Do as I say now."

Dawn's eyes narrowed and she glared at him a moment before she turned and disappeared into the shadows near the stairs.

Cree turned to face the woman who had disrupted not only his night but his life. "I will see you have shelter and food as your father did for me, and one way or another I will have the truth from you."

"Thank you, my lord," the woman said with a bow of her head. "I knew an honorable man as yourself would not turn his child away."

13

"That is yet to be determined," Cree said. "Sloan will see you settled."

Sloan stepped forward as Cree turned away from them.

"Your name?" Sloan asked.

"Tallis."

The name resonated in Cree's head. He had heard it before, but where?

Chapter Three

Cree sat hunched over the table with his hands wrapped around a tankard of ale, the crackling fire in the hearth behind him warming his back. Though summer would be with them for several more weeks, the castle contained a chill no matter what season of the year. He wondered if a chill would replace the heat he had seen in his wife's eyes before Tallis had arrived.

He scowled and downed another swallow of ale.

"Fortifying yourself for the confrontation with your wife?" Sloan asked and swung his leg over the bench to join Cree at the table.

"Watch your tongue," Cree warned.

Sloan filled a tankard of ale for himself. "You know Dawn will not let it be."

"Do not remind me of her stubbornness."

"Something you two have in common." Sloan ignored how Cree's scowl deepened, and he continued. "Dawn will want answers just as you do. I do not recall this woman, but then I was not with you at all times. You and I both have bedded many women along the way, so there is no point in asking if there is a possibility that the child is yours. I do, however, agree with you that Tallis is too beautiful of a woman not to remember."

Cree's nostrils flared and his eyes narrowed. It disturbed him more and more that his wife had heard him claim the woman a beauty. It must have felt like a slap in the face to her or at least that was what he felt he had done to her.

Dawn would always be the most beautiful woman in the world to him, even with her plain features, and she had to know that. He had told her often enough. Still, though, his words had to have hurt her and if there was something that upset him beyond reason was the thought of hurting his wife.

"Do you recall Tallis at all?" Sloan asked.

"There is something familiar about her name," —Cree shook his head—"but nothing else."

Silence fell between the two men, each lost in thought.

Sloan finally spoke. "Go to your wife and finish what I interrupted."

Cree wanted to make love to his wife more than anything, but the events of tonight had cast a dark shadow over him, and he did not want to bring that to his wife.

He finished the last of his ale with one swallow and stood. "You ordered men to watch the woman?"

"Of course, though you know as well as I do she will not lack visitors. The women of the village will hear of this soon enough and be curious to meet her."

"Tell Elsa to go see Tallis and the lad and let them know she is the healer in the village if they should need anything," Cree ordered. Once Elsa heard that, she would know that Cree wished to be informed of anything concerning the pair. Elsa was an exceptional healer and a loyal friend.

16

"Old Mary might get to Tallis first," Sloan warned.

"Then I will learn more of the truth," Cree said and walked to the stairs, thinking of the old woman who some thought a witch. She shuffled when she walked and her hands were gnarled with age and yet her mind was sharp and her aged eyes saw more clearly than those younger than her. Most of all, she was a true friend to Dawn.

Cree stopped at his bedchamber door. He did not want to discuss this matter with Dawn, not just yet. He knew she would have other ideas. He could always distract her with a few kisses and intimate touches that would have them making love in no time. But he did not want to make love to her to distract her.

He opened the door and charged in ready to take on whatever awaited him as he had done in battle, and stopped abruptly. His wife lay asleep on the bed naked, a blanket wrapped around one leg. He walked over to the bed admiring her body. His hand itched to cup her full breasts, tender with milk for their twins, and he so wanted to stroke her narrow waist and down over her hip, and damn if the tangle of soft, dark red hair between her legs did not beg to be explored.

He shook his head. It was better she was sleeping. One of the twins would have her up in a few hours to feed and she would barely fall asleep when the other one would wake. They never seemed to feed together and his son Valan was a hungry lad, demanding more than his sister Lizbeth.

Dawn needed her rest, and she did not need the added burden of this woman claiming that he was the father of her son.

Once Cree disrobed, he joined his wife in bed. No soon as he reached out to wrap her in his arms, she turned and snuggled into them. Her one leg slipped between his legs, settling near his manhood and he groaned silently. This was going to be a difficult night.

~~~

Dawn looked down at her daughter suckling at her breast and smiled. She was so relieved to have had her daughter born with a voice. She had feared passing her affliction on to her child. And while some women complained about their babies crying too much, Dawn was happy each and every time her daughter cried, not that she cried much. She seemed a content baby, unlike her brother who was as demanding as his father.

Dawn smiled, thinking of Cree. She had intended to talk with him when he returned to their bedchamber last night, but then thought better of it. He would be stubborn and refuse to discuss the matter of the woman and child, who she unwaveringly claimed Cree fathered.

The news had been a shock to hear as she stood in the shadows last night in the Great Hall. And though the lad could be Cree's son, he would be a bastard son and that was a terrible fate to bestow on any lad. She had to learn more about this woman to determine if her tale was true or false and if false, why so?

As usual Lizbeth fell asleep as soon as she had drank herself full and Dawn returned her to her cradle, next to her brother. They had placed the twins in separate cradles when first born, but both had cried endlessly and it was only when Dawn had laid them beside each other did they stop.

Cree had ordered Paul, her best friend Lila's husband and a fine carpenter, to craft a double cradle for the twins. The twins had slept peacefully once in it and Dawn wondered if they would always be so inseparable.

With both babes sleeping and the sun up, Dawn had no intentions of returning to her bedchamber. If she did, Cree and she would make love, not that she did not want to. She actually ached to, but she preferred to learn what she could about the mother and child first before Cree could distract her. And since he refused to discuss the matter with her, she would have to find out about it herself.

Flanna stopped her when she entered the Great Hall. "What is this I hear about Cree having a bastard child?"

Flanna had been the cook in the kitchen, and Dawn a servant there, before Cree took control of the village, claimed the land and all its holdings and was granted the title, Earl of Carrick, by the King. Now Flanna was in charge of the keep's servants and Turbett's, Cree's cook, had complete control over the kitchen and had won Flanna's heart. That was why she and Flanna were more friends than servant and master, though it was that way when Cree was present.

Dawn gestured that she knew little of the situation.

Flanna leaned in close and whispered, "I will find out everything and let you know."

Dawn smiled, nodded, and patted Flanna's arm in appreciation. Flanna had eyes and ears everywhere and she had helped Dawn before, so she was glad to have her help again.

"Sit," Flanna urged, "I will have food brought to you."

Dawn motioned as if she carried a basket.

"You want food to take along with you." Flanna nodded, understanding her and as she hurried off said, "I will have a basket made ready."

It was not long before Flanna returned with a full basket and Dawn smiled and nodded. The woman knew her well and had packed enough food for more than one person.

"I brought this shawl for you. There is a slight chill in the misty morning air," Flanna said, draping the finely weaved blue shawl over Dawn's shoulders.

Dawn squeezed Flanna's hand in thanks and gestured that they would talk later and headed out of the keep. A light mist settled over the village along with a slight chill, and Dawn hoped that the sun would soon break through and rescue the day. There was much work to be done in the fields and Cree had planned on going to see how the clearing of the land was going for the new castle and village not far from here. She wondered if he would alter his plans due to the woman's arrival and news.

Dawn rapped on Old Mary's door.

"Welcome, Dawn," the old woman sang out and Dawn entered.

Old Mary always had a knowing about her and Dawn had been glad for it. The old woman had helped her to stay strong in the hardest of times and she would always be grateful. Though age had stooped her over and slowed her down, her mind was remarkably spry, as if it had not aged a bit.

"These old bones protest more each day," Old Mary said with a laugh. "Sit, I have fixed a nice hot brew for us."

Dawn would never be able to spring a surprise visit on the woman. She always knew when someone would visit. She always knew things before they happened and Dawn wondered if she had known about the woman and lad.

Old Mary chatted about what a lovely day it was going to be as she filled their tankards with a minty brew and Dawn took food from the basket to place on the table.

"Meat pies, my favorite," Old Mary said eagerly waving at Dawn. "Sit, sit, the pies are best when warm."

Dawn wished she could feel as equally enthusiastic about the pies, but she was hungrier for anything Old Mary could tell her about the situation than food.

"There is not much I can tell you about her," Old Mary said as if hearing Dawn's unspoken question. "She poses no true threat, but then you would know that yourself, for you know Cree would never allow her to. As for the truth of her claim? I can tell you the child was conceived from love. The rest is for you to find out."

Dawn's shoulder slumped with the weight of Old Mary's words.

The old woman reached out and rested her gnarled hand on Dawn's. "You, above all, know what a harsh world this can be for anyone who carries a burden upon them. And your generous heart has lifted many a burden off others. But this is not your burden to lift—it is your husband's." She smiled. "Though, knowing you, sweet child, you will help him lift it."

Dawn patted her heart, then hugged herself.

"I know you love Cree with all your heart and your babes as well, remember though, this woman feels the same."

A catch to her heart had Dawn gripping at her chest. Could this woman possibly love Cree?

"Love can be troublesome," Old Mary said, then took a sip of her drink. "Nothing is perfect and true love has a way of being tested from time to time, but then true love has a way of surviving even the harshest of tests." After she took another sip of her brew, she said, "You brought enough meat pies for the young lad his mother, did you not?"

Dawn smiled and gestured.

Old Mary grinned. "Aye, you are right, I know you well. Now be off with you. The woman and lad were settled in Dunmore's cottage, since it has become too small for him, his wife, and his growing brood of soon to be six."

Dawn's smile grew thinking of the large family that seemed forever cheerful.

Old Mary laughed softly. "You already have a good start on the large brood you will have one day." Her laugh turned hardy. "Though, I do not know if Cree will survive all the births."

Dawn felt a soft laugh bubble inside her, though it could not be heard. She slipped the basket over her arm, gave the old woman a hug, and left the cottage.

The mist was dissipating and the chill already gone. The sun would soon be shining and it would be a lovely summer's day to enjoy. And Dawn intended to enjoy it, for no matter what the woman told her, it would make no difference. Cree and she loved each other and nothing—absolutely nothing—could change that.

Chapter Four

Dawn approached the door of the cottage with apprehension. Part of her was eager to learn the truth and another part did not want to know. It disturbed her even more that she felt a twinge of jealously toward this woman. Giving birth to the twins had made her feel that she had given something to Cree that no one ever had, and it had made the birth of her babes special. Now with the possibility that Cree may already have a son, the twin's births seemed less important.

She smiled and shook her head. That was a foolish thought. Nothing could make the birth of the twins less important.

What if he had loved this woman?

The thought startled her and sent more than a twinge of jealousy racing through her. She did not want to think that Cree could love another woman let alone make love to her. Though, one was a possibility if the lad proved to be his, but had love been involved or had it simply been a night of lust that meant nothing to him?

Dawn knew only Cree could be the one to answer that and the time would come, whether he liked it or not, when she would have her answer.

Fortified with curiosity, Dawn's apprehensive steps turned eager and she hurried to the front door and knocked.

24

The woman's eyes turned wide upon opening the door and seeing Dawn standing there. She shook her head as if trying to regain her senses, then acknowledged Dawn with a respectful bob of her head and said, "My lady."

Dawn smiled and raised the basket, then pointed to the woman.

"For me?" she asked.

Dawn nodded and also placed her hand in front of her as if demonstrating a small height.

"For Aidan as well." The woman grinned, pleased with herself for understanding Dawn's gesture. She stepped aside. "Please come in and meet my son."

Dawn grew alarmed when she saw that the lad lay in bed, looking pale, his eyes fluttering between wake and sleep. She turned a concerned expression on the woman.

"The trip here has been difficult and the last couple of days he has not been feeling well. He needs rest."

Dawn's hands started flying, for she felt he needed more than rest, a brew to start with and perhaps a chest poultice.

"I am sorry, my lady, but I do not understand you."

Dawn held up her one finger, pointed to the door and then back again.

"You are going to go and come right back?"

Dawn nodded and hurried out the door. She took only a few steps when she spotted the woman she needed...Elsa. She hurried to the plump woman and took her arm and gave a tug.

Elsa understood there was someone in need and quickly followed Dawn.

Upon entering the cottage, Elsa eased the startled woman's concern when she saw her take a protective stance in front of the child in the bed. "I am Elsa the healer and was on my way here to see if I could be of any help to you and your son after your long journey."

The woman's shoulders slumped as if in relief. "I am Tallis and this is my son Adian. He has not been well for the last few days. He is but two years and the journey has not been an easy one. I would appreciate any help you could give him." She stepped aside, giving Elsa permission to approach the lad.

The lad stirred when Elsa laid a hand on his head and gave a small cough.

"Has he had the cough long?" Elsa asked.

"A day now," Tallis informed her with concern.

"He is warm to the touch and we do not want him growing warmer. He also needs a chest poultice to keep that cough from getting worse," Elsa explained.

"What can I do to help?" Tallis asked.

"Sit with Dawn and rest, while I prepare what I need, then I will show you what to do to help your son."

Tallis loving brushed her son's hair off his forehead, kissed it, then placed her cheek to his before joining Dawn at the small table.

Dawn felt her heart ache for the woman. Anytime a child took ill a mother worried, and she silently prayed that the little lad would get well soon.

Tallis squared her shoulders and lifted her chin after taking a seat at the table. "I mean you no disrespect, my lady, but I felt that my son had a right to know that his father is the mighty warrior Cree."

Dawn nodded as if she understood, though she wore no smile. She gestured to the woman slowly and as clearly as possible.

"I am sorry, but I do not understand you."

"Repeat it, Dawn, and I shall tell her what you said," Elsa said as she took items from the pouch that hung from a belt at her waist.

Dawn nodded and gestured once again, and Elsa spoke. "You understand that my husband will question your claim and seek proof?"

Tallis looked to her son, his pale face bringing tears to her eyes. "The proof is there for him to see."

Dawn shook her head and moved her hands, and once again Elsa spoke for her. "It will not be enough for him. He will want more information from you. Tell me about the day you met him."

Tallis seemed reluctant to answer, but after another glance at her son, she spoke. "He appeared at my family's croft one day, requesting shelter and food." Her cheeks flushed red. "I could not keep my eyes off him—he is so handsome—and his eyes lingered on mine as well. I could not deny the attraction between us and I cannot say I regret it. It was but one night we shared and I shall never forget it. The memory remains in my heart and soul and keeps me warm and safe through difficult times." Tallis bowed her head to Dawn. "Forgive me, I do not wish my words to hurt you."

Dawn shook her head as if she understood and yet her words did sting, though she reminded herself that they still needed to be proven true. She rolled her hand, urging Tallis to continue.

Tallis patted her chest. "I wanted him. I could not help myself. That night I took food and drink to him in the stable and sat to talk, though he never invited me to do so. I did not leave until sunrise and even then I did not want to go. I never wanted to leave his loving arms and I—"

Though Tallis had quickly stopped herself from saying more, Dawn knew what she had intended to say... she still missed his arms and she imagined Tallis missed much more.

Tallis suddenly rushed to finish. "I am grateful for the time I had with him. He was mine for one night only. He belongs to you now."

The door burst open and Cree stepped in, the breadth of him filling the doorway. His eyes went directly to his wife.

Tallis hurried out of her chair and over to her son, the smoldering anger in Cree's dark eyes frightening her.

Elsa spoke before anyone could. "The lad is ill, my lord."

Cree's eyes went to the lad, looking small and vulnerable in a bed that was not that big but looked as if it devoured him. "What is wrong with him?" he demanded.

"The start of a fever and it appears there is a heaviness in his chest," Elsa answered and Tallis gasped.

"See to his care and make sure they both stay away from others until you are certain that it is not something that can spread," Cree ordered.

"I am well," Tallis insisted.

"But what of other children?" Cree said. "I have seen villages where only the children perished from an illness. I will not chance the lives of the children here." He looked to Elsa. "Keep me abreast of how the child does."

Elsa nodded. "As you wish, my lord."

Cree went to his wife, placing his hands flat on the table in front of her and planted his face a breath away from hers. "Did I not tell you to let this be?"

Dawn scrunched her brow and tapped her cheek, as if she was trying to recall.

Cree chuckled low, though it sounded more like distant rolling thunder of an approaching storm.

Dawn knew no way of quelling such a storm, but she had had practice, though truthfully she had not always been successful, in quelling her husband's temper. There was one thing that always worked best with him—the truth. The scrunch in her brow faded and her eyes softened as her hand moved to rest against his cheek for a moment, then she dropped her mouth open slightly, traced her finger slowly over her lips, and then did the same to his, letting him know that she longed for his kisses.

His dark eyes instantly sparked with heat. "Outside now," he whispered roughly, though he did not give her a chance to disobey. He grabbed her arm and hurried her to her feet. He turned to look at Tallis. "This is between you and me, and I will see it settled soon, for I will have the truth from you."

Tallis remained silent, her heart beating wildly with fear.

Cree all but dragged his wife out of the cottage and once outside he kept her walking. He wanted a private place to speak with her, or so he told himself. She had sent him to the edge of his patience with her gentle, loving touch and when she let him know that she missed his kisses he had tumbled right off. Now he wanted nothing more than to strip his wife bare and let her know that he missed more than just kissing her.

He marched her through the village, though they were not far from the keep. Clan's people stared and mumbled among themselves, the sight of their mighty chieftain with a firm grip on his wife not uncommon to see. All knew that Dawn had a propensity to disobey the mighty warrior, and he more often than not forgave her. This, however, was different, for news spread quickly in the village and most everyone already knew of the woman who had arrived with her son, claiming the lad to be Cree's and all could not help but wonder what would happen.

30

Sloan approached as they neared the keep.

"Do not bother me now," Cree warned as Sloan got closer.

"Then I am to tell William that the new castle plans are to wait another day?" Sloan asked as he stopped not far from the couple.

Cree swore beneath his breath once again. There had been far too many delays already on the castle that would rest on a summit overlooking the Kyle of Tongue. It would be a good stronghold and a good, safe place for his family and clan. And he wanted as little delays as possible since it would take a year or possibly more to complete.

Dawn tapped his arm and smiled, patting her chest and pointing to him, letting him know she would like to go with him.

"What of the twins?" he asked.

Dawn gestured that she would look in on them before they left and reminded him there were women who helped with the feeding since his son was always hungry.

"Valan is going to be a strong one," Cree said with pride. "He will always protect his sister."

Dawn smiled and nodded, though in her heart she could sense that her daughter Lizbeth had a quiet strength about her that would serve her well.

Cree nodded. "Aye, you will come with me, then I will not have to worry about what trouble you are getting yourself into."

Dawn's smile grew and she planted a quick kiss on his cheek before hurrying off.

31

"Do you truly believe that whether Dawn is with you or not that she would not involve herself in something that would bring you worry?" Sloan asked with a laugh.

"She is a challenge," Cree said with a slight grin.

"And that is just one of the numerous reasons you love her."

"And only her," Cree said his eyes watching the door to the keep close behind his wife.

"Are you sure you do not want someone sent to make inquiries about Tallis and her tale?"

Cree shook his head. "She will tell me the truth."

"What if she does not?"

Cree turned a scowl on Sloan. "I will see that she does."

"I have seen you force the truth from men," — Sloan shook his head— "but never a woman."

"One way or another I will get the truth from her," Cree assured him.

"And what if the truth is not what you want to hear?"

Cree had asked himself that same question and he still was not sure of the answer, and so he had none to give Sloan. "Are the men ready to leave?"

"They await your word," Sloan said familiar with Cree's abrupt way of letting one know he would no longer discuss the matter.

"We leave soon," Cree said and turned and walked over to the steps to the keep. He had been annoyed when Sloan had intruded upon him and

Dawn for the second time, but now he was pleased he had. This brief outing would give Dawn and him time together, away from interferences, from gossiping tongues, and from a matter that could have consequences on his family that would be difficult to prevent.

Chapter Five

Dawn was amazed by the amount of land that had been cleared on the summit where the castle, their future home, would be built. She was also curious about what looked like a foundation to a structure that had once occupied the area.

"Vikings."

Dawn's heart pounded as she turned to look out over the river that flowed lazily below the summit, fearing for a moment she would see Viking ships approaching. That, however, was not possible, since Viking attacks were now tales of the past, though the telling of them continued to instill fear.

She turned once again, this time to face William the young man who had drawn the plans for the castle.

"A Viking stronghold sat here once. It fell into disrepair once it was abandoned, the weather and years claiming the rest. Cree has instructed that the stones remain as a reminder that the Vikings did not succeed in keeping claim on this land."

Dawn smiled and motioned with her hands, William familiar with her gestures.

The young man grinned as he answered, "Aye, Cree will keep claim of this land and all his sons and theirs to follow."

Dawn spread her hand out toward the river.

"It is a beautiful sight from up here. And the river is plentiful with sea trout and salmon. The land itself is home to pheasant, grouse, deer and more. And the seals can be quite entertaining on the beach below. It will make a good home."

"That it will."

William turned and gave a respectful bob to Cree. "My lord."

"I see now why you made those adjustments to the castle plans, but there are a few others I wish to discuss with you."

Dawn wandered off as the two discussed the changes. Usually she would insinuate herself into the conversation, curious as to how the drawings would change since her fingers itched to draw more often than not. However, she could think of little else then Tallis and her son. Or was it the fact that when Tallis spoke of Cree, she sounded as if she loved him and always would? And try as she might Dawn could not help but feel angry at the thought.

The woman had no right loving Cree. He belonged to Dawn and no one else. And though the woman claimed she meant only for her son to know his father, was she hoping for more from Cree?

Dawn tried to shake her concerns and doubts away, but they were stubborn and stuck to her like the persistent fleas that plagued the animals.

"How many times must I remind you not to wonder off on your own?"

Dawn stopped and took in her surroundings before turning to face her husband. She had been so engrossed in her thoughts that she had not realized that she had taken a worn path, leading down the side of the summit. Through the trees, a few feet ahead, she spied the sandy shore.

She turned, forcing a smile, and held her hand out to her husband and turned her head to the shore.

"A brief look and we return," he ordered. "There is work to attend to." Keeping a firm grip on her hand, he led her down the remainder of the path and onto the sandy shoreline.

This time Dawn's smile came easily. She could imagine bringing the twins here to dig in the sand. Swimming was another matter for it was well known that the water's temp did not vary much between winter and summer, and only the hardy, or perhaps foolhardy, dared to tempt it.

The shore, however, would provide a good place for picnics, games, drawing in the sand, fishing, and so much more. Her smile grew as she pictured at least six or more children playing together, laughing, having fun, she and Cree joining in with them.

Her smile faded as she imagined a lad standing off in the distance, removed from the fun and she felt a grip to her heart. She knew the lad was Adian.

Cree knew by her knitted brow that something concerned her and it was not difficult to know what it was. "I told you I would see to this matter. You are not to worry."

Though Cree spoke as if angry, she knew her husband well enough to know it was more out of concern than annoyance. But he needed to understand that she needed to talk with him about it.

She laid a hand to his chest and then to hers, letting him know that she loved him and before he could respond, she continued gesturing.

"I know you want to discuss the situation, but I do not. I will see it done and that is all you need to know."

Dawn shook her head, letting him know that would not do.

"I will not argue this with you, Dawn."

She gestured again, telling him that she would not argue either, but she would have her way.

"Will you now?" he said as if challenging her.

Dawn stamped her foot and tossed her chin up.

His eyes narrowed and in the next instant his arm went around her waist and he yanked her hard against him, his face an inch from hers. "It will be as I say."

Dawn was not surprised that passion shot through her, hardening her nipples, fluttering her stomach, and causing her to turn wet with the want of him. It had been too long since she last had him inside her and she ached to feel the strength of him pounding into her relentlessly and bringing her endless pleasure, not to mention earth shattering climaxes. She simply could not get enough of her husband.

Did Tallis feel the same?

The thought angered her and made her want to show Cree that he belonged to her and her alone. She reached down and slipped her hand beneath his plaid and grabbed hold of him, smiling when she found him rock-hard.

37

Cree gave a low growl, then scooped her up and walked to a secluded spot and went down with her on the warm sand, his mouth devouring hers with a kiss.

The hungry kiss fired their passion and their hands roamed eagerly over each other.

After a few moments, Cree tore his mouth away from hers reluctantly. "Fast and hard it will be, for we have no time to linger."

Dawn nodded vigorously. Fast, hard, slow, easy, she did not care as long as he buried himself deep inside her. She eagerly yanked her dress up while he pushed his plaid aside.

"HONK! HONK!"

The strange noise startled them both and had Cree jumping to his feet, his hand going to the hilt of his dagger.

Dawn sat up, pushing her dress down and smiling when she caught sight of a pair of seals a few feet away.

"Go away!" Cree shouted, waving his hand.

The one seal bravely moved forward and responded with a resounding, "HONK!"

Dawn laughed, though it could not be heard.

Cree cast an eye to his wife, knowing she would find this amusing and sure enough her body shook with her silent laughter. "It is not funny."

In a sense, it was not funny...the pair had disturbed their lovemaking, but they were too cute to be mad at them. Besides, Dawn sensed why they were there and she gestured to her husband.

"What do you mean we are trespassing on their spot? This is my land. If anyone is trespassing it is them." He wanted to kill the pair for having interrupted them, though he never would. They were harmless creatures and while he could be cruel, never would he harm defenseless creatures.

He watched his wife scramble to her feet and before he could warn her to keep her distance from the pair she was at their side. The one held his flipper out to Dawn and she smiled broadly as she rested her hand against it. Then the other one did the same.

Dawn stretched her hand out to the spot where she and Cree had been and the pair gave her a nod and ambled past Cree without a nod or acknowledgement to stretch out in the warm sand, the sun bathing them with glorious warmth.

Before he could voice his objections, Dawn gestured to him and his heart swelled with love. "Aye, you are right. The twins will love it here and they will love the seals." He walked over to her and slipped his arm around her, easing her against him. "Tonight, wife, you are mine and mine alone, and there will be no interruptions."

Dawn tapped her chest rapidly to let him know how happy that made her.

He kissed her quick. "I am going to make you very, very happy tonight."

She smiled and hugged him, laying her head against his chest.

He tightened his arm around her. "You belong to me. You are mine." He lifted her chin so that their eyes met. "I love you."

She could not help but wrinkle her brow, pat her chest, and shrug.

"Are you asking me if I love you and only you?"

She nodded.

He released her and took a step back. "Did I not tell you to leave this be?"

She pointed between them both and to her mouth.

"There is nothing to discuss. This is between that woman and me"

She shook her head vehemently and jabbed in the air at him and then herself.

"No, this does not concern us."

She through her hands up frustrated, then shook her finger at him and pounded her chest.

Cree went to her side and stood in front of her, his hands fisted at his sides. "Do you love me?"

Dawn gestured without hesitation that she did.

"Do you trust me?"

Dawn once again did not hesitate, she nodded.

"Then obey me on this and let it be or I will take you over my knee and take my hand to your naked backside."

The image of him doing just that, though with a tender touch, brought a wicked smile to her face and she closed the distance between them, her finger drawing an X over her heart.

Cree's loins fired to life as the image of her spread naked across his knees, his hand coming done on her round backside, flooding his senses. He grabbed her wrist and leaned down to whisper, "It is a promise you have that my hand will find your backside this night."

Dawn shivered at the sinful thought.

He took her arm. "You have distracted me from my work far too long."

Dawn smiled and pressed close to his side as they made their way back up the path to the top of the summit. She stopped once or twice to look at some plants, then gestured for him to go ahead while she kept herself and her thoughts occupied with collecting a few plants she thought Elsa might want.

Cree hesitated at first, then said. "Stay right here until one of my warriors join you."

She nodded.

He shook his finger in her face. "I mean it, Dawn. I will not worry about you when there is work to be done."

She promised with her finger tracing a cross over her heart, then gave him a quick kiss before he walked off. She had no intentions of disobeying him, she had done enough of that already and the day was young yet. She became engrossed in her foraging and did not realize the warrior had joined her until she almost stumbled over him.

It was only when she saw that the sun had moved in the sky that she realized a couple of hours had passed. It had been a while since she had spent some leisurely time in the woods and she was pleased to have had this time to herself.

The warrior followed her back up the path and she smiled when she caught sight of Cree deep in talk with William. The sight of him never failed to thrill her or touch her heart. She truly loved this man and that love grew stronger every day.

He turned and stretched his hand out to her. She ran to him and he wrapped his arm around her.

"Time to go," he said and hugged her close.

Cree kept a conversation going as they rode at a leisurely pace, focusing on their new home while purposely avoiding the problem that had presented itself this morning. He was not ready to discuss it with her and he was not ready to admit that there was something familiar about Tallis, though he could not place it. In time, he would remember and in time she would tell him the truth—he would convince her of it.

"Land needs clearing for the village and each section of the village will be built at different intervals. I plan on having Elsa's cottage close to the keep in case you or the children are in need of her."

Dawn was wise to her husband's ways and was aware that he talked as he did to distract her from thinking of anything else. She did not mind, for she loved when he shared plans with her and asked her opinion, which he did both—often.

She gestured with a question that he was quick to answer and they shared their return journey home in relative compatibility.

They barely reached the rise that led to the village when one of Cree's warriors rode toward him at a fast pace.

Cree brought his horse to a stop, raising his hand to let the others know to follow suit. Then he waited until the approaching warrior reached him.

The warrior brought his horse to a sudden halt a few feet from Cree and did not wait to be granted permission to speak. "A troop of fifty or more is but a short distance away and they carry more weapons than necessary for a mere visit."

"Have trackers been sent out to see if more follow?" Cree asked.

"Aye, Sloan had them sent out as soon as word came of the troop's approach and I was sent to inform you," the warrior said.

He did not bother to ask if his men were in place, he knew the answer. His warriors were well trained and whether a small or large troop approached, their actions would be the same. They would prepare to defend their home to the death.

"Then let us be ready to greet them," Cree said and turned to Dawn. Without a word, he leaned over, grabbed her around the waist, yanked her off her horse and onto his, dropping her in front of him and keeping a firm arm around her before taking off down the rise.

Chapter Six

All was in readiness when the troop arrived at the keep. Warriors stood ready as did villagers, everyone familiar with their assigned task should an unexpected battle break out. Anxious and alert eyes followed the troop through the village and to the stairs of the keep where Cree stood waiting on the top step.

Dawn stood inside the keep just behind the tall door, keeping it slightly ajar so that she could hear what was being said. Cree had ordered her, most vehemently, to remain in the keep until he instructed otherwise. She understood that he was protecting her from possible harm, but she would have much preferred to be at his side and see for herself what was happening.

"If you step one foot out that door, I will see you confined to our bedchamber for the remainder of the day," Cree ordered without glancing back at the door, and then silently cursed, imagining her response.

I would not be alone for long.

Dawn smiled, certain her husband knew her well enough to know her reply. Her smile faded as the sound of approaching horses grew louder. Their arrival could prove to be nothing, but for some reason she did not believe that.

Cree watched as only ten men came to a stop at the foot of the stairs. Never would he allow a whole troop to enter his village. The remainder waited outside the gates, his warriors keeping a watch on them.

One man guided his horse forward and addressed Cree respectfully. "Earl of Carrick, I beg your forgiveness for my unannounced visit. I am Terran Fitzbane, brother to the Earl of Brimsborne, and I come here in search of a woman."

Cree looked him over, though his eyes never moved. He was thick of body and of average height, but held himself well, his wide shoulders drawn back and his chin up a notch. His deep voice resonated with confidence and the wrinkles around his eyes only added to his fine features. Gray strands mingled with brown and sharp blue eyes remained steady on Cree. Terran Fitzbane was not a man to disregard lightly.

"Go on," Cree said.

"The woman is quite a beauty and travels with a young lad about two years. She has a false tongue and is not to be trusted. She uses the lad as a pawn, attempting to convince any earl, chieftain, any man with a title that the lad is his bastard son. Once she gains some wealth from one, she moves on to the next."

"What do you want with such a deceitful woman?"

"I care not what happens to the lying whore. I care only for the safety of the child. The lad is my brother Giles, Earl of Brimsborne's only heir."

"You are sure of this?" Cree asked.

"I am," Fitzbane said with a firm nod. "Devin was my brother Giles' only son. He wed a local chieftain's daughter and she gave birth to a son. About three months ago, Devin and his wife went to visit her family and were attacked on the way. The lad was never found and Giles has never stopped looking for him. It took time, but we finally tracked him to the whore who continues to use him in her lying scheme. Time is of the essence here. My brother lay dying and his last wish is to see his grandson take his rightful place as heir to the Brimsborne title and holdings."

"What makes you think she and the lad are here?" Cree asked cautious of the man's tale.

"She traveled with a companion for a while, but once the man took ill, she left him quick enough. We luckily came across him just before he succumbed to his illness and he confessed all to me. Please spare me more woe and tell me the child I seek is here."

Dawn rested her head against the wood door, frustrated. This certainly complicated matters. Cree would never turn the lad over to this man without knowing for sure if his tale was true. If it was, it would certainly solve the problem, but if not—the problem just got bigger and could possibly prove harmful.

The thought sent her scurrying. Until the truth could be learned, the lad needed to be protected, especially with him being ill. Dawn hurried through the Great Hall, through the stone hallway that led to the kitchen, then ran through the busy area so fast she doubted anyone realized it was her. She made her way around the back of the keep and along the edge of the woods that ran behind it until she could enter the village without being noticed. Then she hurried off to the cottage where Tallis and the lad were staying.

Cree stared at Terran Fitzbane. He had met many a man who could lie convincingly, especially when wealth and land were involved. He had also met men who would do anything for their family, their clan. The same could be said about women. Cree could not be certain which man Terran Fitzbane was or which woman Tallis was, but one thing was certain...the lad was an innocent in all this and he would not be going anywhere until the truth was discovered.

"A woman and lad arrived here and she is claiming the child is mine," Cree said.

Fitzbane grinned broadly. "Thank the heavens, my nephew has been found. Please present him to me and I shall take my leave. I shall also take the woman off your hands as well and see that she suffers for her misdeeds."

Cree scowled and Fitzbane drew his head back sharply as if avoiding a blow.

"Until I can determine the truth the lad and the woman remain here," Cree said in a tone that was not meant to be challenged.

Fitzbane looked ready to argue, but held his tongue, thinking on his words before he spoke. "I ask you to reconsider since my brother has little time left."

"That is unfortunate," Cree said, "but my decision remains."

"My brother is a good friend of the King and his majesty would not take kindly knowing that you kept his friend from seeing his grandson before he died."

"Your threat is useless, since the King is well aware that it is more important that he remains in my good graces than I in his. You are welcome to camp outside the castle walls until this matter is settled to my satisfaction." Cree turned, dismissing the man.

"You insult me by not extending the hospitality of your home while—"

Cree swerved around. "Obey me or leave, the choice is yours." Cree turned once again and whispered to Sloan. "Get the woman and child into the keep without anyone seeing them and send Neil to me."

"I will not leave without the child," Fitzbane called out.

Cree turned around slowly, a deep scowl etched into his handsome face.

Fitzbane once again drew back as if avoiding a blow.

"I will determine the fate of the lad and you will leave when I order you to or suffer the consequences."

Anger rose up in Fitzbane, sending large red blotches to stain his face. He whipped his horse around clumsily and rode off through the village, his few men following him.

Cree entered the keep, expecting to find his wife behind the door. When he saw that she was not there, he went off in search of her, swearing beneath his breath as he did.

~~~

Dawn did not bother to knock, she threw open the door to find Tallis sitting beside her sleeping son on the bed, her hand loving stroking his brow with a wet cloth.

"He grows warmer," Tallis said with worry.

Dawn wished she had time to comfort and reassure her, but that would have to wait. She had to get the two to the castle. She hurried over to Tallis and began gesturing.

"I do not understand, though I fear you may be telling me that we have to leave."

Dawn nodded and began gathering the things Elsa had left for Tallis to use on her son and putting them in a basket.

"But Adian is too sick. Please just let us stay until he is well enough to travel," Tallis begged.

Dawn shook her head, and then realized her gesture would be misunderstood. She gestured again, shaking her hands, then pointing down at the floor trying to make Tallis understand that she was not forcing her to leave.

A knock at the door had both women jumping. Dawn motioned to Tallis to stay by Adian and she went over to the door and opened it slowly. Dawn reached out and grabbed her best friend Lila by the arm and yanked her in, slamming the door shut.

"What is wrong?" Lila asked. "I saw you slinking along the edge of the woods to get here. Does it have something to do with the troop of warriors that arrived?"

Dawn began gesturing, Lila having understood her since they were young.

Lila looked to Tallis. "Someone has arrived claiming the lad is not your son."

Tallis's face turned pure white.

"Dawn wants to get you and the lad inside the keep where you will be better protected."

Tallis stood. "I thought she wanted us to leave."

Lila shook her head along with Dawn. "No, she wants you moved to the safety of the keep. Gather what you need and Dawn will take you and the lad there."

The three women worked as fast as they could, gathering what was needed and wrapping up the lad in the blanket to carry to the keep.

Dawn gestured to Lila.

"The men had yet to leave the last I saw," Lila said and when Dawn turned to Tallis, Lila interpreted her gestures. "We will need to keep to the edge of the woods and make our way around the keep and through the kitchen so that no one sees us." Lila interjected. "I spotted Dawn because I know her well and knew she would be sneaking about to find out what was going on. But you have no worry. No one will see you." Lila went back to interpreting. "You will stay in the keep until the truth is determined."

"Adian is Cree's son," Tallis insisted, hugging the small lad wrapped snugly in the blanket tightly to her.

Lila looked to Dawn and smiled as she spoke Dawn's gestures. "Then you and Adian have nothing to worry about, for Cree will protect his children with his life."

Tears gathered in Tallis's eyes. "I am sorry. I never meant to hurt anyone."

Dawn patted the woman on the shoulder and urged her toward the door.

Lila opened the door just a crack to look out. "We need to hurry. It looks like Sloan and some warriors are headed this way, though the crowd of villagers is slowing them."

Dawn wondered if Cree intended to put a heavy guard around Tallis and the lad. He had seemed adamant about not allowing the pair in the keep, but that was where they would be most safe and Dawn intended to see them safe.

Lila went out first and purposely caused a distraction so that Dawn and Tallis could slip away without being noticed.

The woods seemed extra quiet as they entered along the edge not far from the keep. Dawn slipped her dagger from her boot, ready to strike in case Fitzbane had men he had sent out to explore. Not that that seemed possible since they had only arrived and Cree kept a heavy guard around their home. But she had learned from Cree to always be prepared.

They were about to turn the corner of the keep when Dawn thought she heard footfalls. She stopped and swerved around with a finger to her lips to warn Tallis to remain silent. She heard the noise again and knew someone was headed their way. She gestured Tallis to brace herself against the castle wall, then she waited until the person got near and jumped out with her dagger raised just in case it was one of Fitzbane's men.

Her wrist was suddenly clamped in a steel-hard grip and her husband turned a harsh scowl on her that had her thinking that she might not get out of disobeying him so easily this time.

"I will deal with you later," he said to his wife and looked to Tallis, giving her a sharp snap of his hand. "Come here, now."

Tallis did as he commanded.

"Give me the lad," he ordered.

Tallis hugged the lad closer. "He is no burden to carry."

Cree went to argue, then shook his head, grabbed hold of her arm, and walked off, tugging the two women along with him. He entered through the kitchen and the sight of him having a firm grip on two women had the servants staring, their mouths agape at the unusual sight.

The servants in the Great Hall did the same, stopping in mid-stride in whatever chore was keeping them busy.

Cree was about to summon Flanna with a shout, but she was there before he could. The woman had the uncanny sense of being there when he needed her and of that he was glad. She served him far better in charge of the keep's servants than as cook in the kitchen, her position when he had first taken control of the village.

"How may I be of service, my lord?" Flanna asked.

"Settle this woman and her son in a bedchamber and see that they have food and drink. Elsa is on her way here to tend the lad, he is not well. See that she is taken to him immediately and that she gets whatever she needs."

"Aye, my lord," Flanna said and nodded to the woman. "This way."

Cree looked at Dawn. "You have gone too far this time, wife."

A small tingle of fear crept over Dawn. Had she truly gone too far?

Cree kept his grip on her and practically dragged her along with him to his solar. Once inside, he dropped the latch on the door so no one could enter and with a quick twist of her wrist had her braced back against the closed door. He slammed his two hands on either side of her head and brought his face within an inch of hers.

"Why is it that you have trouble obeying me and others jump at my command?"

She scowled like he usually did, shivered, and tapped his chest, then smiled, tapped her chest and shook her head.

"So others fear me, but you do not?"

She nodded and gestured again, pretending to hit herself about the face, then shook her head and once again tapped his chest.

"You believe I would never strike you."

She gave a firm nod, as if declaring it so.

He shifted his body closer until it almost touched hers, but not quite. "There are other ways to punish you."

Her smile held a hint of laughter as did her eyes.

"You find it amusing that I could tempt you senseless yet leave you unsatisfied?"

She nodded, her smile remaining strong. She pointed to him and then to her and fisted both her hands and held them tight against her chest.

"You think we both want each other too much for me to deny us pleasure?"

Again she nodded with confidence.

"I denied pleasuring myself with you once before, or do you forget the time Colum forced you to spend with me in that miserable hut?"

Her smile slipped away and she looked at him with questioning eyes.

"You never realized how much I wanted you then?"

She shook her head, remembering how fearful she had been of him.

"Your fear yet courage taunted me and grew me hard far too many times." He rested his brow to hers. "You obeyed me then, at least sometimes you did."

She pressed her hand to his chest and then to hers and turned a sorrowful look on her face, offering a heartfelt apology.

He lifted his brow off hers and took hold of her chin. "I know you well enough, wife, to know that you apologize for any hurt you caused me, but you do not apologize for your actions."

She could not argue the truth, so she did what seemed the most natural thing to do...she kissed him.

He returned her kiss, his ache for her deep and never-ending. He would always ache relentlessly for her.

He tore his mouth away and took hold of her shoulders. "You do realize your punishment?"

Dawn nodded, confident that once their passion took control there would be no stopping either of them, no matter Cree's intentions. She reached out and tugged the strip of plaid down off his shoulder to fall at his waist. Eager to get her hands on his naked chest, she quickly stripped him of his shirt.

She barely got her hands on him when his hands began to tug at her garments and before Dawn knew it, she was completely naked in front of him. He did not give her a chance to divest him of his plaid. He spun her around and braced her back against the front of him.

She sighed silently with anticipation when he moved his plaid out of the way and pressed his hard manhood against her backside. She shuddered with the feel of him firm and thick against her and could not wait until she felt him enter her. It had been too long.

His hands roamed over the front of her, tormenting her nipples as he nibbled along her neck, sending gooseflesh rushing over her.

"I could devour every inch of you and not get enough of you," he whispered.

She encouraged him with a vigorous nod and continuous taps of her finger to his arm. They had established shortly after first meeting that one tap meant yes and two taps meant no. Continuous taps needed no explanation.

His hands worked their way down her body, caressing the sensuous curve of her hips, the soft, small roundness of her stomach left after the birth of the twins . It was as if he was touching her for the first time, learning the nuances of her body that giving birth had left her with and he found her even more beautiful.

"Your body is more gorgeous that I remember," he murmured in her ear.

His words touched her heart and she tried to turn in his arms, wanting to hug him tight and never let him go, but his firm hold kept her as she was.

"You will stay as you are. I am not finished touching you," he whispered and nipped loving at her ear and down along her neck.

Dawn shivered from the exquisite pleasure he was bringing her, thrilled with his intimate touches and lovingly whispered words. It had been far too long since they had been this intimate and it made her realize just how very much she missed it.

She gasped, the sound reverberating in her head since it could never escape, as his fingers worked their way through the thatch of dark hair between her legs and came to rest on the small bud that he began to tease so artfully. His thumb continued to work its magic while he slipped a finger inside her and after only a few moments she squirmed in his arms, trying to stop him. She would come if he continued on and she wanted him inside her when she did.

He tightened his grip on her and continued to tease. Finally, she gripped his hand and rubbed her backside against him, letting him know that it was him she wanted inside her.

He released her abruptly, spun her around, took hold of her with two hands at her waist and carried her over to the desk.

Though it took only a few steps to get there, it felt like an endless journey. All she could think about was being sprawled across his desk and him pounding into her, making her come again and again and again.

He set her on her feet in front of the desk, released her, and took a step back. "Your punishment...do not disobey me again."

Dawn stared at his back as he walked to the door. He could not be doing this. He could not mean to leave her in this state or himself. He was hard, rock-hard. He wanted her as much as she wanted him. He was not only punishing her, but himself as well.

How did she respond? Did she run after him and beg him? She certainly wanted to, but pride kept her from taking a step, though could not prevent tears from gathering in her eyes.

Keep going. Do not look back, Cree warned himself. She had to learn, for her own safety and his sanity that she had to obey him. And since all else had failed, he had no choice. She had to be punished, even if he suffered along with her.

His hand fell on the latch.

Tears.

He felt her tears. He did not know how, but he felt them and the pain in her heart, for it was his pain as well.

"Damn!" he yelled and turned.

Chapter Seven

Dawn stood, a single tear rolling down her cheek.

"Damn you," he shouted and tore his plaid off his body as he went to her.

Dawn fought back the other tears that gathered in her eyes, but they were coming too hard and strong. They burst like a broken damn, running uncontrollably down her cheeks and she thought to turn away, not wanting to appear weak in front of him. Instead, she let her love and passion for her husband take reign and threw her arms wide, eager to have him in her arms and his strong, hard body wrapped around hers.

Cree felt as if he should have himself whipped for bringing tears to her eyes. He loved Dawn for who she was, courageous and challenging and a woman that loved him beyond all reason, as he did her.

His heart soared and the blood pulsed rapidly in his manhood, turning him harder, when she threw her arms wide to let him know how much she wanted him. Damn, if he had not punished himself more than her.

He grabbed her around the waist, planted a fiery kiss on her lips before sending the few things on the top of the desk flying with his arm and dropping her down on it. He grabbed her backside and inched her down to the edge of the desk, spread her legs, and drove into her hard, knowing he would make her come in an instant. And she did.

Dawn almost bucked off the table she arched her back so high from the pleasure of his entrance and to the climax that hit her with such force. Endless shock waves of pure passion rocked her body over and over and just when she felt them settle, Cree drove into her harder, sending her reeling toward another climax.

Cree was astonished that he was so close to climaxing so fast. He wanted to linger in the never-ending passion that gripped both their bodies and souls. He wanted to bring her endless satisfaction. He wanted her to know how much he loved her.

Her body arched again and she pounded the table with tight fists as one surprisingly strong climax followed another.

Cree could hold back no longer. He burst like a fiery ball that sent sparks shooting throughout him and he groaned with satisfaction. He dropped down over her, though only allowed his body to brush hers and kissed her gently.

"I do not want to pull out of you yet, I have missed the feel of you far too much."

Dawn tapped her chest and wrapped her legs around him, squeezing.

He groaned and lowered his brow to hers. "You will grow me hard again if you keep that up."

Dawn grinned, took hold of his face and kissed him gently, slipping her tongue into his mouth to tease and taunt as she squeezed even tighter. It didn't take long for both their passion to spring to life again and another climax to come swift and hard.

They were barely recovered when a knock sounded at the door.

"Go away," Cree shouted. "I do not care who you are or what you want."

"You might want to reconsider that," Sloan shouted back. "Word just came that another troop of Fitzbane's warriors, about one hundred of them, are camped three day's ride from here."

Dawn pushed at Cree's chest, urging him to go.

He got off her reluctantly, though kissed her before he did and helped her off the desk.

He dressed quickly and she did the same.

She went to the door with him and before he reached for the latch, she took his hand and pressed it to her chest and then to his, then stretched one hand out to her side.

"And you will always have my heart too." He kissed her gently, then opened the door."

Dawn sent Sloan a smile and hurried past him.

Sloan looked to Cree. "Perhaps you will not be so grumpy now."

Cree shot him a scathing look.

"Or maybe not." Sloan stepped in the solar and turned a grin on Cree when he saw the contents of the desk scattered on the floor.

"Not a word," Cree ordered.

"You wanted me, my lord."

Both men turned to see Neil standing there. He was a seasoned warrior with a scar on his right cheek, a reminder of one of the many ferocious battles he had fought. Cree waved him in. "I have a mission for you Neil."

The three talked in whispers, though the door was closed.

Cree had no doubt that he could get the truth from Tallis, in time, but there was no time. He needed the truth now and he needed to be certain it was the truth.

"I understand, my lord," Neil said when Cree finished detailing the mission.

"Take but two men with you and let no one know who you are, and time is of the essence."

Neil nodded. "Then I best be on my way."

Once Neil closed the door behind him, Sloan said, "You realize that Fitzbane intends to take the child at all costs."

"A foolish decision on his part," Cree said. "I want extra guards posted around the keep, now that Tallis and the lad reside here."

"I had it done as soon as I discovered she and the child were here."

A knock sounded at the door and Sloan walked over and opened it.

"Come in, Elsa, and tell me how the child fares," Cree said when he saw who it was.

Elsa stepped in. "The brew and poultice has not yet had time to work, my lord, and though he remains warm to the touch, he has not grown hot and feverish. A good sign. But I must warn that his little body will not do well if he does not remain in bed."

"The lad will stay here and in bed until you say otherwise," Cree assured her and turned to Sloan. "I will join you in the Great Hall shortly."

Cree waited until the door closed behind Sloan, and then asked, "Are you certain Dawn is well enough for her to resume her intimate wifely duties?"

"Only she can truly tell you that, though I would say from the delight in her eyes and the wide smile she wears that you have your answer."

Cree could not hide the smile that teased at the corners of his mouth.

"Dawn is with the mother and child now, trying to convince the woman that you will not turn her and the lad over to Fitzbane. The woman is continuously telling Dawn that you are the lad's father, almost as if she is trying to convince herself that it is so."

"You sound as if you do not believe her."

"There is something about her story that does not ring true."

"And what is that?" Cree asked, knowing Elsa to be a very observant woman.

"Tallis keeps telling Dawn how kind and loving you had been to her and in the many years I have known you; you have outwardly shown kindness and love to only one person...Dawn."

Her words lingered in his head once she was gone. He had had no time for kindness and had never given thought to love. Neither had ever served a purpose to him.

Then he met Dawn, a woman without a voice and with plain features, and it was not long before his heart that had been as silent as she was voiceless had begun to spark, feel, and love, but before Dawn there had been nothing.

It was a thought that continued to plague Cree as he walked to the Great Hall.

He gave a shout once there. "Flanna!"

The woman appeared in seconds. He was pleased by her attention to duty and how perfectly she ran the keep's servants. She was also a good friend to Dawn.

"My lord," Flanna said with a bow of her head when she approached him.

"My solar needs...tidying."

Sloan chuckled behind him and Cree sent him a scathing look.

"Aye, my lord, I will see to it right away." She turned and hurried off, her head bowed so no one could see her wide smile.

"It is time to learn more about Terran Fitzbane and to keep a closer eye on him," Cree said. "Extend an invitation for him to join us for supper tonight."

Sloan rubbed his hands together. "Tonight's meal should prove entertaining."

~~~

Dawn sat cradling her daughter in her arms as she fed from her breast. The babe had laid quiet, gurgling and smiling to herself when her brother

64

Valan had fed. Unfortunately Valan did not do the same when it was Lizbeth's turn. He let out a cry now and again and twisted his little body as if annoyed.

"He will quiet down once his sister is snuggled safe beside him," Cree said, entering the nursery and hunching down next to where his wife sat in a chair with their daughter. "She is a quiet one, though lets herself be heard when she wants to."

Dawn nodded, smiling with pride and still reeling with relief that her daughter had not been born with her affliction. Of course there was the possibilities of other daughters being born that would suffer her fate, but for now she would not worry about that. Now she would dote on her daughter who had a strong voice.

Dawn tickled under Lizabeth's chin to wake her so that she would take more milk. She seemed satisfied with far too little, though when she roused her, she would take more. Dawn did not mind that it took longer to feed her than Valan since she cherished the time she spent with them both.

"I have invited Fitzbane to supper this evening. I thought it would be good for Tallis to join us. Bringing them together, may help bring out the truth."

Dawn nodded, then shook her head.

"A nod followed by a shake of your head is a bit confusing."

Dawn pointed to Lizbeth who had fallen asleep again, and then pointed toward the door, then back at the babe, shaking her head.

"You do not think Tallis will leave her son?"

She nodded, pointed to herself, then Lizbeth and Valan, and shook her head and made a face as if she appeared ill.

"You would not leave them if they were ill," he said, though it was no surprise to him. He always knew Dawn would make an excellent mum. He stood. "She will attend supper whether she wants to or not. Elsa can look after the lad and that should keep her mind at ease."

Dawn nodded, knowing she could not change his mind and feeling that perhaps it would be good to bring the two together and see what it brought.

Cree bent over and gripped the back of his wife's neck with his hand, giving it a gentle squeeze as he rested his brow to hers. "I cannot wait to slip inside you tonight." He brushed his lips over hers and she startled him and brought a smile to his face when she slipped her hand beneath his plaid and cupped him gently.

He kissed her quick. "I must take my leave, for I do not want my children to see their father ravish their mother."

She produced a dramatic frown, and he laughed as he left the room.

Dawn settled the two twins before going to her bedchamber to freshen and change for the evening meal. She was glad when Flanna showed up a few minutes after entering her bedchamber, her thoughts so jumbled she wondered how she would ever get herself ready.

"I thought you could use a nice soak in the tub," Flanna said and waved in the servants carrying a metal tub. While they saw to filling it with buckets of heated water, Flanna whispered, "I have news to share."

Dawn was eager to climb into the tub and soak her worries away, though she was more eager to hear Flanna's news.

As soon as they were alone, she striped and got into the tub, the sigh so loud in her mind that she could not understand how no one else could hear it.

Flanna got busy scrubbing Dawn's hair with heather-scented soap. "Neil left on a mission for Cree and there is talk it concerns Tallis and the lad. He took two men with him and they were not wearing their plaids. Tongues also wag that Terran Fitzbane will not leave here without the lad and that it may come to war if Cree does not turn the child over to him."

Dawn rested her head back in the water, Flanna running her fingers through it to rinse the soap out of her hair. When she sat up, she questioned with a gesture.

Flanna shook her head. "No the villagers are more than willing to fight if the lad is Cree's, but with Fitzbane claiming the lad is his nephew, it has left doubt in many. "

Dawn let Flanna know that Cree would see it settled.

"I have no doubt he will. What is disturbing everyone is...*how* he will settle it."

Chapter Eight

Dawn laid her finished braid over her shoulder onto her chest, her dark red hair shining from the recent scrubbing. She ran her hand over the soft pale blue frock that Flanna had helped her get into. Never had she thought to own anything so beautiful, but every time Cree sent William on a trip concerning the building of his castle, the man returned with bolts of cloth that Cree had ordered him to purchase for her. Her wardrobe was growing and so would her daughter's.

A knock had her turning and going to the door to open it, to find a red-eyed, crying Tallis.

"I cannot do this, please do not make me," Tallis pleaded.

Dawn understood her plea. She did not want to go to the Great Hall for supper and have to confront Terran Fitzbane. Dawn scrunched her brow and shrugged her shoulders, wanting to know why.

Tallis rung her hands as she answered, "I fear he will convince Cree that I am not being truthful and I will lose my son to him."

Dawn stepped out the door, closing it behind her and took Tallis's arm and walked with her to the bedchamber where her son lay sleeping. She did not want to take a chance and have Cree see them talking. Here they could talk in private since Elsa had yet to arrive to stay with the lad for the evening.

Tallis went to the chair next to the bed and sat, her hand going to caress her son's head. Proper etiquette caused her to jump up and apologize. "I am sorry, my lady, please sit."

Dawn shook her head and pointed for her to sit, and Tallis did not argue. Besides, Dawn did not think Tallis had the strength to continue to stand. The woman looked exhausted and it made Dawn wonder when the woman had last slept.

She pointed to Tallis and brought her hands together to press to her cheek as she tilted her head a bit.

Tallis easily understood her. "I do not know when I last slept. We were on the road for days and when Adian began to feel ill, I carried him." Tears began to fall again. "I cannot lose him. He is all I have left of—" She brought her hands up to cover her face and catch the plethora of tears that burst free.

Dawn went to her side and wrapped her arm around the woman's heaving shoulders and let her cry for a few moments before tapping her shoulder.

Tallis looked up at her, wiping her tears away, though some persisted in continuing to fall. "I am so sorry, my lady. I have brought you such a heavy burden to bear. I never meant to hurt you. I wanted simply to protect my son."

Elsa entered just then, her brow wrinkling with concern. "What is wrong?"

Dawn gestured before Tallis could respond, explaining that Tallis felt a bit feverish and that she did not think it was wise that she join the others for supper this evening. She knew she was taking a chance with Elsa, since she was completely loyal to Cree, he having saved her life. She only hoped Elsa would understand.

Elsa pressed a hand to Tallis's brow. "She feels more chilled to me and from the look of her I would say she is exhausted. I think a hot bath and bed are best for her."

Dawn patted her chest and nodded, letting Elsa know that she agreed.

"I will see to it," Elsa said, "and you will see to telling Cree."

Dawn left a relieved Tallis in capable hands and as she walked down the stairs, she wondered over Tallis's words. Was Adian all she had left of a night with Cree or had she been referring to something else? And why did she continually apologize to Dawn for hurting her? It made it seem that all that had happened had been intentional on her part, as if it had all been planned for some time. That did not make sense, unless it was as Fitzbane claimed and it was all a ruse that she played on many men.

It was possible, but Dawn did not want to think of Tallis using the lad for such a deplorable scheme. She appeared to truly love the lad or was it an act? It was unfortunate the lad had taken ill, for much could be learned from him.

She would keep attentive at supper this evening and see if there was anything she could learn from Fitzbane to piece this puzzle together.

First, however, she needed to inform Cree that Tallis would not be joining them.

She found him in the Great Hall speaking with Sloan as his warriors began to fill the trestle tables. They appeared ready to enjoy the evening meal, especially with Turbett's food being so tasty, but anyone familiar with Cree's warriors knew they were always on guard, always prepared.

Heads nodded and smiles were sent her way as she approached her husband. His eyes showed their approval when they met with hers, but it was the spark of passion that lit in his eyes that made her smile grow and her heart thump just a bit faster.

Cree had learned many years ago not to let anything illicit a response from him. He never allowed anyone to know how he felt or what he thought, giving him the advantage. With Dawn, however, it was proving more difficult to do. His heart leaped whenever he saw her, his loins often tightened, and he was finding that he was smiling far more often than he ever did. He had truly and unbelievably fallen deeply in love with her. He held his hand out to her, eager to have her in his arms. She took his hand and he tucked her in the crook of his arm, wanting to keep her close.

She did not want to linger on the news she had to deliver, so she gestured quickly that Tallis would not be joining them.

"Why?" Cree asked so abruptly that it had Sloan moving away from the couple.

Dawn turned so that her gestures were kept private and she explained how exhausted Tallis was from her journey. She finished with the complete truth...the woman just did not have the strength to confront anyone. She quickly added that Elsa was tending her.

Cree was annoyed. "Exhausted or not, her appearance could have helped with determining the truth of this unfortunate situation. You felt sorry for her when you should have encouraged her to obey me." He brought his nose down to almost touch hers. "But then you do not obey me, so why should she?"

Dawn pressed herself closer against him and kept her gestures where only Cree could see them, pretending to whip at her chest, then held two fingers up, and gave a tilt of her head back as if looking upward.

"Are you telling me that I should punish you twice for your disobedience, once we are in our bedchamber?" He could not keep the annoyance from his voice since the image of taking his hand to her bare, soft backside hit him like a battling ram, tightening his groin.

She nodded, running her hand over his chest.

"Be careful, wife, or the punishment may be more than you can handle."

The merriment filling her dark eyes let him know that she found his remark humorous.

There was no time for a response—though Cree promised he would definitely respond later when they were alone—Terran and two of his men entering the Great Hall.

The room did not fall silent, nor did glances fall on them. Cree's warriors kept talking, giving them only a cursory glance, as if they were unimportant.

"Our guest has arrived," he said and with a hand to her waist he turned, though kept her close by his side. "Fitzbane," he acknowledged with a nod once the man stood in front of them. "My wife...Lady Dawn."

"A pleasure, my lady," Fitzbane said with a slight nod.

Dawn returned his nod. There was always an awkward moment when she was first introduced to people and they were unaware of her affliction. Of course, her husband did not help matters since he never informed anyone that she lacked a voice— bless the man—for he never thought of her as voiceless. Actually, there were times he told her that she talked too much.

It took a while after his men joined some of Cree's men at a nearby table and Fitzbane accompanied her and Cree to the dais to sit that he realized she could not speak. Dawn gestured to Cree and he had answered her and it was at that moment it had struck the man. Dawn saw the surprise in his eyes and she wondered if he was the type of man who expected his wife to remain silent unless he granted her permission to speak.

Platters of food were soon laid upon the tables and ale and wine flowed generously. Talk continued, though more eating than talking was done.

"The food is delicious," Fitzbane said, sopping up the last of the meat pie gravy with a big chunk of bread. "I thought perhaps you would have had Tallis join us for the meal, so you could see her for who she truly is."

"I am not blind, Fitzbane," Cree said.

"Of course not, but I hear that she can be quite persuasive. If you allow me to talk with her, I am sure this matter could be settled most hastily."

"Perhaps, but there are questions I have for her that she has yet to answer. After she does, then maybe I will grant your request," Cree said. "Tell me about your brother. How long has he been ill?"

Fitzbane talked much about his brother's lingering illness and how he had never been the same after his son Devin's death, also how he had searched endlessly for his grandson, hoping to see him before he died.

"I will do anything to grant my brother his dying wish," Fitzbane insisted.

"Even bring him a lad that is not his grandson?" Cree asked.

"Never would I do such a thing. I will return Adian home to his true grandfather."

"Adian is the lad's true name?" Cree questioned.

"Aye, he is named after Giles and my father."

Dawn listened with interest, having realized what Cree had.

"Why would a woman who stole a child keep his true name?" Cree asked.

The question seemed to startle Fitzbane and he appeared to struggle for an answer, finally saying, "Well, she is a whore with barely an intelligent thought. I can only imagine how the poor lad has suffered being in her company." His eyes suddenly widened as if struck by a thought. "You say the lad is ill, she could be the cause of his illness. I demand you keep her away from him so that she can do him no further harm."

Cree leaned over close to Fitzbane and with a harshness that sent a shiver through the man said, "Make a demand of me again and I shall personally demonstrate how I successfully extract information from anyone who dares to lie to me."

Fitzbane hastily and wisely offered an apology. "Forgive me, my worry for my nephew has caused me to lose my manners, I meant no disrespect. And please, I beg of you, let me see my nephew."

Cree leaned back in his seat. "In time."

Tension lingered as conversation turned to general matters and after a few moments Fitzbane said, "Excuse me for a moment while I see to my men. While you have been more than generous with food and drink, I do not want my men indulging much longer."

Dawn gestured to Cree as the man made his way to the table where his men sat.

"I was thinking the same," Cree said. "Why would he explain to me the reason he would talk to his men? He either is foolish or lying, which begs the question...is he plotting something?"

Dawn made a cross over her chest and shook her head.

"You are right. He is not to be trusted," Cree said pleased that his wife was as astute when it came to judging people as he was.

Fitzbane returned to the dais and a few minutes later his men stood and left the keep.

Dawn hoped the night would not drag on endlessly, not that she had to remain in the hall. She simply wanted to go to bed with her husband...though not sleep. She wondered if she excused herself if it would give her husband the incentive to do the same.

She covered her mouth as she pretended to yawn, then laid a hand to her husband's arm and gestured that she would retire for the night.

"Aye, the night does grow late," Cree said and stood to extend his hand to his wife.

Fitzbane stood as well. "It does grow late and I should take my leave."

Dawn nodded to both men and left them, knowing Fitzbane would no doubt have something to say to Cree. She made her way upstairs and thought to undress and wait naked in bed for her husband, and then she smiled, deciding to let him undress her.

It was only a few minutes later that she heard his strong footfalls approach the door, though it surprised her when he passed by their bedchamber. She went to it and peeked out and saw Cree enter the room Tallis and her son occupied. She wondered why he had not stopped and told her he was going to speak with Tallis or even why he would speak with her so late. He had to have known the woman would be sleeping after she had informed him how exhausted Tallis was. Besides, he knew she would be eagerly waiting for him. Had it been something Fitzbane said to him that had caused him to find the need to question Tallis immediately?

She knew she should not be annoyed. Cree would tell her about his visit with Tallis. She simply wished that he would have stopped and told her. Her annoyance growing over a day that had presented endless problems and worries that were yet to be solved had her pacing. Finally, she decided she could not wait for Cree to return. Besides, the longer it took, the more she imagined she had reason to worry and that was foolish.

Wanting a reprieve from her troubling thoughts, she left the room, hurried down the stairs, through the Great Hall, and outside into the night. The night sky was clear, the stars brilliant, but she did not take time to admire them...she hurried along.

Old Mary would know she was coming to visit even at this late hour. The woman always knew when Dawn needed to talk. The door to Old Mary's cottage sprang open before Dawn could knock.

"I have a brew waiting," Old Mary said with a smile.

Dawn gave the woman a hug. She was like a mum to her, always being there for her when she needed her and there for her when she had not known she needed her, and she loved her dearly.

"It has been a difficult day for you," Old Mary said as she settled her old bones into a chair at the table while Dawn poured them each a brew. "You are lucky that you know that your husband loves you more than life itself or you would be worried now."

Dawn dropped down in the chair. Old Mary knew just what to say, knew how to remind her of what was important.

"Cree is different than most men and shows his love to you in different ways that most women would not understand and many would not find acceptable. You love each other for who you are not who either of you want the other to be. That is what true love is about, accepting and respecting the person you fell in love with."

Dawn sipped at her brew, letting the truth of the old woman's words sink in.

"You are part of him now, connecting in a way that no other ever could. He cannot hurt you without hurting himself and the same for you."

Dawn thought about earlier in his solar and how he intended to punish her by leaving her aching for him. But the punishment was also his and he did not allow either of them to suffer. Old Mary was right. They were connected like no other and always would be.

Old Mary laughed softly. "Even now he does what he must before returning to you, for once he does he knows that he will not be able to leave your side."

Dawn's eyes shot wide. Why had she not thought of that? Of course Cree had not stopped to tell her that he needed to talk with Tallis, for if he had he would not have left their bedchambers.

Old Mary reached out and rested her hand on Dawn's. "Do not let doubt rob you of the truth. Confront it and put it to rest before it can do harm to you or Cree."

Dawn smiled and squeezed Old Mary's hand, grateful for her wise advice.

"If you push aside what you know in your heart is true, it will leave room to discover what is not."

Dawn nodded and gestured as if she held a small child in her arms and then scowled which represented her husband, and she shook her head.

"Cree is not father to the lad Adian," Old Mary said and Dawn confirmed with a nod. "And how do you know this?"

She gestured repeatedly, knowing Old Mary would clearly understand her. She had since Dawn was a child.

"You finally realize that Tallis loves another and it is he who she speaks about the night the lad was conceived. And why do you know this?"

Dawn felt a catch to her heart and gestured slowly.

79

"You saw in her what you had once felt in yourself," Old Mary said softly.

Dawn nodded, wishing she had realized it sooner.

"Do not batter yourself because you have just now realized the truth. Love always interferes with sound reason and sometimes it needs to. Is love not interfering with Tallis's plans?"

Dawn's brow knitted in question.

"The woman cannot hide the love she has for the man who fathered her child. No matter how hard she tries, it continues to surface just as yours does for Cree. All is not what it seems and no matter what way one views the problem the woman and child are in danger. But I believe you have sensed that from the beginning or you would not have disobeyed your husband or fought to keep them both safe."

Dawn was about to smile but an expected yawn stole it.

"Go now. Your husband returns to your bedchambers soon."

Dawn gave Old Mary another hug before leaving and thanking her for having eased the burden she had been carrying all day.

Dawn could not wait to return to the keep and share her thoughts on Tallis with her husband, though she was more looking forward to being wrapped in his strong arms. She hurried her steps, though she stopped a few feet from the keep and glanced up at the night sky. She had no time to be bothered with it before, but now her heart was lighter and the beauty of the stars so bright in the sky whispered to her.

She stared up at their brilliance and smiled at the ones that winked repeatedly at her. It was a glorious night and she wished Cree was here right now to share this moment with her. The thought of him had her hurrying along, eager to see her husband.

The attack came so quickly that she barely had time to respond. She was grabbed around the waist and dragged toward the woods.

Chapter Nine

No hand bothered to cover her mouth. Why should it when she could not scream for help, though in her mind she did and with such force that she wondered how it could not be heard. She tried desperately to rip at the hand that held her, but the muscled arm would not budge.

Suddenly, she was thrown back against a tree trunk, a hand gripping her throat.

"The mighty Cree was wise in choosing a wife who could not speak, for then he does not have to listen to the endless harping of a woman. It even saves him from coming to her rescue since he would never hear her cry for help."

Dawn glared at Fitzbane as she tried frantically to loosen his hand at her throat, his grip so harsh that she could barely breathe.

He let her struggle for a while before he ordered, "Stop, or I will choke the life from you and be done with it." He squeezed harder.

Dawn had no doubt he would and so she stilled.

"Listen well, you will—"

Shouts, voices, and footfalls drew close and she prayed someone would find them.

Dawn was released as fast as she had been grabbed and she fell to her knees, grasping for breath. She struggled to her feet, not wanting to take the chance Fitzbane would return. She was glad she had, for once she reached the steps of the keep those who had frightened Fitzbane off were nowhere to be seen.

The Great Hall was also empty and as Dawn took the stairs slowly, she wondered over telling Cree of her ordeal. He would grow furious and go after Fitzbane, starting a possible war between the clans. But was it fair not to tell him?

She entered their bedchamber glad he had yet to return. It was not for her to judge what actions should be taken against Fitzbane for his attack on her. That was Cree's decision. He ruled this place; his word was law.

She gave a thought to going to see if the twins needed feeding, but the women who cared for them throughout the night no doubt had them well in hand. Besides, the long day and its endless ordeal had finally taken its toll on her. She removed the combs from her hair to let it fall free, slipped out of her garments and climbed into bed naked to wait for her husband.

~~~

Cree entered his bedchamber to find his wife sleeping, her dark red hair spread around her neck and shoulder like a silky cape. Her body was tangled in the covers, though one or two naked limbs peeked out and the tip of a nipple tempted him. He could not blame her for not being able to remain awake. The day had been a demanding one on her and yet she had dealt with it with kindness and a generous heart.

If it had been a man who arrived claiming he loved Dawn, he would have killed him on the spot. He shook his head, recalling how she had heard him say that he would remember a woman as beautiful as Tallis, but he had said it only to see her reaction, to see if perhaps it would somehow illicit a remark that would help him learn the truth.

Cree slowly disrobed, thinking on what he had just learned from Tallis. After this evening spent with Fitzbane, he had an idea of what the truth might be and he had wanted Tallis to confirm it. At first, she had vehemently stuck to her story about him being the lad's father until he told her what he believed to be the truth. She finally broke down and told him everything.

The problem now was...how did he protect them from harm?

Finding an answer would have to wait until morning. He wanted nothing more than to climb in bed and wrap his arms around his wife.

When he was finally completely naked, he climbed into bed and gently took her in his arms. She snuggled against him and it was difficult for him not to wake her and make love to her.

He stroked her back, his hand drifting down over her soft backside. He smiled, recalling how when he had warned her about punishing her for disobeying him that she had suggested she would not mind his hand at her backside. It had turned him hard as the thought of it did now.

Stop touching her, he told himself, but he did not listen. She felt too good and it had been a long month since he had last stroked her so intimately. He closed his eyes and let himself enjoy the feel of her.

They sprung open when only a short time later her hand moved between his legs and began to caress him, turning him harder and harder. He had not meant to wake her, but since he had...

He slipped his hand between them to stroke her as intimately as she stroked him. It was a pleasure to lay there in the quiet of the night touching each other, stoking their passion, eagerly anticipating what was yet to come.

"I have missed this between us," he whispered and kissed her softly.

She tapped his arm, letting him know she felt the same and so pleased he had wakened her, in more ways than one, with his touch.

Cree had no intentions of rushing as they had done earlier today in his solar. This time was for taking it slow, lingering, and enjoying every kiss, caress, and climax they would share.

When she tossed her head back and her caress turned to strong tugs that threaten to bring him to climax, he knew it was time to make her come at least once, so that they could linger longer in this divine pleasure.

He eased her on her back and wished he had stoked the small fire in the hearth so that there was enough light to see her more clearly. She was a mere shadow and he loved to watch her face as she exploded in climax. Later he would see to it, and then make love to her again.

He was careful with her breasts, having learned that they could be tender if it had been a while since she fed the twins. So with his hands on either side of her head, he hovered just above her as his knee eased between her legs to spread them apart.

When she felt him nudge at her legs, she spread them wide, eager for him to slip into her and she sighed silently with pleasure when he did. He belonged there; he belonged to her. The thought suddenly turned her possessive and she wrapped her legs around him, forcing him deeper inside her.

"Hungry for me...are you?" he asked, obliging her and sinker deeper and deeper with every thrust.

She tapped his arm repeatedly.

He knew her well and the stronger the taps came the closer she was to coming. He cursed himself again, for he wished he could see her face and the way it contorted with pleasure when she burst in a climax.

He drove into her over and over and she grabbed his arm squeezing it as a climax gripped her entire body, sending a repeated shudder racing through her.

Dawn did not want the spiraling passion to ever end and she startled and grew angry when Cree suddenly pulled out of her. She went to grab his arm in protest, but he flipped her over before she could. In the next instant, he slipped his arm under her stomach and yanked her up so that she was on her knees, then he entered her from behind.

His hands took hold of her backside and held it tight as he slammed into her again and again, intent on making her come not just once more but repeatedly.

Dawn kept her hands braced firm on the bed, dropped her head back, and squeezed her eyes shut as her husband's hard thrusts reignited the climax that had yet to fade completely.

"I am going to make you come until you are consumed by pleasure, and collapse."

She smiled and pushed her backside hard against him.

He stopped a moment. "Is that a challenge to see who lasts longer?"

She pushed against him once.

He laughed and began again to move inside her only this time slow. "You will never win this one, my love." His one hand slipped around her leg to tickle her small nub senseless.

Damn, she yelled silently, though it reverberated in her head. He was not going to play fair. She smiled at her husband's wicked ways, and thought to do the same.

She kept her hands planted firmly on the mattress and gave a good thrust back against him as she squeezed his manhood tightly, causing her own pleasure to soar.

"Damn," he yelled and Dawn grinned wide.

She came quickly a few moments later and harder than the first time, which left her body spent, but she would not surrender and collapse, giving him victory. Besides, she was enjoying herself far too much to end it so soon.

She teased him with a roll of her hips and another thrust against him, and he thought he would come right there and then, but he held it back. Besides, he wanted her complete and utter surrender. He would have it no other way.

He stopped his thrusts to regain control and leaned over her to kiss and nibble along her back as his hand gently cupped one breast, weighted with milk, a drop of it slipping out as his finger teased the hard nipple.

Dawn tossed her head from side to side, passion racing through her like never before, urging her toward another climax.

"Good lord, I have missed the sweet taste of you," he whispered, and then slammed into her so hard that she burst in a blinding climax.

Cree felt her legs grow weak from the shudders that wracked her body with a fierce climax and he quickly slipped his arm around her stomach to keep her on her knees as he let himself join her in a gut-punching climax that forced him to roar with pleasure.

They both collapsed together on the bed, Cree on top of her, his arm still around her waist. He was still inside her and he waited until the last shudder ran through both of them before he rolled on his side, taking her with him to rest her back against him.

Dawn laid her hand on his arm and tapped it repeatedly and softly.

"You enjoyed that?"

She nodded her head vigorously.

He laughed and gave her a squeeze. "I am glad, for I loved every moment of it."

She gave his arm a gentle squeeze, letting him know that it pleased her to hear that as a deep yawn took hold.

She was wrapped snuggling against him, so he felt her yawn. "The day has been long and eventful. You need sleep and in the morning I will tell you what I learned from Tallis."

While Dawn would have loved to have heard the news there and then, she was simply too exhausted and much too comfortable in her husband's arms to want to do anything else but sleep. Her tired body agreed and in minutes she was lost in a deep slumber.

Cree pulled a light blanket over them and spent from their lovemaking, besides being pleased that intimacy had been restored between them, he fell asleep.

~~~

Light filtered through the two glazed windows, stirring Cree awake. He or Dawn usually woke with the sunrise, though not today. The sun was already up and so would he be shortly, having to see to the matter of Tallis and her son. First, however, there was the matter of waking his wife whose naked

89

backside was planted snugly against him, which of course aroused him.

He would wake her slow and gently. He caressed the side of her face as he eased her hair away from her neck so he could nibble at it. His hand stilled when he saw the bruise that marred her lovely skin and when he saw that the bruise looked to go around her neck, he eased her on her back to have a better look.

His dark eyes filed with rage and he could not help but shout, "Dawn!"

She woke with a start, her wide eyes greeted by her husband's furious ones.

He rested a gentle hand to her neck. "Who left these marks on you?"

Dawn scrunched her brow, wondering what he was referring to as she tried to bring herself fully awake and comprehend what he meant and why he was so angry.

"Who dared to choke you?" He all but ground out, trying to keep his temper at bay.

Choke. She recalled then that Fitzbane had almost squeezed the breath out of her, evidently leaving the evidence for all to see.

"What happened? When? Why did you not tell me? Why—"

She pressed a finger to his lips and moved to sit up.

Cree quickly sat up, helping her to do the same.

She looked down at her breasts heavy with milk and knew that she must feed the twins soon, but first she had to calm her husband. She feared he would rush off and do Fitzbane deadly harm and that would lead to a battle and possibly war between the clans.

Dawn took her time explaining what had happened, prefacing with...you must not let your anger rule over reason. But as she told him what had happened, the rage in his dark eyes grew. She explained that no one had been about when she entered the keep and that she had planned on telling him but had fallen asleep. And their lovemaking had made her forget all about it.

Cree got out of bed when she finished and started dressing.

Dawn was quick to do the same, fearful of her husband's intentions. She grabbed his arm when he turned to walk to the door. She wanted to know what he intended to do, and she gestured her question to him.

He caressed the bruise at her neck, his fury growing ever stronger. "My greatest fear is just what happened to you last night. You were attacked, almost choked to death and you could not call out for help. And it happened here—home—the place that should be your safe haven. My warriors will hear about failing to protect you and their home...and Fitzbane will die for touching you."

He turned to go and she grabbed his arm once again, but he yanked it away. She hurried in front of him and braced herself against the door, preventing him from leaving, not that she truly could. She only hoped to talk some sense into him.

She tapped at the side of her head and pointed to him.

"I do not need to think." He grabbed her around the waist and lifted her out of the way, opening the door. "I do what must be done to protect and keep safe what is mine." His hand shot out to take hold of her chin. "And make no mistake, you are mine. You belong to me and no one— absolutely no one—lays a hand on my wife."

Chapter Ten

Cree clenched his hands at his sides as he hurried down the stairs. Rage consumed him; there was no stopping it. He was out for blood and he would get it. The image of Fitzbane choking Dawn and she helpless to scream out for help would not leave his mind, adding to his determination to see Fitzbane pay for what he had done to Dawn.

He heard his wife rushing down the stairs behind him and he stopped and turned. He reached out, his arm coiling around her waist, and halted her in her tracks before she could collide with him.

"Leave this be and go see to the twins," he ordered and she shook her head adamantly. "You will obey me on this, Dawn."

She threw back her shoulders, threw her chin up, and shook her head even more stubbornly.

"One of these days I am going to punish you good for refusing to obey me," he said and took hold of her hand. "But for now, since you are intent on trying to stop me—an impossible task—you will come along and see what happens when someone dares to harm you."

Dawn cringed when he shouted several times for Sloan as they entered the Great Hall, certain his angry roars had set the rafters to tremble.

Several of the warriors who occupied various tables stared at him in fear and one got up and rushed out, returning a few moments later with Sloan in tow.

"My lord," Sloan said with a bob of his head while keeping a safe distance from an angry Cree.

Cree released Dawn's hand and drew back her hair for all to see the bruises that circled her neck. "Tell me how this was allowed to be done to my wife last night in her own home," he roared.

All the warriors got to their feet, ready to follow Cree into battle if necessary.

Sloan turned and addressed Dawn. "I am so sorry this has happened to you, my lady. I do hope you are not in pain."

Cree muttered several oaths beneath his breath, realizing that in his anger he had failed to inquire about her well-being. "Are you in pain?" he snapped which angered him all the more for sounding annoyed at her.

Dawn shook her head and began to gesture.

Cree shook his head. "You cannot be serious to blame yourself for this. This is your home and if you want to visit with Old Mary late at night you should be able to do so without fear of harm coming to you."

Dawn continued to argue, letting him know that she should have been more careful with an unfamiliar troop here and have informed someone that she was leaving the keep.

"This is not your fault. Extra guards were posted and should have had eyes on all that went on here last night." He turned a furious glare on his men. "You all will answer to me for this."

Each of them bowed their heads and a few shivered.

"This was my responsibility," Sloan said. "I will find out who failed to do their duty and why."

"And I will see to their punishment," Cree said, "but now I will see to punishing the person who dared to touch my wife." He turned to Dawn. "You will stay in the keep until I return." He looked to Sloan. "Assign two warriors to see that she obeys me."

Dawn had no chance to protest. Cree hurried out of the keep his men following, except for the two who walked over to her and remained close. Her mind went crazy as to how she would escape them.

After pacing the room a few minutes, she was relieved to see Old Mary enter.

The old woman pushed the hood of her cloak off her head and smiled. "The sun kisses the earth with warmth today, but these old bones still feel chilled. Elsa asked me to stop by and look in on the woman and the lad that arrived yesterday and let her know how they are doing."

Dawn wondered why Elsa did not send one of the women who helped her tend the ill.

"Show me the way," Old Mary said, slipping her arm around Dawn's. "I can never keep track of the various rooms in this place."

Her remark was what made Dawn realize that the woman was up to something since Old Mary knew the keep well enough and her mind was much too sharp to lose her way in familiar surroundings.

The two warriors followed close by up the stairs and positioned themselves outside the room as soon as one checked to see that there was no way she could escape them.

Tallis stood there watching all of them anxiously and not leaving her sleeping son's side.

Once the warriors left, Old Mary looked at Dawn. "Fitzbane needs to die, though not at the hands of your husband...yet."

Tallis gasped. "I have prayed for his death since the accident."

Dawn scrunched her brow at the woman.

"Dawn wants to know what you mean," Old Mary said.

Tallis dropped down on the chair by the bed, her hand going to rest protectively on her son. "I confessed all to your husband last night, I had no choice. He had realized the truth and I could no longer deny it."

She seemed hesitant to go on, but Old Mary encouraged her to continue, "Tell us everything so we may help."

"I am Devin Fitzbane's wife and Adian is his son. Devin discovered that his uncle Terran plotted to become chieftain of the clan. He knew his father was blind when it came to his younger brother. He thought Terran could do no wrong and served him well. Devin feared for all our lives and decided to take me and Adian to my family's home until he could prove to his father what Terran had planned.

"We were attacked on our way there. Devin was quick to send me off with one of the Fitzbane warriors loyal to Devin and his father. The last I saw of my husband was him fighting off the band of mercenaries sent to kill us." Tears began to fall and she wiped them away. "I have been in hiding since that day. Douglas, the warrior who saw me to safety, looked after Adian and me. It has been difficult these past three months, always running and hiding. Finally, we came upon a deserted cottage tucked away in the woods. Douglas intended to settle me there and go and see about Devin and if Terran was still searching for us."

Her tears began to fall harder. "I had taken Adian into the woods to collect berries when Terran arrived at the cottage. I heard Douglas's screams as Terran tortured him for information, though I often think that he screamed to alert me to Terran's arrival. I took Adian and ran. That is when I decided there was only one man who could protect my son." She looked to Dawn. "Cree was a warrior I knew Terran would not stand a chance against, so as I made my way here, I devised a tale. I am so sorry. I never meant to hurt you, but I had to protect my son. I love him so much and he is all I have left of Devin." She smiled. "He and I have been in love since we were young and our families fully approved of our union. We were so happy." Her smile faded and her tears flowed.

Dawn's eyes were teary as well and her determination to help the woman had grown ever stronger with each word she had spoken.

Old Mary spoke as Dawn gestured. "You and Adian are safe here. Cree will protect you both. Right now, I must find a way to get past the guards outside the door and get to my husband before he makes the situation worse. If he kills Fitzbane, all could be lost. We need to prove he means you and Adian harm."

"I thought the guards were for me and Adian," Tallis said with relief.

'No, my dear," Old Mary said. "You see Dawn has a way of not always obeying her husband and many times for a good reason. But I think I have an idea of how Dawn can manage to escape the pair."

Dawn grinned, knowing she could count on Old Mary.

A few minutes later, Dawn and Old Mary left Tallis and proceeded down the hall, the two guards following.

There had taken only a few steps when Tallis threw open the door and called out, "Hurry fetch, Elsa. Please hurry!"

Dawn shoved one of the guards and waved her hand, urging him to do as Tallis said.

He turned to the other guard. "Do not let her out of your sight."

The other guard nodded and stepped closer to Dawn who turned to go to Tallis when suddenly

Old Mary reached out and grabbed Dawn' arm, and then her own chest.

Fighting for a breath, Old Mary managed to say, "Healing pouch. My cottage. On table."

Dawn hugged the old woman to her while Tallis came running to her side.

Old Mary repeated the words again, though with more difficulty.

Tallis looked up at the guard who stood there staring at them helplessly. "Go to her cottage and get her healing pouch and hurry."

He shook his head. "I cannot leave Lady Dawn."

"I will not let her leave," Tallis assured him. "And do you truly think she would leave the old woman like this. Go. Hurry. The other guard will return soon enough."

It was Dawn's tear that had the guard hurrying off and as soon as he was out of sight, Tallis and Dawn helped Old Mary up."

"Be off with you," Old Mary ordered Dawn.

Dawn hugged her, the thought of one day losing the old woman having bought genuine tears to her eyes. She took off, taking the stairs carefully, hoping the other guard had not yet found Elsa. She stuck to the shadows of the Great Hall once she entered and was just about to enter the stone hallway that connected the kitchen to the keep when the other guard returned with a worried Elsa in tow. Dawn shrunk back into the shadows as they passed by not too far from her.

Once they were out of sight, she ran down the narrow hall and straight through the kitchen and out the open door, oblivious to the workers who stared at her with wide eyes.

~~~

Cree approached Fitzbane's campsite, his anger growing with every step he took. He saw Fitzbane scramble to his feet from where he sat on a blanket talking with two of his warriors who stood along with him and quickly stepped in front of him.

The other Fitzbane warriors were quick to rest a hand on the hilt of their swords, but before they could form a protective circle around Fitzbane, Cree's warriors were on top of them, forcing them to remain standing as they were.

Cree wore no sword. He did not need one. He intended to use his hands on the man just as Fitzbane had done to Dawn.

Sloan slowed his steps beside Cree as he continued forward. He knew Cree would not want his help, but he would be there in case he did need help...an unlikely prospect.

"Is there a problem?" Fitzbane called out from behind his two men.

Cree did not answer him. He just kept advancing on him.

"Stay your ground," Fitzbane whispered to the two men.

Cree did not halt in his steps, he keep moving toward Fitzbane, his fist flying out to knock the one warrior out with one solid blow while a mighty jab to the other warrior's knee with his foot dropped him to the ground. Then his hand shot out, wrapping around Fitzbane's throat, lifting him up so that his feet dangled just above the ground.

Fitzbane clawed at Cree's hands, barely able to breathe.

"You are going to die for touching my wife and I am going to enjoy beating the life out of you." Cree dropped Fitzbane to the ground and before he could get a good footing or catch his breath, Cree delivered a vicious blow to his jaw, sending him reeling.

Fitzbane stumbled like a drunken lout and Cree did not wait, he grabbed him and landed one vicious blow after another and not to only his face. When Cree released Fitzbane, he fell to the ground on all fours. He raised his head and blood ran from his mouth and nose and his one eye was beginning to swell.

Cree raised his booted-foot and gave Fitzbane's backside a hard kick, sending him sprawling to the ground. He did not wait for the man to recover. Cree leaned down and grabbed Fitzbane by the neck and dragged him to his feet.

"I am going to squeeze the life out of you like you almost did to my wife," Cree said with an angry hiss.

Fitzbane's one eye was almost closed now, blood spilled from his mouth and was caked around his nose and once again he clawed at Cree's hand, fighting to breathe.

Cree squeezed tighter as Fitzbane gagged and clawed in desperation as Cree began to slowly choke the life out of him.

Someone grabbed Cree's arm and he threw the person off him.

"Cree!" Sloan shouted.

The panic in Sloan's voice had Cree turning and there on the ground lay his wife. He released Fitzbane, the man collapsing to the ground as Cree hurried to Dawn.

Sloan was helping her to stand when Cree reached them and pushed Sloan aside, taking hold of his wife.

"Did I not tell you to stay in the keep?" Cree snapped his arm firm around her waist. He shot Sloan a scowl. "Once we are done here, find the two idiots who let her escape them and see that they are given extra guard duty for a month."

Dawn winced, feeling terrible about the two guards' punishment.

"Are you hurt?" Cree demanded, running a quick glance over her.

She shook her head and gestured at Fitzbane who remained on the ground and shook her head again.

"Fitzbane gets what he deserves," Cree said loud enough for all to hear.

Dawn shook her head again.

"It is not your decision."

She tapped the side of her head.

"I have thought about it and it is a fitting punishment," Cree said. "And you will not interfere with what I decree."

He was right about that. It was not right of her to question him in front of his warriors and his foe. She needed time alone with him to make him see reason. So, she did the only thing that she could think of...she suddenly swayed in place, laid her hand on his arm and rolled her eyes back and dropped into a pretend faint.

Cree scooped her up before she collapsed completely. He yelled to Sloan. "See that Fitzbane is locked in the hut and place six men around it. And corral all his warriors here at the camp and keep them surrounded while I see to me wife. Who truly better have fainted."

Dawn popped her eyes open as soon as he took the last step up the keep stairs.

Cree looked down at her with a scowl. "A brief moment to have your say is all I will grant you." A few steps into the hall and he placed her on her feet. "Be done with it."

Dawn did not waste a moment, she began gesturing, hoping his anger would dissipate at least a little and he would realize the truth of her words. After only a few gestures, his brow knitted and she knew he was giving what she said thought, so she continued.

When she finally finished, Cree turned away from her to pace for a moment. "You are right. There could be others helping him to achieve his goal. Killing Fitzbane would not necessarily free

Tallis and her son. More needs to be learned from Fitzbane and his brother Giles notified of his devious plan."

Dawn was relieved to see that she had made him see reason.

"When that is all done, then I will kill him," Cree said.

Chapter Eleven

Dawn sat on a blanket with Tallis shaded from the sun under a large oak tree while Adian plucked at the grass beyond the blanket. The twins slept soundly in a cradle Dawn had brought outside for them to enjoy this glorious summer day. It was sunny and warm with a light breeze, no time to be spending indoors.

"It is amazing how much he has improved in a week's time," Tallis said with a smile as she watched her son.

Dawn gestured to her, patting her own cheeks.

Tallis laughed. "Aye, I have improved myself, but how could I not, having enjoyed such delicious meals? Turbett works magic with food." She reached out her hand to rest on Dawn's arm. "I am forever grateful for what you and Cree have done for me and Adian. I still cannot believe that others, who Giles believed loyal to him, also plotted with Terran against him." She shook her head. "I am so glad Cree kept Terran alive and found out the depths of his plans, including that he was poisoning Giles, his own brother. When Giles had taken ill, Devin and I had our suspicions that he was being poisoned, but we could not prove it. I am so very glad that Cree sent men to help Giles rid himself of his foe and that as soon as it is safe, I will be able to return home. And again I am sorry for the hurt I caused you."

Dawn shook her head and gestured.

"Dawn says no apology is necessary. She also would do whatever was necessary to keep her babes safe. Wouldn't we all?"

Dawn turned and greeted Lila with a smile.

"I hope you do not mind if I join you," Lila said.

"Please do," Tallis said. "I have so missed the company of other women."

Dawn scooted over for Lila to sit and as soon as she placed Thomas, her almost year old son down on the blanket, the lad crawled over to Adian and joined him in plucking the grass.

The women talked and laughed away almost two hours. It was not until Adian and Thomas began to fuss, needing a nap, and the twins started to stir with hunger that the three women got to their feet to take the children inside and see to their needs.

Dawn stopped when she turned and raised her hand to shelter her eyes from the sun, having caught the sight of riders up on the rise.

"Who is that with Cree?" Lila asked, shading her eyes to get a better look herself. She smiled. "It is Neil. Elsa will be glad he has returned. But who is the other man?"

The three women watched as the men approached the village, not surprised to see several of Cree's warriors following behind them.

Cree had been secretive earlier this morning when he told her he would be gone for several hours. She had asked him where he was going and he had told her to meet Neil who was on his way home from a mission he had sent him on.

Dawn watched with pride as the small troop entered the village. Any time Cree returned, villagers stopped what they were doing to stand and stare at him. He always made such an imposing figure, though none as imposing as the first day he had been brought into the village a captive of the then liege lord, Colum. His wrists had been tied, chest bare, and he was tugged along by a rope that Colum held while riding his horse. Yet Cree had walked with confidence and not an ounce of fear. And when his eyes met hers, she had shivered with fear, though now that she thought of it...it may have been with passion.

She smiled at the wicked thought and was glad he had returned, for she was looking forward to retiring early this evening with her husband. Or perhaps a quick trip to his solar would prove satisfying.

"Oh my God! Oh my God!" Tallis screamed, then scooped her son up in her arms and ran toward the riders. "Devin! Devin!"

The stranger, a tall, slim man with fine features, among the troop stopped his horse and dismounted slowly, a distinct limp to his gate as he tried to hurry to his wife.

Tallis continued to call out his name as if she could not quite believe it was truly him and when she reached him, he threw his arms around her and a now crying Adian.

Cree continued past them, directing his stallion toward Dawn.

Lila turned with tears in her eyes to Dawn. "Cree is a good man and the village was lucky the day he invaded it and claimed it. And I am glad he fell in love with my best friend. You deserve a good man."

Tears pooled in Dawn's eyes as Lila walked away, grateful for her friendship and her love.

"Are those happy tears trying to escape?" Cree asked, dismounting and slipping his arm around his wife's waist.

Dawn smiled and nodded and pointed past him.

"You want to know how I found Tallis's husband."

She nodded again.

"You forget I was once a mercenary. I had Neil make contact with one mercenary in particular that I had a long history with and had him inquire into the attack on Giles' son. He was generous with his information since Neil offered a generous fee for it. I wanted to know who paid the group to kill the Fitzbane family and prove what I had suspected...that Terran Fitzbane was behind it. Neil tracked the band down and to his great surprise found Devin Fitzbane alive, a slave of the mercenaries, and he negotiated a price to buy his freedom."

A tear fell down Dawn's cheek and Cree wiped it away. "Happy?"

She scrunched her arms against her, letting him know she was very happy.

"It also helped that I finally recalled why the name Tallis sounded familiar to me. About two years I happened upon an old acquaintance of mine who told me he was just about to carry out a mission he would have been handsomely paid for when it was suddenly aborted. The mission had been to take the life of a woman named Tallis. I can only assume that Fitzbane tried to eliminate Tallis before she could give birth. Why he aborted the mission, I could not say."

Dawn tapped her chest, excited and began to gesture.

"Tallis delivered her babe early." Cree nodded. "That would explain it. Why pay to have Tallis killed when she no longer carried the Fitzbane heir. It is good this has all been discovered. Tallis and Adian are finally safe."

The twins cried out at that moment and Dawn gestured as if shoveling food into her mouth.

"They are hungry," Cree said.

Dawn nodded.

Cree gave his wife a quick kiss. "So am I."

~~~

The evening was a cheerful one with Tallis and Devin reunited. Food, ale, and wine flowed as plentiful as conversation. Devin ate like a starving man, and though it was obvious he had suffered much the last three months, he did not speak of his ordeal.

"I think I will eat myself ill, the food is so delicious," Devin said with a laugh.

"Eat your fill and then some if you wish," Cree offered. "And you are welcome to remain here until you feel strong enough to return home."

"You have been more than generous to me and especially to my family. I will not continue to impose on your kindness. Besides, I wish to return home and see that my father is well and make certain I rid the clan of those who conspired against us, though I will forever be in your debt."

Tallis had not been able to keep her hands off her husband. She was forever touching him, resting a hand on his shoulder or on his arm, as if making sure that this was no dream and he was truly there with her.

"It will be good to be home again, though I fear that your father will not do what is necessary when it comes to his brother Terran," Tallis said. "He will never be more than what he is now, an evil man, and I fear your father will not see that."

Devin agreed with a nod. "I have thought the same myself."

"Have no worry," Cree said, "Terran will not be returning home with you. He dared to harm my wife and I will see him punished."

"Again I am in your debt," Devin said with a respectful nod. "My father has a good heart and I have no doubt he would forgive his brother as he has over the years."

"A mighty chieftain can have a good heart, but never a foolish one or his clan will suffer for it.

Evil deeds and disobedience must be punished and rules obeyed or discord will prevail and eventually chaos will rule. Remember that and you will be a good chieftain one day."

Cree turned to his wife and Dawn smiled. He did not have to say a word to her, she knew his thought. He was letting her know that he had not forgotten that she had disobeyed him.

Dawn leaned closer to him as if she were about to whisper to him and crossed her wrists.

"Aye, you are right. I should tie you up and punish you," he whispered, and then scowled, the image arousing him. "One of these days..." he shook his head, the image growing much too clear and he growing much too hard.

Dawn's smile grew and she crossed her heart several times and he wanted to throttle her since it was as if he heard her clearly.

Promises. Promises.

Dawn gestured that she was going to feed the twins and afterwards she would retire and wait for him in their bedchamber.

He silently cursed his thoughts of her naked in bed waiting for him since it did not help his arousal any. And naturally, time could not go fast enough after that. It was only an hour later, though it felt much longer to Cree that Devin and Tallis bid him good evening and retired to their room. Cree took a few moments to talk with Sloan, then made his way to his bedchamber.

He was eager to make love to his wife and could not take the stairs fast enough. He was surprised that he did not find her in their bed naked, waiting for him. She stood by the hearth in a delicate nightdress, the fire light creating a silhouette of her body beneath.

She was a beauty and the thought brought back a memory that had haunted him since the day he had spoken the words.

He walked over to her and slipped his hand around the back of her neck and tugged her to him to meet his lips that swooped down in a hungry kiss. His tongue shot into her mouth, catching her silent gasp before turning her senseless with his demanding kiss.

After only a moment, he pulled his mouth away from hers. "There is something I must tell you."

Her heart slammed in her chest, seeing his eyes fill with pain and she worried over what he was about to say.

"That day that Tallis arrived and you heard me say that I would have remembered a beauty such as her...I never meant those words. I meant only to see her reaction and what I could learn from it. When I turned and saw you there, I learned what I never expected to learn."

She scrunched her brow.

He kissed her lightly. "I learned that I would rather suffer the tortures of hell than to have you believe that I think another woman more beautiful than you. There is no woman that can come close to your beauty."

Dawn's heart soared with joy and she smiled so wide she was sure it devoured her entire face.

Cree smiled along with her, pleased to see how happy he had made her. Her smile faded suddenly and he grew worried. "What is wrong?"

She patted her chest and hung her head.

"What are you sorry about?"

She tapped his chest, then his mouth, and then herself and shook her head.

Cree nodded slowly. "For not obeying me." He turned and walked away from her to sit on the end of the bed. "You disobeyed me several times in a matter of two days and you forced me to punish the two guards who failed to keep you safe and in the keep."

She nodded and gestured again.

Cree shook his head. "No, you do not deserve their punishment. Their failure earned them their punishment."

She patted her chest.

He nodded. "Aye, you deserve to be punished for what you did. But what your punishment will be is what weighs heavily on me."

Dawn hung her head for a moment, then slipped her nightdress off her shoulders and let it fall to puddle around her feet. She took slow steps toward him.

Her beauty grew him hard in an instant.

She stopped beside him, smiled, and lowered herself over his knees, presenting her bare backside to him.

Cree smiled as his hand came softly down on her bottom, and said, "We are both going to enjoy this punishment, wife."

The End...not quite.

Highlander's Promise
A Cree & Dawn Short Story #2

by

Donna Fletcher

This is a work of fiction. Names, characters, places, and incidents are either the product of the author's imagination or are used fictitiously, and any resemblance to actual persons, living or dead, business establishments, events or locales is entirely coincidental.

Visit Donna's Web site
www.donnafletcher.com
www.facebook.com/donna.fletcher.author

Chapter One

Cree grabbed his wife around the waist, yanked her off the top of him, and rolled so that she lay beneath him. "Are you trying to kill me or yourself riding me that hard?"

Dawn turned her head, a tear falling from her eye.

"Damn," Cree mumbled and slipped off her to take her in his arms and tuck her naked body as close against him as he possibly could. "I know you do not want me to go, but I have no choice. The King commands it."

Dawn eased away from him to speak with her hands, having lacked a voice since birth, but her husband was accustomed to her way of speaking as long as she did not go too fast, a habit of hers when she grew angry or upset.

She pointed to him, then to her, and then brought two of her fingers together tightly and shook her head.

"I know we have not been separated for any length of time since we first met, but it cannot be helped. I must see to this matter for the King. I will only be gone two maybe three weeks. Believe me when I tell you I do not want to go. I do not want to leave you and the twins, but I will leave you well-protected. You have nothing to fear."

117

She patted her chest frantically and then his.

"Do not worry about me. I will see this mission done and return to you, and then you better be ready to ride me as hard as you have tonight, for I will be going mad having been without you for so long."

Dawn ran her hand along his jaw and mouth, outlining his lips with her thumb, and then pressed her cheek to his. She could not fathom being separated from him for that long and knew that a part of her would go with him, and she would not feel whole again until he returned to her.

"I love you, Dawn," Cree whispered in her ear. "You are my heart, my soul, every breath I take. Without you there is no life. There is no me. We are one... always and forever."

Tears ran down her cheeks and she wrapped her arms around his neck. She loved this man more than she ever thought it was possible to love. She wished she could speak aloud and tell him how she felt, but that would never be, so she spoke not only with her hands but also with her heart.

She took gentle hold of his hand, pressed it to her cheek, feeling its warmth, then placed it against her chest, holding it there for several moments, her eyes focused intently on his as she did so, then she slowly moved it off her chest to press against his.

Cree smiled. "You gave your heart to me shortly after we first met in that dark hut, frightened as you waited for me to emerge from the darkness. I could smell your fear and sense your courage. I have kept your heart tucked safely with me ever since, and I always will."

She cuddled closer to him, holding on to this moment—this night—for as long as she could, for tomorrow he would take his leave and she so feared she would never see him again.

"I promise I will come back to you, Dawn. You have my word," Cree said.

Dawn looked into his eyes, tapped his chest hard, then slapped her hand to her chest, and then to his.

"You most certainly will not come after me if a sorrowful fate should befall me, and I will have your word on that."

Dawn tightened her lips and stubbornly tucked her hands against her chest.

"I mean it, Dawn. Give me your word you will do nothing foolish."

Dawn pursed her lips tight and shook her head.

"I warn you now, wife. If you ever do anything so foolish, I will see you punished for it."

Dawn shook her head again, letting him know she did not care what he said.

"Disobey me, wife, and I will lay you naked across my knees and give you a good thrashing."

Her smile was so broad, he knew she laughed inside and knew why. "All right, so we both know you enjoy that, but I will think of some other befitting punishment for you."

Her hands moved ever so slowly and a tear slipped from the corner of her eye.

Cree wiped it away. "You do not care as long as I am home safe with you."

Dawn nodded and kissed him gently. It did not take long for the kiss to turn demanding and soon they were once again making love, knowing sunrise would come too soon, along with their goodbyes.

Chapter Two

Dawn shook her head as the scream rose up in her throat and echoed in her head. She grabbed her chest, the pain tearing at her, and glared at Sloan while fighting to keep her legs from collapsing out from under her. She did not struggle against the tears that ran from her eyes or wipe them away. They would never stop falling anyway.

Lila ran to her side and wrapped her arm around her, crying along with her best friend.

Dawn felt the hurt deep down in her heart.

"I am sorry, Dawn," Sloan said. "This should have never happened. Cree went as an emissary to King Alexander. Parlan Minnoch had no right or cause to take Cree prisoner. And with Minnoch castle impenetrable, it will be difficult to free him. I have sent word to the King that he demand Cree's immediate release."

Dawn's hands moved slowly, it being too much of an effort for her to lift them.

Lila interpreted. "And what happens to my husband while the message is being delivered to King? Does Cree languish in Minnoch's dungeons? Does he suffer the tortures of hell? Or does he..."

Dawn's hands stopped moving, not able to bring herself to admit that Cree could die.

"The only thing I can think to do right now is to return to Castle Minnoch with more men and attempt to negotiate Cree's release, while seeing if there is a way to free him if negotiations should fail." Sloan took hold of Dawn's hands, his heart aching for her when he felt how they trembled. "I will bring Cree back to you."

"Come, let me take you to your chambers away from this commotion," Lila said and led her from the Great Hall as Sloan shouted orders and warriors began to gather, all ready and willing to help rescue Cree.

Flanna, overseer of the keep and friend to Dawn, entered the bedchamber shortly after Lila and Dawn, tears brimming in her eyes. "I will see that a soothing brew is made for you."

Dawn shook her head while Lila nodded.

"He will escape," Flanna assured her, squeezing Dawn's chilled hand. "Did he not escape when taken prisoner here? There is no dungeon that can hold Cree."

Dawn wanted to believe Flanna, but she recalled overhearing Cree talking with Sloan before leaving on the mission.

"Parlan Minnoch is not a man to be trusted. He will pledge allegiance to King Alexander, and then stab him in the back when a better opportunity comes his way. He has no honor and no morals. His castle is a stronghold that few can breech and once inside escape would prove difficult. This mission will not go easy."

Escaping here, Dowell, from a hut that barely remained standing was far different from escaping a cell in the dungeons of Castle Minnoch. Besides, Cree had planned all along for Colum, the liege lord of Dowell at that time to capture him. His capture this time had not been planned.

"You should rest," Lila advised.

Dawn shook her head and gestured with her hands.

"Aye, go be with the twins. I will wait here for Flanna and bring the brew to you."

Dawn nodded and before going to the door, she gave Lila a firm hug.

"Cree is like no other man," Lila said, hugging her friend just as firmly. "He will come back to you."

Dawn nodded and left the room, her fear trailing after her.

The twins Valan and Lizbeth were napping, both having fed a short while before Sloan had arrived, Valan being hungrier than his sister as usual, and of course he fussed until Lizbeth was placed beside him. Five months now and his sleep was still restless if his sister was not next to him.

Three weeks and Dawn had barely slept without Cree beside her. The bed was not only empty, but so was her heart. She could not imagine endless nights ahead without him or the twins not seeing their da ever again. Their faces would light up with joy when he took them in his powerful arms. Valan would make sounds as if trying to speak to him, but

Lizbeth would simply lie content staring at him and each time the two stole his heart a bit more.

A tear slipped from her one eye, and there and then she knew what she had to do... she had to go rescue Cree.

~~~

It was late when she made her way to Old Mary's cottage. Lila had long since returned home to her husband Paul and baby Thomas. Sloan was much too occupied with his plans to pay her any attention and Flanna too busy seeing that the servants kept the horde of warriors supplied with food and drink.

Dawn walked in without knocking, knowing the old woman would be expecting her. As long as Dawn knew Old Mary, she had had a knowing about her and it was that knowing she would seek tonight.

It did not bode well seeing tears in Old Mary's eyes, for the last time she had it was when Dawn's mum died. Dawn shook her head, letting her own tears fall as she went to Old Mary to be wrapped in her frail, but loving arms.

After a few minutes of endless tears, Dawn eased away from her so that she could speak with her hands. The old woman and her mum had taught her to use her hands to make herself known, so Old Mary understood her gestures better than anyone.

Dawn hands moved with determination, letting Old Mary know that she intended to go rescue Cree.

124

Old Mary nodded. "Fate is a strange creature. Sometimes she is generous in showing me things and other times..." She shrugged. "She shows me nothing, but then she had shown me that you and Cree would have many children and so far that has not changed. So I would say things bode well for Cree's return." She chuckled at Dawn's quick response. "Aye, I agree. Cree must survive so that you can make him suffer for putting you through this pain." Her aging eyes turned serious. "This will not be an easy task for us."

Dawn tilted her head in question, pointing to Old Mary.

"You cannot go alone. You need someone to speak for you, and you most certainly cannot allow anyone to think that your loss of voice is permanent. It is becoming widely known that Cree has a voiceless wife, so we must take precautions. I will go with you."

Dawn shook her head vehemently.

"Do not waste time arguing with me or telling me I am too old and feeble for the arduous journey. Besides, who pays attention to an old woman? And who will save you from Cree when he sees you have come to rescue him?"

Old Mary was right about Cree being furious with her for endangering her life to rescue him, but that did not matter to her as long as she could free her husband and see him returned home safely.

"You need to find out Sloan's plans so that we do not cross his path and jeopardize our mission. No doubt he will attempt to negotiate with Minnoch for

Cree's release. The thing is... what does Minnoch want or gain from taking Cree prisoner?"

Dawn shook her head, having thought the same but having found no answer.

"One thing I have sensed about this situation is that we have no time to waste. For some reason, we must hurry and see this done as soon as possible. Go and find out what Sloan plans and when he will take his leave. He cannot know what you intend to do, so we cannot depart until he does. Now go and do what must be done."

Dawn hurried out of the cottage, feeling anxious over Old Mary's warning that they could not waste a moment. If she felt they must rush, then something was very wrong and that frightened Dawn. With hasty steps and a fearful heart, she returned to the keep, eager to be on her way to rescue her husband.

~~~

Dawn rode beside Old Mary in the cart. Their garments were worn and patched and had an odor about them that kept anyone from getting too close. The cart carried a bundle of rags smelling almost as badly as their garments. To anyone they would appear two peasant women, trying to sell what little they had to survive.

She had watched the surrounding countryside for the last five days with little interest, thinking of her departure from home. She had told Lila and Flanna the truth. Lila had tried to talk her out of

126

going, but Flanna had not. Dawn had finally convinced Lila when she asked her if she would do the same for Paul if he were in such a situation.

Dawn had instructed the two women that as soon as her departure became known they were to let everyone know that she and Old Mary went to join Sloan in his attempt to free Cree. And they were to make it clear to the remaining warriors that they were not to follow. They were needed at the keep to protect Cree's children. As far as the twins, Flanna and Lila would help look after them and Lila would help feed the twins along with other women in the village.

The hardest thing for Dawn had been hugging her *bairns* good-bye, rubbing her cheek against their soft, tiny ones and tapping their chests lightly to let them know she loved them.

Old Mary directed the lone horse off the well-traveled rode and behind a large tree. "It is time. We must do this now. We reach the castle by dusk as planned."

Dawn nodded and got down off the cart and went around the cart to help Old Mary climb down.

"Cree is not going to like this," Old Mary said, shaking her head, "but having given it endless thought, it is the only way for you to remain safe."

Dawn nodded and grabbed a pouch tucked under the seat of the cart. She pulled a long strip of cloth out of the pouch, then pulled a dagger from her boot and handed it to Old Mary.

Old Mary hesitated. "If there was another way—"

Dawn gave the old woman's stooped shoulder a squeeze, letting her know it was all right.

"This will hurt," Old Mary warned and Dawn once again gave the old woman's shoulder a reassuring squeeze.

They had discussed the plan over and over, Old Mary asking her repeatedly if she was certain she wanted to do this. There had never been any doubt in Dawn's mind. It was a necessary part of the plan and she would do anything to see their mission successful. Dawn nodded, squared her shoulders, and lifted her chin high.

Old Mary placed the dagger to Dawn's neck. "I must do this slowly so as not to make a mistake and cut you too deep, especially with these gnarled fingers of mine. And you must not dare move. Stay as still as a statue."

Dawn gestured for her not to worry. There was little she would not do or pain she would not suffer if it helped to free her husband.

"You are a courageous one, Dawn," Old Mary said and slowly began to run the blade across her soft flesh, careful not cut where her life's blood flowed.

Dawn cringed and shut her eyes against the pain. She fought to keep still and fought to stop herself from grabbing Old Mary's arm to end it. This had to be done. It was the only plausible excuse for her not being able to talk. It could not be faked, for sentries at a town's gatehouse were known to ask many questions and if one of Minnoch's warriors should yank the cloth down and find nothing, she and Old Mary would join Cree in the dungeon.

She opened her eyes once Old Mary was done and a few tears fell from them.

"You must love Cree very much to face his wrath when he discovers you allowed your throat to be cut to rescue him," Old Mary said, letting some of the blood run down and stain the top of Dawn's garment. Then she gently wrapped the worn, but clean, drab strip of cloth around Dawn's neck and ran a thinner strip over it to tie and hold the bandage in place. She smiled as the blood soaked through in spots. "I do not think it will leave a scar, but I cannot be certain."

Dawn shook her head as she tapped her chest.

"I know you do not care, but Cree will, for it will always be a reminder of what you suffered for him. Now come, we cannot waste another minute. We must reach the village of Loudon's gate before it is closed for the night."

They were soon on the road again, the cart ambling along as if the two women were in no hurry to get anywhere. When they were actually desperate to reach their destination and find a way to free Cree.

~~~

Dusk was just beginning to settle when Dawn and Old Mary approached the gatehouse. Both women stared at the high gray stone walls sounding the town and the wall walk where several sentries stood.

Old Mary's words came back to Dawn. *It will not be an easy task.*

Old Mary brought the cart to a stop at the gate. Two guards of fair size approached them, each carrying a spear and neither looking too pleased to see them.

"What is your purpose in coming to Loudon?" the one asked and took a step back after getting a whiff of them. The other guard followed suit.

"A day or two of rest, if you please, before we move on," Old Mary said, nodding as she spoke.

"What happened to her?" the other guard asked, pointing the spear at Dawn.

"Her husband took a knife to her for talking too much and now she cannot talk at all, so he threw her out," Old Mary said.

"If she cannot talk, how do you know that is what happened to her?" the one guard demanded.

"She is my granddaughter and I got tossed out with her."

The guard on Dawn's side stepped closer, wrinkling is nose against the foul odor, and pointed his spear at her. "Raise your chin."

Dawn did as told.

The guard used the tip of his spear to tug the cloth down, revealing the wound that began to bleed from his weapon roughly tugging the cloth away from it. He cringed and shook his head. "Disgusting and probably well-deserved. Take the path on the right to the end, and you are not to stay for more than a day or two. We need the room for those who soon will be arriving and are willing to pay to see the execution," the guard said and waved them through.

"As you say, kind sir," Old Mary said and drove the cart through, the gate closing shut for the night behind them.

Dawn gripped the sides of her skirt. *Execution?* Who was being executed? And why had Old Mary not asked.

As if reading her thoughts, the old woman whispered, "The less interest we show the better. Now pay attention. We need to know our surroundings."

The village was quiet, but then autumn had arrived with a chill, chasing many inside their cottages once night fell. Dawn took in all she could, though it was difficult not to take her eyes off the castle in the distance as the cart ambled down the path. It rose like a mighty beast, the narrow windows more like eyes that spied on all and somewhere deep in its bowels was her husband.

"Do not stare," Old Mary whispered.

Dawn quickly lowered her head, fighting against the tears that threatened her eyes. She forced them away since tears would not help save her husband.

Old Mary kept her voice low. "Those in need are not the only ones to seek shelter here for the night. Thieves pick on the most vulnerable and the soldiers here care little if they do. We must stay watchful."

Dawn nodded.

Old Mary brought the cart to a stop at the far end of the village, where other travelers were already camped. Some were asleep under their wagons and some lingered by the campfires they had lit, eating what meager food they possessed. A few men cast curious glances their way, one man blatantly rubbing himself when his eyes settled on Dawn.

She ignored him and was grateful for the dagger she carried in her boot. She hurried off the cart, then went to help Old Mary down.

"Away with your hands," Old Mary snapped loudly. "It is bad enough your husband threw you out and me along with you. I will not see my skin rot as yours does beneath your garments."

Dawn lowered her head and scratched at her arms as she backed away, understanding Old Mary's intentions. No man would touch Dawn if he believed he would be left with rotting flesh.

"See to the horse," Old Mary ordered.

Dawn hurried to tend the animal and after that she got a small fire going, worried that the night chill would cause Old Mary's bones to ache. They ate a small amount of food, taking care not to let anyone see they had more. They were saving some for barter and some for Cree once they freed him, if either proved necessary.

"In the morning, I will ask around and see what I can find out," Old Mary whispered as she stretched out on the blanket Dawn had spread on the ground, knowing her bones would surely protest tomorrow.

Dawn could not sleep. She was not only concerned for their safety. She was worried for Cree. Sloan had avoided given her an explanation as to why Minnoch had taken Cree prisoner or what plans the man had for her husband. Did he mean him harm? The guard's words came back to haunt her. *Execution.* Could it be Cree who was going to be put to death? And if so why? It made no sense to her, but she had learned that men needed little reason to do harm to others, though women were also not exempt from doing harm, her own birth mother having been one of them.

She yawned and closed her eyes, only to open them moments later. The camp remained quiet as did the village. The only movement was the sentries on the wall walks. It would not be easy to free Cree from this place with sentries patrolling the wall walks and the gatehouse closing at dusk. The only way would be to sneak him out in the cart during the day. But how did she get him out of the dungeon with enough time to spare before someone discovered him gone?

Dawn slept on and off throughout the night and the more she pondered over how to free Cree, the more she lost hope. It was when the sun rose on a new day that hope returned to her, for she knew there and then that if she did not free her husband... she would join him in his cell.

Chapter Three

"Word has gone out. He is going to be beheaded."

Old Mary laid a hand on Dawn's leg to calm her. It had not been long after everyone in camp had woken that talk had turned to the infamous prisoner held in Minnoch's dungeons.

"Wagers are being taken that Cree will break free before that," someone said.

Laughter circled the small group of men talking and one voice was heard saying, "That is a fool's wager. No one escapes Minnoch's dungeons."

Another chimed in, "Death is the only escape from that hell hole."

The small band of men dispersed after agreeing they would wait and see who won the wager for themselves.

"We need to hurry," Old Mary urged and Dawn nodded eagerly.

Dawn refused to let the grim talk defeat her or think that the suddenly gray skies were an omen of doom. If anything, knowing her husband's fate made her more determined than ever to free him, nothing would stop her now.

It was market day in the village and the stalls were busy with people trading their wares. Everywhere Dawn and Old Mary went talk was of the prisoner Cree and his fate. Wagers were being made, mostly in Minnoch's favor.

"Make way for Lord Minnoch! Make way!" a solider shouted and people scurried out of the way.

Dawn turned to take a look and grabbed Old Mary's arm, rushing her behind a cart. It was not the sight of Minnoch that made her take cover, though one look at him did instill fear. He was fair in height, thick in muscle, his head completely bald and a vicious scar ran from the top of his brow down to the corner of his eye. His features were not appealing, though they were memorable in an ominous way. No, it was not Minnoch she hid from, it was the two men who rode behind him... Sloan and Elwin.

Several warriors formed two lines on either side of one of several wooden doors that ran along the stone wall of the keep. The door opened and a guard appeared. He gave a respectful bob of his head to Minnoch and limped to the side. Two of Minnoch's warriors entered before him, followed by Sloan and Elwin and two more of Minnoch's warrior's trailed behind them.

The door closed and several warriors stepped in front of it.

Old Mary whispered to Dawn. "Stay here and watch."

Dawn gave Old Mary a quick glance as she trailed after the guard who had limped away, then she turned her attention to the closed door and waited.

~~~

Cree heard several footfalls approach long before the group reached his cell. He was on his feet when the cell door swung open and when the guard entered with a torch, he stumbled back upon seeing Cree standing there as powerful as ever.

Sloan entered along with Elwin, Minnoch following them in.

Minnoch approached Cree. "Tell your men why you are rotting in my dungeon."

"Tell them your lies yourself," Cree said.

Minnoch turned and spat the words out with anger. "He stole from me."

"What lies do you spew?" Sloan demanded.

"Not lies," Minnoch said and stretched his hand out to one of his soldiers. The man dropped something into Minnoch's hand. "I left him alone in my solar for a moment and I returned to find he had broken the seal on my chest and had these in his hands."

Cree was the only one who did not glance at his hand. He knew what he held, rubies and emeralds that Minnoch himself had taken out of the chest in his solar.

"King Alexander insults me, sending a thief to see if I am truly loyal to the crown. I will show the King just how loyal I am by beheading the man who no doubt would steal from the King himself," Minnoch said.

While Elwin drew everyone's attention by protesting loudly, Cree looked to Sloan and without a word being exchanged, gave Sloan a barely noticeable nod.

"Your complaints are useless. This thief will die in three days' time and Loudon Village will celebrate," Minnoch said.

"I will have time alone with Lord Cree," Sloan demanded.

Minnoch laughed. "So you can attempt to plan an escape? I am no fool. Say your good-byes, for the next time you see him will be when the axe comes down upon his neck." He turned to one of his men. "Take them out of here."

Sloan and Elwin protested loudly as they were led out, while Minnoch remained behind with two warriors.

"The King underestimated me as did you. I will see you dead and claim your lands as mine and the King will have no choice but to grant me them for ridding him of such a dishonorable warrior." He turned to go, then stopped and turned to face Cree once more. "As for your wife, I have wondered what it would be like to poke a voiceless woman." He laughed and turned to go.

"Minnoch," Cree said with such command that the man could not help but turn and face him. "I am going to enjoy killing you."

Minnoch could not stop the shudder that ran like a cold chill through his body when for a brief moment he believed that Cree would see him dead, and he was relieved when the key turned and clicked in the lock behind him.

~~~

Dawn glanced around while she waited, taking in all she could, from the constant stream of sentries on the walk wall, to the double guards at the dungeon's entrance and the continuous presence of guards wherever one looked. From what she saw, the prison was a stronghold and she wondered how she would ever get inside let alone get Cree out.

The door suddenly swung open and Sloan burst out, Elwin behind him, both men angrier than she had ever seen them.

"You cannot be serious," Sloan said, turning on Minnoch when he joined them outside.

"Cree stole from me and will pay the price... death. I will lay claim to his lands just as he did with Dowell, and the King will thank me for it."

"You falsely accuse Cree and plan to behead him before the King can even be made aware of it, and you think the King will be pleased? And you think the King will allow you Cree's lands? Are you a fool?" Sloan asked as if he could not believe the man's ignorance.

Minnoch took a brisk step toward Sloan. "Never dare to call me a fool again. Your chieftain will suffer the executioner's axe in three days' time. I will seize all his holdings and as for his wife and children? Their fate will be at my discretion. And if you think the King will bother himself with such a trivial matter, then you are the fool. I will pledge my fealty to King Alexander and he will be glad of it."

Dawn pressed her hand tightly against her stomach, his words roiling her insides until she thought she would lose what little she had eaten this morning. She could not believe his words. Cree condemned to death and she and the twin's fate left to Minnoch? It could not be allowed to happen.

"And if you think to attack me, think again. I have more than enough warriors to defeat you," Minnoch said with the confidence of one who had already tasted victory.

Dawn knew that Sloan would not stand by and see Cree beheaded. He had brought more warriors with him when he returned and she had no doubt he had informed clan leaders loyal to Cree of the situation. The problem was time and Minnoch was using it to his advantage. It would take time to amass enough warriors to breach these castle walls. Sloan would not wait. He would attack and attempt to free Cree and no doubt Sloan and Cree's warriors would be slaughtered along with him. Cree had to be freed before it was too late.

"You will regret this, Minnoch," Sloan said and he and Elwin hurried off.

Minnoch lingered, talking to his guards and Dawn slowly wandered closer, hoping to hear what they were discussing and hoping it might be of some help in freeing Cree. When she realized one guard had begun to stare at her, she casually moved away... but not soon enough.

"You there!" the guard shouted and that was when Dawn realized it was the guard who had been at the gatehouse and had pushed her neck bandage down with his spear.

Dawn froze, knowing she had no other choice but to obey.

The guard said something to Minnoch and he grinned like a man who was about to do something that would bring him much pleasure.

"What are you doing?" Old Mary said, coming up behind her and slapping her in the back of the head. "Have you not gotten us into enough trouble?"

Two guards followed Minnoch as he approached the women. "She has no voice?" he asked of Old Mary.

"No, sir," Old Mary said with a bob of her head. "The fool could not keep her mouth shut, so her husband slit her throat and kicked her out of the house."

"Why not simply cut her tongue out?"

Old Mary shrugged. "I cannot speak for him. I do not know."

"I have use for her, two days should do, and then I will return her to you," Minnoch said.

Old Mary was quick to try and dissuade him, knowing he was not a man to trust. Once he had hold of Dawn, she might never see her again. "She is not a clean one, sir. Her skin rots in private places."

"All the better," Minnoch said with a laugh.

"Please, sir," Old Mary begged with tears in her eyes. "She is my granddaughter and she is all I have. Please do not hurt her."

Minnoch laughed again. "That will be up to the prisoner Cree. He either accepts the generous gift I give him or I give her to the soldiers."

Old Mary looked to Dawn. "You please the prisoner whatever way he wants." She hugged Dawn and whispered, "I give you my word, I will come for you and Cree tomorrow night."

"Take her!" Minnoch ordered.

The soldier poked Dawn with the opposite end of his spear and Dawn trembled as she made her way to the door in the stone wall, though it was not out of fear. She was going to be exactly where she wanted to be... with her husband. And tomorrow night, she and Cree would be free, for when Old Mary gave her word, she kept it.

Dawn stepped through the door and made sure to take in everything she could, though with the guard continuing to prod her in the back, hurrying her along, did not give her much time to see as much as she would have liked to. Besides, the place was dank and dark with barely enough torches to light the passageway. They passed the guards' quarters and from what she could see there were many. How Old Mary would get them out, she did not know? But Dawn trusted her word.

With a guard in front of her and the one with the spear behind her and Minnoch following them, they made their way down a flight of stairs and into a narrow passageway with two cells on the left and two on the right, and Dawn's stomach roiled from the foul odor. She was grateful they did not stop. The thought that Cree would have to endure such a horrid stench turned her stomach even more. They continued on, taking another set of stone stairs down. The deeper they went the more worried Dawn grew. How would they ever get out of this place?

They entered another passageway, two torches barely casting sufficient light on the area. The guard in front of her stopped and the guard with the spear took tight hold of her arm.

Minnoch stepped to her side and Dawn was surprised to see two more guards enter the narrow passage and flank the door of the lone cell with a narrow slit at the top that could barely be seen.

"I have a very special gift for you, Cree... a woman to entertain you for a couple of days. And since I am aware that you like a woman who has no voice, I found you one. Have a look."

Minnoch did not wait for Cree to respond, he gave a nod to the guard who held her, and he and the other guard yanked and tore at her garments until she stood naked before them.

Dawn shut her eyes, no man but Cree had ever seen her naked and the only solace she took in suffering such an indignity was that it would possibly save her husband's life. Nothing was more important than that.

"You are lucky, Cree, she has a fine body, one I would not mind plowing, but I like to hear a women scream when I take her." Minnoch nodded to the one guard.

He quickly drew a dagger from the sheath at his waist and sliced the bandage at her neck, letting it fall to the ground.

Minnoch laughed. "Her husband grew tired of her endless chatter and slit her throat then threw her out. She is all yours now, though if you do not want her she can service the guards for the night." He nodded to a guard by the door.

The guard inserted a key in the lock and swung the door open.

One of the guards shoved her toward the door, though it looked more like a yawning black hole she stumbled toward it.

"Your choice, Cree," Minnoch said with a laugh.

Silence hung heavy, not even a breath was heard as all eyes looked upon the black hole and waited.

A hand suddenly shot out of the darkness, grabbed her arm, and yanked her in. The door slammed shut, the key clicking in the lock.

Chapter Four

Dawn was never so glad to feel her husband's arms close tightly around her and she pressed her cheek against his naked chest. She fought back the tears that threatened to spill. She would not cry. She would not let Minnoch bring her to tears.

"I do not hear you plowing her, Cree. Do I need to send one of my warriors in there to show you how it is done?" Minnoch said and laughter echoed in the passageway.

Cree lifted her and she barely had time to get her legs around his waist before he slammed her back against the door so that it creaked in protest, then he pretended to take her, pounding his hand viciously against the door as he held her firm against him with his other hand. He grunted repeatedly, and then let out one last, long grunt.

"I will be sure to let your wife know how you spent your last few days and do my best to console her," Minnoch said and loud laughter soon drifted off as the passage emptied.

"I am going to take great pleasure in killing that bastard," Cree whispered angrily near his wife's ear. His voice softened, though the anger did not leave it when he asked, "Have you been harmed?"

Dawn tapped his arm twice, answering no.

Cree quickly shifted her in his arms and carried her deeper into the dark cell, walking without the slightest hesitation, as if he could see the small space clearly. He lowered them both to a spot on the ground, settling her on his lap, tucking her close and keeping firm hold of her. He turned silent, saying nothing.

Dawn knew her husband well. She could see, sense, and feel when things troubled or angered him. Then there were those times when his wrath surfaced and no one—absolutely no one—would dare go near him, except Dawn.

She felt that wrath smoldering in him now and she did the only thing she could think of... she took his hand and pressed it firm against her chest, then she pressed it to his chest, and she repeated the gesture over and over and over. *I love you. I love you. I love you.*

His fury tempered, but did not fade.

"And my love for you runs as strongly as yours does for me, wife, which is why I am both overjoyed and furious to hold you in my arms. You have much to explain, but first..." He took hold of her chin, tilting it up and brought his lips down on hers.

His demanding kiss stole her breath, her heart, and her soul, and she got lost in it. Time and place did not exist, only the two of them and their hearts that once again beat together as one.

When it ended, he rested his brow to hers and whispered, "Good God, Dawn, what are you doing here?"

It was not easy gesturing in the dark and his frequent interruptions did not help.

"You came to rescue me? You endangered yourself over a fool's errand?"

She continued.

"Old Mary is with you? Are you two daft?"

After several more interruptions, Dawn pressed her finger to his lips, ordering him silent.

He let her finish, then pressed his finger to her lips.

She smiled. She loved that he treated her as if she truly had a voice, but then she did. It was just heard differently than others.

"If we were home the keep's rafters would tremble with how loudly I would chastise you. Do you not have faith in me? Do you think me weak?"

Dawn tapped his arm twice and twice again as she shook her head. A tear trickled from her eye as she took her hand and pretended to chop at the side of his head, reminding him of the beheading.

"I have lost my head to only one person... you."

Her body shook with laughter, though a shiver from a sudden chill quickly stole it from her.

"Damn," Cree muttered and ran his hand up and down her back, trying to rub warmth into her. "They gave me no bedding, no blankets. I have nothing to wrap you in."

Dawn patted his arm.

"My arms are not enough to keep you warm and if you catch a chill and die on me, do not think it will stop me from coming after you and punishing you for not obeying me."

Dawn laughed again, then sighed and snuggled her body comfortably against him.

"How can you be content here in this wretched place?" he asked, feeling her body ease in his arms.

She tapped his chest, then hers, and shrugged.

"As long as we are together, it does not matter to you?"

She tapped his arm once.

With it being dark, it took a few hand gestures for him to understand what she asked next. "You want to know how I planned to escape?" One tap to his arm had him continuing, though not answering her question. "And what of your plan? How do you expect to get both of us out of here?"

Dawn gestured slowly.

"Old Mary will rescue us tomorrow? You cannot be serious."

Dawn nodded and tapped his arm once.

"An old woman bent and gnarled with age will free us from the bowels of this place?" he asked incredulously.

Dawn nodded again.

He was about to argue with her when they both heard footfalls approach.

Dawn's arms went around her husband, holding him tight.

Cree felt her fear of being taken from him and his anger soared. He quickly shifted her body so that she straddled him, keeping his back to the door and tucking her head against his chest. His hands went to her backside and he lifted her up and down in a motion that made it seem she was riding him. And he snapped, "Harder women! Harder!"

Light suddenly filtered through the narrow slit in the door.

"Minnoch will be pleased to know you are enjoying your gift." A snorting laugh faded along with his footfalls.

Cree waited a moment to make certain the guard was gone, only then did he lift his wife and rest her in his lap again. His arms hurried around her and feeling that her back had chilled again began rubbing warmth back into it.

He pressed his warm cheek to her cool one and whispered in her ear. "You feel how hard I am, how much I want you. But then you are well aware that my desire runs strong for you all the time, and you make no secret of your desire for me. But as badly as I want you, never would I make love to you in such a horrid place and for others to see." He felt her cheek rise against his in a smile and he felt her nod. She eased away from him and it took him a moment to understand her gestures, then he smiled. "You are right. This is the second time you were locked away with me and expected to please me. I recall how much you feared me when first meeting you."

She gestured again.

"What do you mean you still fear me?" he demanded. "If you feared me you would obey me and your presence here in this cell proves you do not obey me."

Dawn pressed her hand to his cheek for a moment before gesturing again.

Cree took her hand and kissed her palm. "Never fear that I would stop loving you. It is not possible. Besides, you belong to me and I keep what is mine."

She thumped his chest, then thumped hers.

He brushed his lips over hers. "Aye, I belong to you and no other. You are stuck with me."

She hugged him tight, letting him know that he was also stuck with her and she would never let him go.

"Old Mary will get us out tomorrow night," Cree said as if saying it aloud forced him to believe it.

Dawn nodded and assured him with gestures that Old Mary would not fail them.

"Tell me how the twins do."

Dawn told him how much they miss him, especially Lizbeth. She told him how her eyes widened and how her tiny head would turn from side to side as if eager to hear her da's voice whenever someone entered the room. And how she would scowl just like him when she did not hear it.

Talk faded between them and they sat in silence, Cree continuing to caress her bare back, arms, and tucking her legs up close so he could keep warmth in them as well.

After a while Cree's hand drifted over her shoulder and up along her neck, then ever so slowly his fingers felt along her throat.

Dawn tensed. She was waiting for this moment and wondered why it had not come sooner.

"Seeing you here in such danger with little opportunity to keep you from harm and get you out of here safely had my anger near to erupting. And when they striped you bare, I wanted to snap every one of their necks, which I intend to still do. But when Minnoch had the bandage pulled off your neck, I felt a fear grip me that I have never felt before. I thought once he saw that you had suffered no wound, he would discover your identity and there was no telling what he would do."

He paused a moment and Dawn could feel his body grow taut with anger.

He ran one finger over the wound along her neck. "Imagine my shock when I saw this."

Her hand went to his to brush it away, but he pushed her hand away.

"No! I want to feel for myself what was done to you. At first when I caught a glimpse of it, all I could think of was how I was going to slowly slit the person's throat who had done this to you and watch him bleed to death. Then an absurd thought came to me. You did this to yourself so that no one would suspect you were my wife."

Dawn nodded, not wanting to implicate Old Mary. He would eventually find out, but now was not the time. She felt his anger rumble deep in his chest and thought better of offering any kind of explanation for what she had done. None would make a difference to him.

He spread his hand over the wound. "I want to lash out at you for being so foolish, though your foolishness also saved you, but if you had obeyed me in the first place you would be home safe with the twins."

She shook her head.

"Do not argue with me, woman!"

Dawn tensed at the harshness of his growling whisper.

"You have placed your life needlessly in danger and took the chance of killing yourself by slicing," —he stopped abruptly— "Old Mary cut your throat, did she not?" He did not let her answer. "She would have never let you do it yourself nor would she let you attempt to rescue me alone, since she knows you well and knew there would be no way of stopping you. Bless that woman for being so wise."

Dawn made no move to respond.

"Will it scar?" he asked the harshness in his voice replaced with concern.

Dawn shrugged, letting him know she was not sure.

"It will always be a reminder—"

Dawn pressed her finger to his lips and gestured.

"Of how much you love me," Cree said when she pressed her hand to her chest and then to his and kept it there. "Your love for me is never in doubt, either is your penchant for disobeying me."

She could not help but smile.

151

"Enjoy this small victory, for it will be your last. I intend to find a punishment that will finally have you doing as I tell you."

Her hands gestured too quickly in response and she had to repeat herself a few times.

"Are you asking me if I will always protect you?" Cree asked annoyed.

Dawn nodded while tapping is arm once.

"How could you even think I would not protect you?"

Dawn quickly thumped her chest, then his.

"You do the same? I think not, since I do not need protecting."

Dawn waved her hand around the cell.

"So help me, wife—" Footfalls silenced him, but only for a moment. "On your knees," he ordered.

Dawn did as he said, thinking how he protected her now, keeping the guard from seeing her naked body each time he pretended to couple with her.

"I win the wager," one guard said. "I told you he would be poking her again. Plow her good, Cree. You do not have much time left."

They waited until Cree pretended to finish, draping his body over his wife as if spent in climax.

When their footfalls faded, Cree took his wife in his arms again and she hugged him tight. Anger stirred in him for what his wife was suffering and somehow he was going to make certain that all those involved suffered worse for it.

Dawn rested her head on her husband's chest. Worry and fatigue were beginning to take its toll on her. She had barely slept since Cree's departure and being with him now, feeling safe for the moment, she found herself growing sleepy.

"Rest," Cree whispered when he felt her yawn and her body go limp in his arms.

Dawn could not fight the fatigue and the safety of her husband's strong arms gave her the will to surrender to it.

Cree rested his cheek on the top of her head, not caring that the scent of her hair was far from appealing. She was here with him now and the ache that had wrenched at his gut since the day he had left her was finally gone. He closed his eyes and let himself enjoy this moment if only for a short time.

Several footfalls woke them, neither of them knowing how long they had been asleep, and Cree was quick to get them both to their feet. This time, however, he did not pretend to couple with her. He pushed her behind his back.

"Say your good-byes. Minnoch says you have had enough fun with her," the one guard said with a laugh.

Fear raced through Dawn and she did her best to stamp it down. She did not want to leave Cree, but she would have a better chance of rescuing him being free than locked in here with him. And standing behind, almost on top of him, she could feel his muscles beginning to grow taut with anger. She could not let him stop them from taking her. It would ruin any chance of freeing him.

She gestured quickly to him.

He whispered, though did not turn around to face her. "Yes, you will go, but if they dare lay a hand on you in front of me, or at all, I will kill them."

She gestured quickly again.

"You will not come back for me," he ordered in a harsh whisper.

Dawn hurried around him as the door flew open.

Cree clenched his hands to stop himself from reaching out and stopping her.

Dawn did not need to force tears to her eyes, they came easily, having to leave her husband locked away in here. She reached out, not caring who was there only wanting them to believe she was grateful to be free.

"Stop your crying, you fool. If you had listened to your husband in the first place you would not be in this mess."

Cree never felt so grateful as he did now, seeing his wife fall into Old Mary's arms, and he sent her a message that left no doubt he meant to be obeyed. "Take the crying bitch and keep her. The smell of her rot disgusts me."

Old Mary draped a blanket around Dawn and gave her a shove. "Get moving. We leave in the morning."

Cree shut his eyes tight and clenched his fists even tighter as the door slammed shut and the key turned in the lock. When he got his hands on his wife he was going to give her a good thrashing. When Old Mary had given her a push, Dawn had held up her hand and two of her fingers were crossed. She was letting him know she would not be separated from him. She was coming back to free him.

Chapter Five

"Keep going, I've had enough of your laziness," Old Mary said, poking Dawn from behind.

Dawn kept the blanket tight around her and was glad for Old Mary's prodding. Hearing her voice, knowing she was there, gave Dawn courage. She hated leaving Cree behind, but knew it was necessary. There had been too many guards and more would have been alerted if Cree had made an attempt to escape.

Her gesture of joined fingers let him know she would return, though she knew he would not be happy about it. It made no difference to her. She would free her husband whether he thought it dangerous for her to do so or not.

When they reached the room where the guards were stationed, one stepped out and blocked their path.

"How about a quick poke before you go?" the guard said his smile revealing rotting teeth.

"Go on and give him a good poke," Old Mary said, giving her a shove.

A foul stench suddenly rose up around Dawn.

"Let me get her cleaned up first," Old Mary said, shoving her aside to reveal a putrid fluid where Dawn had stood.

Dawn cringed while hiding her smile, familiar with the smell of water fouled by decaying fish guts. How Old Mary came by it or knew she would make use of it was something Dawn would not question, though she was forever grateful.

"Be gone with you," the guard shouted, gagging at the stench.

Another guard hurried Old Mary and Dawn along the passageway and practically tossed them out the door.

Dawn was surprised to see that it was night.

"Hurry, we do not have much time," Old Mary urged, pushing Dawn toward the shadows of the nearby trees. She pulled a sack form beneath her tunic and handed it to Dawn. "Hurry into these." Her voice grew soft. "I saw that Cree was well enough, but what of you? Are you all right?"

Old Mary had always worried over her and she assured the old woman that she was fine, though anxious to free Cree.

"A plan is set and we must see it done," Old Mary whispered.

Once Dawn was dressed in less foul smelling garments, Old Mary took her arm and walked out of the shadows.

"My bones ache, lass. Let us return to camp and rest so we can leave by morning," Old Mary said for those close enough to hear.

Dawn grew anxious. Old Mary was letting anyone who could hear her know they were leaving tomorrow, which meant she had a solid plan that could very well free Cree.

When they reached where they were camped, they found that their cart had been ransacked, its contents strewn about. They pretended to be upset, though it mattered little to them. Nothing worth stealing had been left. Dawn had tucked the food pouch beneath the cart and Old Mary had kept her pouch of herbs tied at her waist.

"We leave at sunrise," Old Mary said as they tossed the last of the smelly rags back in the cart.

"Make it the crack of sunrise," said a warrior passing by. "We need the room for those willing to pay to watch the beheading in two days."

Old Mary sat poking at the fire with a stick and complaining how useless Dawn was. It was when some nearby men began talking loud enough to drown her out, as if tired of hearing the old woman grumble that Old Mary began to whisper to Dawn. "Listen well, I have found a way into the prison and I believe I have a plan that will work."

Dawn felt hope rise and squeeze at her heart.

"I convinced the guard with the limp that I can cure him of his ailment with my special brew and healing touch. I offered proof with a taste of my special brew and laid my hands on his sore leg muscles with strength enough to ease his ache. Both were enough to alleviate his pain some and have him believe I could rid him of the cursed pain completely. I told him I would need a quiet place where I could work on him with no interruptions."

Dawn's heart began to quicken.

"He told me of a jail door that only he has the key to. I am to go there when the village is well

158

asleep for the night and he will let me in. I will prepare a brew and as soon as he falls asleep, I will let you in and we will get Cree out," —Old Mary hesitated a moment— "I must remain there and see him wake, so he does not think anything is wrong and alert others. Besides, we cannot leave until sunrise when the gate opens. You must get Cree to the cart and hide him beneath the heap of rags. I will return just before sunrise and we will be at the gate as it opens and we will leave this retched place."

Dawn squeezed her hand and Old Mary held it there, for she would not take a chance of anyone seeing Dawn gesture to her.

"I know you worry for me, but I worry just the same for you and Cree. Together we can see this done, and then God help the fool Minnoch, for nothing will stop Cree from killing him."

~~~

The rain brought thunder with it and many took shelter beneath their carts or wagons and some sought shelter in whatever structure they would not be thrown out of for the night. It made it that much easier for Old Mary and Dawn to sneak around, since few would venture out in the rain.

Old Mary left Dawn in the night shadows, her garments beginning to soak, as she tapped at the door. The guard quickly opened it and ushered Old Mary in, giving a hasty glance around to make certain no one saw them.

Dawn waited impatiently, her insides quivering and her heart thumping much too fast. This rescue had to succeed. Nothing could go wrong. Nothing. This would be their only chance. It seemed like forever before the door opened and Old Mary waved her in.

"We have little time, Old Mary said. "He will sleep for only so long and we must be careful not to let the other guards know of our presence."

Dawn gestured quickly.

Old Mary shook her head. "The other guards do not come up this far, since this area is where the food is delivered, and then carried down to the cells. Once you reach a certain section you will recognize it and know where to go from there." Old Mary handed her a ring of keys.

"Make haste and be as silent as your voice." Old Mary hugged her. "I will be here waiting for you and Cree, and we will be gone from this place before you know it."

Dawn did not waste a minute. She kept her steps light as she walked along the, stone hallway, keeping close to the wall and the shadows. It was not difficult to stay in the shadows since the wall torches let off little light. When she reached a staircase that joined another, she recognized where she was and took the steps carefully. And just as carefully and quietly, she made her way through the passageway that held the four cells, two on either side that she had seen when she had first come this way. She did not want to think of the poor souls that were locked behind the doors. There was nothing she could do for them. She was here for Cree.

She reached the second staircase and her thumping heart began to pound madly in her chest. Soon, very soon she would be with Cree again and this time he would leave with her. Footfalls suddenly approached and she braced herself against the dank wall, letting the darkest shadow she could find consume her.

The footfalls grew louder and in a few seconds a guard walked past her, so close that she feared he would be able to smell her, but then the already foul odor in the air no doubt helped to disguise her own unpleasant scent.

Once he passed by her, his footfalls no longer heard, she hurried to the lone cell and gently shoved the key in the lock, opened the door, and slipped in, closing the door behind her.

An arm snagged her around the waist and yanked her back against his hard chest while a harsh whisper sounded in her ear, "You disobey me yet again."

Dawn pressed a finger to his lips and with quick gestures let him know he was to follow her lead.

He was about to say something when footfalls sounded again, no doubt the guard returning this way. In one swift motion, Cree drew them both into a corner of the cell and there they remained wrapped around each other as the guard approached. As soon as the guard made his way passed the door, they slipped out, locked it, and

Dawn lead him up the two flights of stairs to freedom.

Cree was not surprised to see Old Mary when they came upon the woman.

"No time to explain," Old Mary said. "You must go with Dawn and stay hidden where she puts you until it is safe to come out. Now hurry."

Again Cree did not argue, though it was difficult to hold his tongue. He followed Dawn out and saw Old Mary gesture to her and his wife shake her head. Old Mary's head kept nodding as she swung the door shut behind them and the key clicked in the metal lock.

Cree looked at his wife. She shook her head, hoping he understood that he was not to worry that it was part of the plan and he did not protest. He continued hurrying along with her, yanking her deeper into the shadows when he caught sight of a sentry along the walk wall.

They waited there, wrapped in the shadow's protective embrace, the sentry not moving. Dawn rested her cheek on her husband's naked chest. It was something she had done often, especially when she nestled beside him at night in bed. But now, this moment, she enjoyed more than ever before since she had thought she might never get the chance to do it again.

Tears stung her eyes when he eased his hand between them and she felt him press his hand to his chest, then to hers and held it there, letting her know how much he loved her. She pressed a gentle kiss to his chest and she felt him shuddered.

162

When they heard the sentry walk off, she reluctantly extracted herself from his arms and hurriedly led the way, eager to have this done and have her husband free of this horrible place and home where he belonged.

The rain had turned to a drizzle and Dawn feared that some of the travelers would return to camp fearful of what little they possessed being stolen. She stopped just before reaching the camp and looked around, nothing appeared to stir. She hurried Cree to the cart and worried he would protest when she shoved at him to climb into it. He hesitated only a moment before doing as she directed, though she could tell by how his dark eyes narrowed that he was not pleased with the situation.

He was too tall for the cart, so he had to curl his legs up near to his chin, not a comfortable positon but a necessary one. She spread the rags over him, arranging them so that they looked no different from before and thinking that no one would suspect the mighty Cree to be cramped tight in a cart, hiding under a pile of foul smelling rags.

She was feeling more hopeful that all would go well with Cree freed from the dungeon, and her heart swelled with joy. Fear, however, continued to linger, for they would not be entirely free until they were beyond the village walls.

Dawn leaned against the side of the cart when she finished, releasing a silent sigh and tensing the next instant when a figure stumbled out of the shadows toward her.

"Heard you gave Cree a good poking, how about giving me one?"

Chapter Six

Cree did not hesitate. He slipped out from under the rags, came around the cart and felt his simmering anger boil over when he saw his wife trying with little success to push the man off her. He wasted no time in coming up behind him and quickly snapped his neck. He had little choice in the matter under the circumstances. Besides, the man dared to touch his wife and that in itself was reason enough to end his useless life.

Dawn pointed at a wagon a few feet away. Cree dragged the man over to it and rolled him under it and onto his side so that he appeared as though he was sleeping. He returned to his wife, wanting to take her in his arms and make sure she was unharmed, but she had already pushed the rags aside and was waving for him to get back in the cart.

Before he climbed in the cart he whispered to her, "When we get home I am going to shackle you to me."

Dawn smiled wide and quickly traced a cross over her heart, asking if that was a promise.

Her smile tempered as his scowl deepened. She would eventually answer to him for all she had done and she was looking forward to it, since his attempt at punishing her usually ended with them making love.

She once again arranged the rags over him and positioned herself on the side of the cart where she could see Old Mary approach. It was only a couple of hours before sunrise, and then they would be on their way.

Dawn remained alert as the time passed slowly and when the first ray of sun rose in the sky, she grew worried. Old Mary had yet to return and she recalled the old woman's last gesture to her.

Leave if I am not there by sunrise.

Dawn did not care what Old Mary had ordered her to do. She would not leave her behind. Her heart pounded when the sun was full in the sky and a minute later Dawn pressed her hand to her chest as she saw Old Mary approach. Dawn could tell that her bones ached by her slow gait. She had to be exhausted, having not slept all night. Dawn wanted to run and hug her, but that would have to wait until later.

"Get moving, lass, you heard the soldier tell us yesterday that we had to be gone by sunrise or he would throw us out," Old Mary said for Cree and those returning to their wagons and carts to hear.

Dawn helped her up onto the seat when no one was watching, and she could feel the fatigue in the effort it took the old woman to climb up even with Dawn's assistance. But when Dawn hoisted herself up next to her, she was not surprised to see the old woman grip the reins tightly with her gnarled hands and guide the horse slowly along the path to the gatehouse.

Dawn wished they could go faster, but they would draw attention to themselves and so the short ride to the gatehouse seemed as though it took hours. She kept her head down and had to keep her hands clasped, they trembled with such worry. She wondered if the guards would poke the mound of rags with their spears and discover Cree beneath. But early morning saw the two guards yawning and more interested in seeing their night watch on the gatehouse done. They waved them through without a word.

Old Mary continued their slow pace, both women's attention caught by the many riders and wagons that began to pass by them, heading to Loudon. A few people called out, inquiring about the prisoner and if a decision had been made to his fate.

"Three days and he is to be beheaded from what we hear, and it is a shame we will miss it," Old Mary said to those excited about the event.

One woman, sitting beside her husband on a wagon seat, produced a gleeful smile when she learned the news. "Luck is on our side, it is. A beheading is always a good sight to see, especially one deserving of it."

Dawn shivered, wondering how people could be so heartless, but then she had thought her husband heartless, having heard horrific tales about his exploits before she met him and got to know what a truly honorable man he was.

167

They could not get away from the walled town quickly enough for Dawn and once again she wished they could travel faster than a snail's pace, though she understood why Old Mary had maintained a slower pace than usual. And when the road emptied of travelers, Old Mary's words confirmed her suspicions.

"Where does Sloan camp?"

Cree explained in whispers and Old Mary followed his directions, after stopping and retrieving the sack that she and Dawn had hidden before they entered the Village of Loudon.

Old Mary directed the cart off the well-worn path, maneuvering it through the woods, hitting bumps and ruts and jostling its occupants so much that Dawn worried Cree would tumble out.

It was not long before several of Cree's warriors suddenly appeared. When they saw that it was Old Mary and Dawn, they turned speechless and, shaking their heads, led them to the camp.

"What are you two doing here?" Sloan snapped sharply as the cart rolled to a stop.

Cree rose up out of the cart, sending the offending rags flying off him. He vaulted over the side with ease to land on his feet and was met with shocked silence.

Dawn smiled, for to her he looked as he did the first day she had laid eyes on him, only his wrists were not tethered with a rope. The muscles in his chest and arms gleamed with a fine sweat, defining their strength. His long brown hair was shot through with gold and the brilliant color of the sun, a distant contrast to his dark eyes that smoldered with anger.

"We have no time to waste," Cree said, looking to Sloan as he stepped around the cart to lift his wife off and stand her next to him. "Minnoch will find out soon enough that I have escaped and he will send warriors to search for me, and I want us well on our way home before he does."

Sloan shouted orders and the warriors got busy breaking camp. Cree hurried into a black shirt, one of his warriors handed him. He slipped on leather straps, crisscrossing them across his chest and shoulders and when they were in place, Cree slid his sword into the sheath on his back. A dagger was placed in his boot and another dagger went in the sheath attached to the strap that sat snug around his waist.

Sloan nodded to Dawn, anger in his voice when he asked, "Her neck bleeds. Who did that to her?"

"I did," Old Mary said as a warrior helped her off the cart. She took a clean stripe of cloth from the pouch at her waist and approached Dawn with it to gently wrap it around her neck and absorb the blood that trickled from a small section of the wound. She looked to Cree as she finished. "Elsa must see to this as soon as we arrive home and I will speak with you about it whenever you wish."

"The time will come for us to talk," Cree said, "but now you will ride with one of the warriors and it will not be an easy journey."

Old Mary smiled. "Life is not an easy journey. We do what we must to survive it." She turned and gave Dawn a hug.

A tear trickled from Dawn's eye as she gestured to Old Mary, letting her know that she was forever grateful, for without her help she would have never been able to rescue Cree. They hugged again and Old Mary walked off with one of Cree's warriors.

"We ride through with brief rests for the horses and food," Cree ordered.

"We have done this many times before, but the women have not," Sloan said.

"They have no choice." Cree turned to his wife and she gestured before he could say a word. He looked to Sloan with a smile. "She says make sure you do not slow her done."

Sloan grinned and nodded to Dawn. "I will do my best, my lady."

Cree's stallion was brought to him and the horse snorted and stomped the ground as eager as Cree to be on his way. A warrior handed him a cloak and he draped it around Dawn and settled his hands at her waist and, with one swift lift, placed her on the horse and quickly mounted behind her.

Sloan rode up beside him. "All is ready."

"The cart?"

"No one will ever find it," Sloan assured him.

"Then let us be on our way." Cree rode out in front, setting a strong pace and his warriors were quick to follow.

They rode for some time before Dawn could no longer keep a concern of hers to herself and she gestured her worry that the twins could be in danger.

Cree tucked her closer against him. "I would never leave them or you unprotected. More warriors were sent to Dowell." Her scrunched brow and shrug let him know that she questioned his response, and he explained. "I made your father aware of my absence and asked him to stand ready to ride for Dowell with his warriors if it should become necessary. Word was sent to him of my capture. By now he and his warriors are well settled at Dowell."

Dawn had not known Kirk McClusky was her father and he did not know he had a daughter, and they both had been pleased to find each other. She felt a great relief knowing her father would be there to protect his grandchildren.

She gestured, asking if Torr, her half-brother, and Wintra, Cree's sister, would be with them, Wintra due to birth a babe in a few months.

"I had your father alert Torr to the situation and to have him stand ready if necessary, but to keep the news from Wintra. If she learned of it, she would want to ride for Dowell immediately and Torr would forbid it, since she is not feeling well."

A scrunch and a shrug made him aware of her question.

"I only heard before I left that Wintra was not feeling well," Cree said, knowing his wife was concerned for his sister, since they had become like sisters themselves. "When all is settled with this, we will visit."

She smiled and nodded, showing how pleased she was with that.

Her smile warmed his heart and he thought about how cold his heart had been before he met her, before he fell in love with her, and how he was forever grateful she had entered his life. His words were simple, but delivered with strength. "I have missed you, wife."

Her smile grew and she gestured slowly so that he would be sure to understand her.

Laughter rumbled in his chest. "Make no mistake, wife, I will show you just how much I have missed you once we are in bed."

Dawn's grin widened as she gestured again.

Cree laughed again. "You are right, a bed is not necessary, though it would make things easier since I intend to see that backside of yours gets what it deserves in more ways than one."

Dawn shuddered and tingles raced through her at the thought of his hand coming down on her backside as she climaxed. She had missed intimacy with him. She had missed everything while he was gone. Her day was busy with caring for the twins and seeing that all ran well in the keep, though Flanna saw mostly to that with little help from her. Without him by her side, life seemed barren and she never wanted to feel such vast emptiness again.

She laid her hand on his arm and squeezed tightly, hoping he understood that she never wanted them to be separated again.

"I feel the same," Cree said easily understanding what she attempted to convey, since his thoughts were the same. "I have been gone from you and the twins far too long."

She nodded vigorously, agreeing. There were many questions she had for him, but one in particular had her more curious than ever. She gestured, pleased that he understood her more often than not.

"You want to know why Minnoch took me prisoner and condemned me to death?"

Dawn nodded eager to hear.

"I wish I knew myself. My capture makes no sense. Minnoch was aware that I had come to speak with him in regards to his allegiance to the crown. It is known that Minnoch had been an ally of Haakon IV of Norway, having lived in that country for a number of years. King Alexander wants to make certain that his ties with Haakon have been severed permanently and his loyalty lies with Scotland. I see no possible reason for Minnoch to falsely accuse me of stealing from him and order me beheaded?" Cree shook his head. "There is something I am not seeing."

Dawn shrugged and motioned as if placing a crown on her head.

"I am not sure what the King will do when he learns of this. It is important that he finds out if Minnoch is loyal to him and with how untrustworthy Minnoch is there is no telling what his explanation will be to the King."

Dawn thought a moment before her hands began moving again.

"I agree. You would think that the King would not trust Minnoch after he imprisoned and was about to behead the emissary he sent to speak with him. But his need for Minnoch may outweigh good judgement."

Her brow narrowed and she tapped his chest.

The king will not dare hand me over to Minnoch, for if he proves disloyal to the King, it will be me the King sends to deal with him."

Dawn chopped at the side of her neck with her hand.

"I should behead Minnoch?"

She nodded firmly.

"We will see, though whatever happens, I intend to see the bastard pay for what he did."

~~~

Dawn was exhausted when hours later they stopped for a brief rest. She could not imagine what toll the last few days and now this hasty ride home had on Old Mary, though one look at the old woman napping beneath a tree told Dawn all she needed to know.

The warriors got busy seeing that the horses drank from the stream and food was hastily dispersed and eaten.

Dawn nibbled on a piece of dried meat in between washing her face in the stream. She could not wait to get home and wash the filth off her, though that filth was part of what had helped her rescue her husband. But the mission was done and it was time to rid herself of the foul odor.

Cree stood a distance away from her, watching. He hoped the wound on her neck would heal so that no scar would be left. If a scar remained, it would always remind him of that moment he saw her through the narrow slot, standing there naked, the fresh wound at her throat, and once again he felt anger twist at his gut.

"You owe her your life."

Cree turned to see Sloan standing next to him.

"Your wife saved you."

Cree scowled at Sloan. "We had a plan."

"It did not include a quick beheading."

"She paid too high of a price."

"I guess that shows just how much she loves you."

"She disobeyed me."

Sloan laughed. "She never obeys you."

"And look what happened because of it."

"Yes, look what happened. You live."

Cree walked off, not wanting to hear anymore and his steps took him to his wife. He was only a few feet away when the pounding of hooves was heard. Cree rushed to his wife as he drew his sword and once he reached her, he shoved her behind him.

Warriors relaxed the hold on their weapons when one of their own appeared.

The rider rode over to Cree as soon as he spotted him. "They know of your escape. Minnoch gathers his troops to come after you."

Chapter Seven

Dawn's legs gave way when Cree lifted her off his horse. He scooped her up and carried her up the steps of the keep and into the Great Hall. "Flanna!" he yelled and the woman appeared as if out of thin air. "Dawn requires a bath, food, and rest, but first get Elsa."

"I will see to everything, my lord," Flanna said with a bob of her head.

Cree looked to Kirk McClusky as he rushed across the room to him.

"Did I hear you say Elsa?" Kirk asked concerned for his daughter. "My daughter requires the healer?" His eyes turned wide when he saw the blood-stained bandage around her neck. "What happened?"

Dawn wanted to answer her father, but she was simply too tired to move her arms.

"She is fine. Let me get her settled, and then we will talk. Until then, go find Sloan, he will tell you what needs to be done." Cree said and Kirk hesitated. "As soon as she is settled, you can speak with her yourself." That seemed to mollify Kirk and with a nod he hurried off.

Cree walked over to the steps and took them up to their bedchamber slowly. His body ached from the endless ride. It was a five day journey to reach home and they had made it just shy of three days. Here at least, he could more easily protect his wife, his children, and his clan.

He entered his bedchamber and at that moment felt he had truly come home, the large bed he shared so happily with his wife, greeting him with freshly dressed linens.

Dawn stirred in his arms and winced when she moved.

"You are home and safe," he said and kissed her brow.

She opened her eyes and looked around, wanting to make sure this was real and not a dream. She smiled happy that it was not a dream, they truly were finally home. She would sleep in her bed tonight in her husband's arms instead of on a horse in his arms.

"Elsa will be here shortly," he said, lowering her to her feet, though keeping a strong arm around her waist.

Dawn nodded, holding onto his arm, her legs not yet firm beneath her, thanks to the endless hours on the horse.

Elsa entered with a basket on her arm, Cree having left the door open.

Dawn could tell that he was relieved to see the woman, not that anyone else would notice. He let no one see what he felt, but she had learned to spot the small signs, a tiny crinkle at the corner of his eyes, a slight flare of his nostrils, a sudden tightness to his lips. They all told her something. At the moment, it was the slightest flare of his dark eyes. He was impatient to hear what Elsa had to say.

"It is good that you all have returned safely," Elsa said as she approached Dawn. Her nose wrinkled when she got closer.

Dawn was quick to apologize for her unpleasant odor.

"That matters not," Cree barked. "See to her wound."

Dawn did not bother to scold her husband for being so sharp with Elsa. The healer understood him better than most and dealt with him better than most.

"Help her to sit," Elsa said to Cree. "She looks ready to collapse."

"She nearly did when I took her off the horse." Cree got her to the chair and eased her down on it, then stepped away once Elsa stood beside his wife.

Elsa gently removed the bandage from her neck.

Dawn saw anger spark in her husband's dark eyes when the wound was revealed.

"I need to clean this, and then I will apply an herb mixture to the areas that are not healing as they should," Elsa explained.

"Why are they not healing as they should?" Cree demanded.

"The cut is deeper in some places and if not properly tended will not heal. But it will, beginning now."

"Flanna walked in with a bucket of fresh water and towels that she arranged on a chest she pulled next to Elsa.

178

He wondered how Flanna always seemed to know what people needed before being asked. She was an asset to the keep and a good friend to Dawn.

Elsa turned to Cree after Flanna left. "Dawn is in good hands. Go do what you must."

Cree walked over to his wife and kissed her brow. "I will join you later."

Dawn smiled and gestured that he better or she would come find him.

He was glad to see she had not lost her strong spirit after all she had been through. He drew an X with his finger over his chest, promising her before turning to Elsa and asking the question that had haunted him since seeing his wife's wound. "Will it scar?"

"I do not know. Only time will tell."

Cree left without saying another word and Dawn's smile faded, knowing her husband was upset.

Dawn gestured slowly to Elsa.

"I believe you are right. Your self-inflicted wound is nothing to your husband's self-inflicted suffering. And the only cure for both is time."

Elsa was right about her wound. Time would tell if any reminder remained of it, but Cree's wound went much deeper. Only revenge would heal the fact that he had been unable to stop his wife from being stripped naked in front of him and that frightened Dawn.

~~~

Cree found Sloan outside, busy fortifying Dowell. He had no fear his warriors would have trouble protecting their home. They had fought many years for the benefit of others and now they fought for their families and own home. The villagers had also been taught to fight when necessary and being life had improved considerably since Cree had laid claim to Dowell, all were willing to fight for him.

"All is ready?" Cree asked, approaching Sloan.

"Aye," he answered firmly. "McClusky is moving his men to our southern border in case Minnoch circles around and attempts to attack from there." Sloan was quick to add, "How is Dawn?"

"Well enough," Cree said.

Sloan let a moment of silence pass between them. "You are going to kill Minnoch." It was not a question. Sloan was confirming what he knew to be true.

"With much pleasure," Cree said. "Is there any word on how long before he arrives here?"

"We have no word on that yet."

"Let me know as soon as you do," Cree said and followed a path through the village.

Night was not far off, dusk now laying claim to the land. Torches began to flicker in the cool air as his warriors went about securing the village.

Cree turned up a path to a small cottage and before he could knock on the door a voice called out, "Enter." He smiled as he opened the door and walked in. Old Mary was sitting up in bed, her wrinkled skin appearing younger from a recent washing, and a mug was cupped in her hand, heat rising from it.

"You are well?" he asked and took a chair from the small table and placed it next to the bed to sit.

"I am, and I have waited for you," she said with a nod.

"You knew I would come here tonight. Did you know Dawn would survive the rescue attempt? Is that why you agreed to join her?"

"As I told your wife, fate is a funny creature. Sometimes she will show you things and sometimes she shows you nothing. I think those times fate remains silent, she feels the decision should be ours alone. And Dawn did not want me going with her. It was I who insisted on accompanying her."

"Whose thought was it to cut her throat?"

"We discussed different options, but none proved as safe as having the actual wound to verify our story true. No one would suspect that someone would slice their own throat. But then no one realizes how much Dawn loves you." After a yawn, she said, "Tell me my punishment so that I may get some much needed sleep."

"I cannot punish you for helping my stubborn wife, for keeping her safe, and for freeing us both. I am most grateful."

"And I am most grateful that Dawn has found a man who loves her with all his heart."

"And I always will."

Old Mary slipped her one hand off the mug and held it out to Cree.

He took it.

"This is different from what you think. Be careful for Minnoch will not stop until he has his revenge."

Cree left the cottage with Old Mary's warning playing over and over in his head, but still it made no sense to him or perhaps his thoughts were not as clear as they should be, not having slept for over two days. There were a few more things he needed to do, and then he would join his wife in bed.

He swore beneath his breath. Simply thinking about crawling into bed with her aroused him and she was too exhausted for him to even be thinking of making love to her. He smiled, knowing his wife, her hands would be all over him once they were in bed, possibly even before it. Good God, he was a lucky man and he hurried to finish his tasks, the last one being a good washing, then he would go see the twins, for he would not go to them filthy and smelly. Finally, he would go be alone with his wife.

~~~

Dawn sat with each babe in her arms, both sleeping contently after feeding from their mum's breasts once again. Though they had no voice to recognize her by, somehow they knew when she entered a room. They cried out and Valan looked as if he would jump out of the cradle to get to her. He was so much like his father. Lizbeth waved her tiny arms, smiled, and made sounds until Dawn scooped her up. She did not know how they knew it was her, but they did and that pleased her.

She cuddled them close and kissed the tops of their heads repeatedly, relieved to be home with them safe in her arms. She had spoken briefly with her da, assuring him she was unharmed and thanking him over and over for being here and protecting the twins. With tears in his eyes, he had told her that he would do whatever it took to keep her and his grandchildren safe. Then he had gone on to brag profusely about the twins. She smiled, happy to have found her da after all this time.

The door creaked open and she smiled when she saw her husband enter quietly. She could smell his freshly washed body from where she sat and she suddenly craved him, fearing it would take more than one night to appease her need for him.

Cree walked softly over to his wife, not wanting to wake the babies, but eager to see his son and daughter again. He hunched down in front of his wife, enjoying the scent of lavender that wafted off her.

He sniffed the air and smiled at her, letting her know how much he favored her scent.

She nodded at him and sniffed the air as well, her smile growing wider, though a yawn was quick to steal it away.

Cree pointed to Valan, and then the cradle. Dawn nodded, handing their son gently over to him. Cree pressed his son close to him and ran a tender hand over his tiny head. His face squished up as if annoyed at being disturbed and Cree grinned, happy to be home, holding him tucked in his arm. After running his finger along his son's soft cheek, he

183

placed him in the cradle. It would not be long before the lad would be looking for his sister to snuggle against.

Cree turned and Dawn lifted their daughter up to him. As soon as he took her in his arms, Lizbeth opened her eyes and smiled so wide it appeared as if she was attempting to speak to him.

"Hello there, my little princess," he said softly. "Da has come home to you."

Her smile brightened, and then she turned her tiny head and pressed her face against his chest and in the next moment she was asleep. He held her close, not wanting to let go of her just yet. He lifted her so that he could press his cheek against her warm, soft one and whispered, "I love you with all my heart, princess, and I will always protect you."

Dawn did not think she could love her husband any more than she already did, but seeing him, the mighty warrior Cree, with such love in his eyes for his son and daughter had Dawn loving him even more.

Valan was already thrashing about when Cree placed his daughter next to his son. As soon as the small lad felt his sister there, Valan settled beside her. Cree placed a blanket over them and turned to his wife, stretching his hand out to her. "Time for bed."

Dawn took hold of his hand, eager for bed, though not for sleep.

The short walk to their bedchamber seemed to take forever to Dawn and once inside she found herself doing something she had not expected, frowning. Why did her husband walk away from her to stand by the hearth, turning his back to her? She expected him to take her in his arms and kiss her breathless. And why was he waiting to disrobe? They had been too long without each other and she was most eager for him to bury himself deep inside her.

She walked over to where he stood, his hand braced against the mantel and scooted under it, to stand in front of him with a wrinkled brow.

He hooked his arm around her waist and turned her away from the hearth. "Your nightdress will catch the flame."

Dawn was quick to remedy the matter. She striped off her nightdress and stood naked in front of him, except for the bandage at her neck. And that was where his eyes rested.

"Does it pain you?" Cree asked with a hint of anger.

She shook her head, smiling.

"You smile when you could very well be left with a scar that will be a constant reminder of—"

She gestured quickly.

"You think it was a small price to pay to free me?"

Dawn nodded, her smile remaining strong.

"Slicing your throat is a small price?" he argued.

She gestured again.

Cree could not stop the laugh that surfaced. "I should be glad that you did not lose your voice?"

Dawn nodded, the corners of her mouth crinkling from inner laughter.

His laughter left a smile and Cree shook his head as he said, "What am I going to do with you, wife?"

Her gestures were slow and precise, leaving no doubt to what she was saying. Dawn felt her bare feet leave the floor so quickly that a gasp caught in her throat as she landed snugly in her husband's arms, tucked against his chest.

Now I am going to show you how much I missed you."

After lowering his wife to the bed, Cree discarded his garments with haste and rested himself over her, though only for a moment. His arm circled her waist and as he rolled to his side, he took her with him, bringing her to rest against him.

Her lips found his as soon as their faces neared and she captured his with a hunger he returned. They had been separated too long, their need now too great to do anything but satisfy it. He had never been as famished for a woman as he was for his wife at this moment. The more he kissed her, the more ravenous he grew, the more demanding his kiss. He warned himself to slow down, be gentler with her, but how does a starving man feast slowly? How does a man who thought he might never kiss his wife again, make love to her again, wake beside her in bed ever again, temper his love for her when he finally joins with her again?

This would be no slow, easy joining, at least not the first one.

186

He rolled her on her back with the weight of his body.

"I cannot wait," he whispered.

Dawn nodded, patted her chest frantically, and spread her legs.

Chapter Eight

Cree silently cursed himself for lack of control especially when he slipped inside his wife and felt himself ready to come. He wanted to take his time, make her come more than once, before he did, and yet, his body betrayed him, demanding immediate release.

He warned himself to go slow, not think about how good it felt to slip in and out of her, but most of all to love her. *Love her.* God how he loved her. And he wanted her to feel and to know how very much he loved her.

"You are mine. You belong to me and always will."

Dawn wrapped her legs around him and squeezed tight, letting him know that he belonged to her and she would never let him go.

He let loose with a roar. She had squeezed him so tight she had made him come and hard. And as he spilled into her, he let out another roar, driving deeper inside her and when he felt her fingers dig into his arms, he knew she was about to climax. He braced his hand on the bed and stiffened his arm to raise himself slightly above her so that he could slip his other hand between their bodies and stroke her sensitive nub.

Dawn tossed her head back and let loose with a silent scream, the climax hit her so hard. She let herself drown in its pleasure and she blessed her husband, for when she thought it done, he plunged into her again and made her come once more with just as much intensity.

They both shuddered as their climaxes drifted off and Cree brought her to rest beside him when he rolled off her.

Dawn snuggled against him, relieved he was home there beside her. With a hint of a smile, she gestured to him.

Cree laughed. "I should rest because you are not done with me yet?"

She nodded.

"We will see who needs to rest first," he said, smiling.

They lay there quiet, wrapped around each other, both happy to be home, happy to make love again, happy the night lay ahead, and in minutes they were fast asleep.

~~~

A rap at the door broke through Cree and Dawn's sound sleep.

"Cree, wake up, it is passed sunrise and the King's troops approach."

Cree shot out of bed and yelled for Sloan to enter as he grabbed his plaid and fit it around him. "How many troops?" he asked as soon as Sloan entered.

"A large contingent."

"Is the King with them?"

"Not that we can see."

"How long before they arrive?"

"An hour maybe less," Sloan informed him.

"Alert everyone to their arrival and see that everything is made ready. I will meet you in the Great Hall in a few minutes."

Sloan nodded and left the room.

Dawn hurried out of bed and over to her husband.

He took her in his arms. "This was not how I wanted to wake beside you this morning." He smiled at her short, quick gesture. "You are right. We woke beside each other and that is all that matters." He kissed her gently. "But I had not planned on sleeping through the entire night."

She smiled, tapped her chest and shook her head, letting him know that she had not as well.

"It would seem we both needed the rest."

Dawn agreed with a nod.

"I promise, tonight will be different."

Her smile faded.

"I am hurt, wife, that you do not believe me," he said teasingly, knowing it was not his words that had stolen her smile.

She tapped his chest, then hers and crossed two fingers tightly and shook her head firmly.

He understood full well what she was telling him. She would not see them separated again. He felt the same, but how could he promise her when

190

he was not sure if he would be able to keep the promise?

"I will do my best not to be separated from you and you will do your best to obey me."

She gestured quickly.

Cree scowled. "You can make no promise to obey me?"

She shook her head and with firm gestures, as if showing her anger, she let him know that she would not let the King himself take him from her.

Another knock sounded before Sloan called out, "Minnoch is a day's ride from here."

"I will be right there," Cree shouted and stepped away from his wife to hurry and finish dressing.

Dawn felt a chill race over her, prickling her arms with gooseflesh. With Minnoch and the King's guard so close, she feared what might happen.

Cree took her in his arms once again. "Do you have faith in me, Dawn?"

She did not hesitate to nod her head.

"Then do not worry and do not make *me* worry." He kissed her quick and left with haste.

Dawn slipped on a robe and hurried off to feed the twins.

~~~

The Great Hall was chaotic with servants bustling about, but Flanna had it well in hand. Delicious scents wafted down the passageway that kept the kitchen separated from the keep and had

191

Cree's stomach grumbling. Their visitors would feast well today.

Cree made his way through the chaos searching for Sloan and when he spotted him, he was surprised to see the Earl of Kellmara standing beside him."

"And do what do we owe this visit, Kellmara?" Cree said when he reached the two men.

Kellmara turned to greet Cree. Age showed in his pure white hair that skimmed his shoulders and on his face, though it did not diminish his handsome features and bold blue eyes. He was tall, though not as tall as Cree and his body muscled and firm for a man his age. Cree could see where his sister got some of her fine features.

"Torr made me aware of your situation and I came to offer my help." Kellmara said.

Cree laughed. "You mean you made sure to put distance between my sister and yourself."

Kellmara shook his head, though smiled. "I would rather fight to the death here, than face my daughter when she finds out that no one informed her of her brother's dire situation." His smile was replaced by concern. "Wintra continues to feel poorly and I am very grateful that my son-in-law is courageous enough not to let my daughter know what goes on with her brother or there would be no stopping her from riding here. But tell me, how may I be of help to you?"

The three men sat at a table and Cree explained the situation to Kellmara.

"This is more troublesome than I thought," Kellmara said. "With the King's troops arriving shortly and Minnoch a day away, there is no telling what could happen. You need to be prepared for anything."

"We are," Sloan informed him.

"Then tell me where my warriors would be most helpful to you."

"It was good of him to come and offer help," Sloan said after Kellmara was given instructions and took his leave. "He did not only come to escape his daughter's wrath once she discovered what was going on. He came because he looks upon you as a son." Sloan did not expect a response and Cree did not give one. "I will see if the King's troops draw near."

Cree sat alone at the table, thinking of what Sloan had said. His mum, a widowed peasant had fallen in love with a titled man and surprisingly he had fallen in love with her. Cree had been astonished to learn that Kellmara had plans to wed his mum and to claim him as his son. But Kellmara's father learned of it and sent him away on what he thought would be a brief journey. His father forcibly kept him away for years and by the time he was able to return home, the woman he loved was dead and her son gone, along with his sister, Kellmara's daughter he had not known about. It had taken Kellmara years to finally find them both.

The village bell tolled, announcing the arrival of the King's guard just as Dawn rushed into the Great

Hall. It pleased her to see Cree's eyes widen at the sight of her. Dorrie had come to her bedchamber offering to help her dress for the arriving dignitary. At one time, she would not have trusted the woman, but unexpected events had turned Dorrie into a friend and now she welcomed her help.

She was glad she did, seeing how pleased Cree was by her appearance. Dorrie had swept her hair up, fashioning it into an intricate knot. Since she refused to wear a tunic over the soft green, wool shift, Dorrie tied a strip of leather around her waist to rest on Dawn's hips, Dorrie had also suggested that she wrap her shawl high up around her neck to hide the bandage, but Dawn would not have it. She was proud for what she had done to save her husband's life and she would not hide it. The shawl went around her shoulders to protect her from the autumn chill.

"How is it that you became more beautiful in the short time I was gone?" Cree said and kissed her lips lightly.

Dawn beamed at the compliment.

Cree offered his arm to her. "We greet our visitors together."

That Cree took pride in her, though she could not talk, made her grateful every day that he had come into her life. To him, she had a voice, and he helped her to let it be heard.

They waited on the top steps as the King's guard approached. Two enclosed wagons trailed the first troop of about twenty men and twenty more

194

men trailed behind the wagons. Several more troops remained in the distance.

Cree and Dawn walked down the steps when a guard walked to the first enclosed wagon and placed a set of steps in front of the door before opening it. Cree was not happy to see Mathias Obern descend the steps. He was one of the King's most trusted advisors. He made sure that the King's orders were followed precisely. He cared not for excuses or reason. The King's word was the King's word and all would obey it even if it proved wrong. That, and he never cared for Cree, since he had not always followed the King's edict, made Obern a thorn in Cree's side.

Dawn felt the muscles in her husband's arm grow taut. He was not happy with the man who approached them. He did not appear formidable, not even reaching her height and with not enough weight on him to lift a Highland sword. His features were pinched, though haughty and one could see at first glance that he thought himself of great importance.

"Cree," the man said, stopping in front of him.

It was not lost on those around them that the man did not address Cree respectfully.

"What message do you have for me from the King, Obern?" Cree said, dismissing him as unimportant.

"I warned the King that you could never be taught civility and I will be sure to let him know upon my return."

"See that you do," Cree ordered, "for it is not civility the King wants from me."

Obern wrinkled his nose in distaste and turned his head away slightly. "We need to talk privately."

"You speak of civility, yet you would be so rude as not to acknowledge my wife?" Cree snapped.

Dawn squeezed his arm gently, attempting to calm the anger she felt building in him. She did not care that the little man had not glanced at her once. She cared more about the message he brought from the King.

"I do not need to meet the peasant woman without a voice," Obern said dismissively. "And do not think to threaten me, Cree, for I have the King's guard at my side. My only concern is that the King's orders are adhered to and I will make certain that is done before I leave here."

Dawn let her hand slip off her husband's arm and she gestured to him, then turned and with a respectful bob of her head to Mathias Obern, she hurried off.

"A peasant woman with manners, remarkable," Obern said and walked up the steps past Cree.

Sloan quickly followed behind Obern, fearful that Cree would snap the man's skinny neck.

Cree did not immediately follow the insufferable man. His eyes were on his wife as she hurried through the village. Obern's slight had not bothered her. She was more concerned for him and that was what she had let him know. That and her playful warning that he better not fall asleep on her tonight.

In the middle of this dreadful ordeal, his wife found time for humor and he loved her for it. He turned and climbed the keep steps to see this done with Mathias Obern so that when Minnoch arrived he could kill him and be done with it.

Obern was already ensconced in Cree's solar while the King's guards were treated to a feast in the Great Hall.

Cree's brow wrinkled when he entered his solar, thinking he may have entered the wrong room. Flanna had done well, making it ready for someone of importance. A table was laid out with the finest linen and an assortment of food was spread out atop it, the bowls and serving dishes placed at various heights to make it more pleasing to the eye. Decanters of fine wine were placed on a separate table along with pitchers of ale. But it was the table set with sweets that Obern seemed to be most interested in, though Cree knew he would not indulge until he made the King's message clear.

Obern sat in one of the chairs that had been arranged near the hearth, extending his slim hands out and rubbing warmth into them. "The Highland weather can chill the bones."

"The Highlands are for the hardy soul," Cree said, taking the chair opposite the man.

"Hardy or not, I have been here long enough and wish to see this done."

So Obern had been in the Highlands for a while, which meant the King had sent him to make sure things went as planned. Cree was not surprised since King Alexander did not care for the fact that the Western Isles continued to hold allegiance to Norway. He had attempted negotiations and possible purchase with the King of Norway, but met failure at every turn. With Minnoch pledging his allegiance to King Alexander and friend to King Haakon of Norway, it could very well help turn the tide in the next negotiations.

"King Alexander sent me to keep watch over your mission and to save it should it turn badly, which I warned the King it would most certainly do. And of course I was right." Obern's posture could not get any stiffer or his chin any higher when he asked, "Why in heaven's name did you steal from Minnoch?"

Cree leaned toward the man. "Accuse me falsely as Minnoch did and the King will need a new advisor. And the question better asked is why would Minnoch see me, an emissary of the King, beheaded without speaking to the King first?"

"I have your word you did not steal from Minnoch?"

"Why would I steal a few gems when I have my own wealth? You well know that, Obern. And aye, I give my word and I never give my word falsely."

"I know King Alexander trusts your word and therefore so must I," Obern said a bit reluctantly.

"Yet you would stand by and watch me beheaded?"

"I would have stopped the beheading if I had been in the area to do so. Unfortunately, I only found out about it two days ago. And I must admit I was surprised to discover that it was your wife who rescued you from death."

"Then you will understand when I tell you that I intend to kill Minnoch."

"That is not possible," Obern said, shaking his head and raised his hand to prevent Cree from speaking. "King Alexander needs Minnoch and his orders are that by no means are you to harm Minnoch. You are to welcome him into your home when he arrives."

"Welcome the man who wants to behead me?" Cree asked not to mention what he had done to his wife and for that alone he wanted to see Minnoch dead.

"I will speak to Minnoch when he arrives and see that he makes peace with you."

"There will never be peace between him and me, that I can promise you," Cree said, trying to contain the rage brewing inside him.

"Peace or not, I will have your word that you will obey the King's orders. You will not harm or kill Minnoch."

"And what of Minnoch? The King needs him so he will not threaten him. I tell you now, I will not stand idle and let him harm my clan or my family."

"The King does what must be done," Obern said.

"Aye, and I do the same."

"The King will have your word on this, Cree. You will not harm Minnoch and you will welcome him into your home upon his arrival."

Cree remained silent.

"This is not negotiable, Cree," Obern said sternly.

"You are right, it is not," Cree said, though he doubted Obern understood what he meant. "The King has my word."

Chapter Nine

Dawn was walking up to Old Mary's door when it opened and Elsa came out, shutting the door behind her.

"She is getting some much needed sleep, after a full meal," Elsa said. "Have you rested well and eaten yet this morning?"

Dawn pressed her hand to her cheek, wondering if her harrowing ordeal had left its mark on her.

"Others may not see the toll your adventure has taken on you, but I do." She hooked her arm around Dawn's. "Rest is called for and food to help restore your strength." She lowered her voice. "There is no telling what will happen with the King's guard here and Minnoch on his way."

Someone shouted out for Elsa and she waved to let them know she would be right there. She turned to Dawn. "Rest when you can, for who knows what the next few days will bring."

Dawn watched her walk off and as she did, her eyes caught what she had been too preoccupied to see... the village was preparing for battle. The younger bairns were huddled in a circle listening to two women tell an adventurous tale of a mighty warrior. It was what was done if battle might be imminent. This way the two women could easily herd the young ones into the safety of the keep.

Several lads carried long, narrow baskets and laid them to rest in various places throughout the village, an innocent enough task. But those baskets held arrows and had been strategically placed for the archers who would need them.

She had known a battle was possible, but watching the villagers prepare made it seem that they sat on the brink of war. She shivered at the thought and prayed that Cree in his strength and wisdom would see a way to avoid it.

Her stomach growled and she realized that with the unexpected arrival of the King's emissary, she had neglected to eat this morning and now it was nearer to mid-day. She paid heed to Elsa's warning. She did need to eat and keep up her strength. If battle did break out, there was no telling when next she would be able to eat.

Dawn noticed the villagers hastily stepped out of the way of the King's guard as a few of them walked through the village. The soldiers made the people uneasy and Dawn could not blame them. They held the authority of the King, which meant they held authority over Cree and that could prove troublesome.

She hurried toward the kitchen in the back of the keep. A few people called out greetings, though most simply waved, too busy with their chores to stop and chat. She rounded the corner of the keep and as soon as she took two steps, she was snagged around the waist and yanked against an unfamiliar body.

"So Cree brought you home and cleaned you up."

Between his slurred words and his breath heavy with ale, it was easy to surmise the man was well into his cups. What startled Dawn the most was what he had said. He had to be one of Minnoch's men and one that was there in the dungeon when she had been brought in. But what was he doing here? Minnoch was a day's ride yet from here, unless he had sent some soldiers ahead to see what they could find out.

"Since you are all cleaned up, how about giving me some of what you gave to Cree?"

Dawn cast an eye to the kitchen door. Why was it closed? It was usually open, but then with all the King's soldiers roaming about, Turbett probably did not want them disturbing him.

"Come on, we will find a place where no one will bother us," he said and burped loudly.

The awful stench drifted down around Dawn and she gagged. She did not wait another minute. She brought her heel down on the man's foot as hard as she could and when he let out a yell, she rammed her elbow back into his gut with a force that sent him tumbling. She turned and ran, but his hand snagged her ankle and she went down hard.

"You're going to pay for that, whore," he said and scrambled over her as he fought off her flailing hands.

This is when she wished she had a voice so that she could scream, but there was no point in wishing for something that would never be. And she was not about to rescue Cree from the likes of Minnoch and his soldiers only to fall prey to one of them again.

She made a tight fist and swung with all her might, connecting with his jaw. He toppled off her and she scurried to her feet and made a run for the kitchen door. It flew open just as she was about to grab the latch, her momentum propelling her through the opening and sending the person there tumbling to the floor along with her.

She heard someone yell to get Cree and when she looked to see who she had fallen on top of her eyes turned wide. Spread out beneath her was Mathias Obern.

"Get off me!" he screamed in Dawn's face.

Dawn was about to comply, worried that she had caused a bigger problem for her husband when she was suddenly lifted off him. She was relieved to see it was Cree who had hold of her.

"Get Elsa," he shouted, ignoring Obern's complaints as he struggled to get to his feet. "Your wound bleeds. What happened?" Fury rose up in him when he had entered the kitchen and saw his wife on top of Obern and when he had yanked her up and saw that her bandaged was soaked in one area with blood, his heart had slammed against his chest.

Dawn took a moment to catch her breath, though as she did, she pointed outside and gestured at being grabbed.

"Someone attacked you?" Cree asked his anger mounting.

"What is going on?" Obern demanded.

Cree did not answer him. He cast a quick glance to Flanna and said, "Watch her." Then he walked outside and over to the man who was stumbling around, trying to get to his feet.

Flanna kept a firm hand on Dawn as they walked out of the kitchen, Obern following behind them and the servants behind him. Sloan hurried past them all and a couple of the King's guards came to stand protectively beside Obern once outside.

"Here let me help you up," Cree said and roughly yanked the man off the ground. When he saw who it was, one of Minnoch's soldiers who had striped his wife naked, he let loose with a vicious punch and sent the man flying several feet.

Cree was on top of him before he could get up, dragging him to his feet. "What are you doing here? Did Minnoch send you?" He did not give the man time to answer. He punched him again. This time in the stomach and he doubled over and fell to his knees.

"Stop! Stop this at once!" Obern ordered.

Cree turned such a vicious scowl on him that the skinny man stumbled back away from him.

"This man dared to put his hands on my wife and he dared to spy on my clan. He will get what he deserves."

"You will not harm one of Minnoch's men," Obern ordered.

Cree cast a look to Sloan and he walked over to stand next to the kneeling man while Cree advanced on Obern with fast strides.

The two King's guards stepped in front of the quaking man and Cree did not hesitate to shove them out of the way, sending them stumbling. Cree's warriors had gathered around and stepped forward to make sure the guards did not get in his way.

"I gave the King my word I would not harm Minnoch. Do not ask anymore of me, little man, or you will learn firsthand why the King seeks my special skills." He glared at Obern as he said, "Go to the kitchen and speak to my cook as you requested."

Obern went to protest.

"Say one word, just one word," Cree warned and Obern trembled so badly that when he turned he stumbled and the guards had to help him to the kitchen. Cree was quick to turn and go to his wife when he heard Elsa.

"You bleed again? This is not good. You need to come with me to my cottage so I may tend this properly," Elsa said.

Cree did not like the look of concern on Elsa's face. He turned to his wife, brushing dirt gently off her cheek. "Go with Elsa and do as she says. I will be there shortly."

Dawn wanted to ask her husband why he gave his word to the King not to harm Minnoch. And would Minnoch do the same and give his word not to harm Cree?

Cree dusted dirt off her nose. "I know you have questions, we will talk later."

Dawn traced an X over her heart.

"Aye, I promise," he said, doing the same.

Dawn gave Cree a quick kiss, and then went reluctantly with Elsa.

Cree motioned Sloan over and two of Cree's warriors went and stood guard by the man who appeared to have lost some of his drunken stupor.

"Minnoch will make you suffer if you hurt me," he called out.

"Say another word and I will slice your throat and watch you bleed to death," Cree said as if looking forward to such a gruesome task.

The man was quick to lock his lips.

"Send for McClusky and Kellmara," Cree ordered Sloan. "I want to know more of what is happening on our borders. Then take this one and get whatever information you can out of him. When you are done let me know."

"What are you going to do?" Sloan asked.

"Send Minnoch a gift."

~~~

Cree entered Elsa's cottage and almost cringed when he saw how red and raw the one area of his wife's wound looked. "It will not heal?" he asked as he entered and stood aside so as not to get in Elsa's way as she worked on Dawn.

"It had at least stopped bleeding until this scuffle today."

Another reason to kill the bastard, Cree thought.

Elsa turned to Cree. "It might be better to sear it closed."

"It will scar," Cree said.

Elsa nodded. "It will, but I worry that it will turn putrid if it doesn't at least show signs of closing soon."

"Sear it then," Cree ordered.

Dawn hurried off the chair, shaking her head. Her hands gestured fast and her face was pinched with anger.

"I will not argue over this with you, wife," Cree said firmly. "It will be done."

Dawn crossed her arms over her chest, narrowed her eyes, and shook her head slowly, in defiance.

Cree inched closer to her. "Do I need to hold you down?"

Dawn held up a tightly clenched fist.

"You would hit me?" he asked, stopping beside her.

She tapped near her wound, and then patted her chest hard.

"You say it is your decision to make?"

Dawn nodded.

"With your choice I could lose you and that I will not have." He slipped his hand around the back of her neck. "You are mine, Dawn, and I will not let you go, not ever. My heart would shatter and life would be meaningless without you, so you will have the wound seared if I must hold you down and see it done."

Dawn pressed two fingers to his lips and with her other hand tapped her chest, and then held two fingers in front of him and pointed to her wound.

His brow wrinkled. "Are you asking for two days to see if the wound begins to heal?"

She nodded.

"You will let Elsa sear it if by then it gets no better?"

She took his hand and pressed it against her chest and nodded.

"Of course I would be with you when it is done. And you give me your word on this?"

She tapped his chest once.

Cree turned to Elsa. "Will two day's wait matter?"

"I cannot say for sure."

Cree cupped his wife's chin. "One day." Though it hurt him to see the disappointment in her eyes, he would not chance losing her. "One day or nothing."

Her shoulders rose and fell in a resigned sighed as she nodded.

He went to kiss her lightly, but stopped and turned to Elsa. "This means no vigorous activity?"

"Nothing that would jostle the wound and cause it to bleed."

Cree kissed his wife and whispered, "It may be best if I sleep elsewhere tonight." He did not give her a chance to argue, since he knew she would. He turned and walked to the door. "I will wait outside for Elsa to finish."

As he walked out the door, Dawn shook her head, her shoulders rising and falling again with a sigh and her lips falling in a frown.

"A scar does not matter to him," Elsa said, "you do."

She pointed to her wound, then at the door, and shook her head.

"When Cree takes his revenge on Minnoch, your scar will no longer be there whether it is visible or not," Elsa assured her.

There was truth to her words. Unfortunately, Cree had been forbidden to seek revenge against Minnoch, so her scar would always hold a reminder that in his eyes he had failed and that she could not have.

When Elsa was done securing a fresh bandage and saw that blood had already seeped through it, she said, "One day will not be enough. Tomorrow I will sear it."

Cree turned and took her hand as soon as she stepped outside. He looked to Elsa in the open doorway and with a nod said, "Tomorrow."

They had taken only a few steps when Sloan hurried over to them. "The prisoner wishes to speak with you."

"I will be right there," Cree said and took his wife's hands. "A warrior will follow you to make certain you remain safe and I will return to you soon."

Dawn gestured.

"Aye, I am sure Old Mary would like to see you as well." He kissed her cheek. "I will meet you there. At least, there you will not get into any trouble."

210

Sloan laughed, Cree shook his head, and Dawn smiled.

Chapter Ten

Dawn did not want to disturb Old Mary, but it was necessary that she speak with her as soon as possible. With hurried steps, she approached the cottage door and was about to knock when the door opened.

Old Mary waved her in. "I should have thought of it before this, but the years dim memories and sometimes make them vanish completely."

Dawn closed the door, not surprised to see the old woman up and about, though mostly not surprised she knew why Dawn was there. She gestured, asking Old Mary how she was feeling.

"That hasty ride home did not help my old bones any, but rest will see to taking care of that. But you need more than rest." She paced in front of the hearth. "I woke from a dream, recalling the time you were very young and took a bad fall, leaving you with a deep gash on your cheek that would not stop bleeding. Your mum was advised to sear it, but she refused to see you left with a scar. It was bad enough you could not speak, she feared a scar on your face would only make matters worse for you."

Dawn must have been very young, for she did not recall the incident.

"Your mum sought the counsel of a wise woman in the woods and the woman told your mum to get honey and apply it to your wound right away, making sure to fill the wound with the honey, then cover and leave it. When the bandage was removed there was barely a scar and with time, it faded completely. Of course, there had been no honey to be had so it took your mum a few days to dislodge a bees' nest from a tree and leave it until the bees vacated it. She suffered several bee stings, but that did not matter to her. You mattered to her."

Dawn felt her chest tighten, recalling what a loving woman her mum had been and how blessed she had been to have had her as a mum instead of the evil woman who had given birth to her. She gestured to Old Mary.

"I miss her too," she said with tears in her aging eyes. "I believe Turbett has beehives." She rustled through a basket in the corner and pulled out a cloth that she tore into strips. "Use these clean cloths as a bandage. The one you wear is stained with fresh blood.

Dawn frowned, feeling at her neck and seeing the blood on her fingers after touching the bandage. Dawn wiped the blood from her fingers on a small piece of cloth Old Mary handed her, then she took the fresh cloth from her and gave the woman a hug. With a quick gesture, Dawn let Old Mary know that she did not know what she would do without her.

Old Mary waved her off, a tear spilling down her wrinkled cheek.

Dawn hurried her steps, but was met with disappointment when Turbett refused to let her have the last of the honey.

"It is for the sweets I promised Obern I would make for him, hoping it might help Cree in some small way." Turbett turned to leave a frowning Dawn and stopped, then turned back quickly. "There is a bees' nest in the woods that fell out of the tree a couple of days ago. The bees should be gone by now. You may find some honey in it."

Dawn smiled and Turbett explained where she could find the nest, then turned and hurried into the kitchen, shouting orders.

Dawn waved at the warrior to follow her.

He stood firm. "No woods today, my lady."

Dawn tried to argue with him and grew frustrated when he stood steadfast.

"What seems to be the problem?"

Dawn turned with a smile to see her da and Kellmara, Wintra's da standing, behind her. She was grateful her da understood her gestures so easily, having had a daughter who had been voiceless like Dawn. It was an affliction that seemed to affect some of the women in his family. Dawn had been grateful that her daughter, Lizbeth, had not suffered such a fate.

Dawn explained to her da.

"Then we will go find the nest and get you what you need," Kirk said and took his daughter's arm.

"Mind if I join you?" Kellmara asked. "I know a thing or two about beehives. Actually, Cree's mother, Colleen, taught me and we will need to be careful for there may still be some bees lingering about."

With the two men to protect Dawn, the warrior did not argue. He simply followed behind them.

Dawn enjoyed hearing about Cree's mum and how much Kellmara loved her. She only wished the pair would have had a chance at a life together. Even now you could hear the love in his voice for the woman that he had lost so many years ago.

They had gone a distance into the woods when Kirk tugged at his daughter's arm to stop.

"Are you sure you are feeling up to this after what you have been through?" Kirk asked with concern.

Before she could answer, the warrior pointed and said, "The beehive is right over there."

Dawn smiled, having been worried that they would not find it.

"You stay back away from it," her father said. "Let me and Kellmara see to this." He turned to the warrior. "You stay with my daughter."

Dawn sat on a tree stump and waited, watching from a safe distance. When she saw her da and Kellmara's heads shoot up and both of them look about, she knew something was wrong. After a moment, her da hurried over to her, a piece of the hive saturated with honey in his hand.

"We heard footfalls not far off," her da said quietly. "Kellmara is going to see if it is anything Cree needs to be concerned about."

Dawn motioned that the warrior should go with Kellmara.

The warrior shook his head. "I stay with you."

She did not bother to argue with him since Cree would see him punished for leaving her side. She gave one last look toward Kellmara before her father took her arm and hurried her off, but the man was already gone.

By the time the three reached the edge of the village, Dawn had suffered three bee stings to her face. Her da's face suffered two stings and the warrior was lucky and had gotten only one on the back of his hand.

"We best go see Elsa," her da said. "She can see to our stings and help coat your wound with the honey."

Dawn had hoped to avoid most everyone until the red welts from the stings faded, though it could take a few hours as it had done the couple of times before when she had been stung.

Her da would not hear it. "Cree will be furious with me if I do not have Elsa tend you."

He would be furious anyway when he saw her face, though she did not bother to tell her da that.

Elsa's mouth dropped open when Dawn and her da entered the healer's cottage.

"Good God, what happened?" Elsa said hurrying over to her.

Dawn's father explained about the bee stings and how Dawn needed the honey applied to her wound.

Elsa's brow wrinkled. "I have tried honey before to heal wounds, but only after the bleeding has stopped."

"Well, now you will be trying it as my daughter wants," Kirk McClusky said with a commanding tone.

Dawn stared at her da. She never had a father to speak for her before and it filled her heart with joy to realize she had one who would speak for her now.

"See to her wound first," her father ordered and took a seat on one of the chairs near the table.

"I will be using the honey on the bee stings as well as the wound. It will help with the itching and pain," Elsa said as she got to work.

Cree burst through the door as Elsa was slathering honey onto Dawn's wound. He stood staring at her speechless. She had three bright red welts on her face, one on each cheek and one on her chin. He turned to Kirk McClusky and shook his head, seeing two red welts on his face, one above his eye and the other on his cheek.

Kirk went to stand and explain.

"Sit!" Cree ordered, pointing at the man, while turning his eyes on his wife.

Dawn was glad her father sat and did not argue with Cree, from the scowl on his face his temper was close to erupting.

Elsa stepped aside when Cree approached his wife. "I leave you for a short time and this is what happens?" He did not expect or want an answer from her. He was not finished speaking yet. He turned to Kirk. "And you—her father—join her in her folly?" Again he did not expect a response and he did not get one. Kirk McClusky wisely remained silent. "Will you ever obey me?" Cree threw his hands up. "A foolish question, since you have yet to obey me."

Dawn heard anger in his words, but saw worry in his eyes. With heartfelt gestures, she let him know how sorry she was for upsetting him.

"You apologize for upsetting me, but not for disobeying me?"

She nodded and a sudden pain shot through the one sting on her cheek and she cringed.

Cree spewed several oaths, reached out and took her hand, and turned to Elsa. "Do something for her." He moved to Dawn's side, out of Elsa's way and while the woman tended his wife, he looked to Kirk. "Explain."

Kirk detailed the whole event and finished with, "I was pleased after all this time of not knowing my daughter that I could finally be a father to her."

Dawn squeezed her husband's hand when he looked ready to argue with her father and was relieved when instead he turned to Elsa.

"Do you think this honey will help heal her wound?"

"I am not sure, but I believe it is worth trying," Elsa said.

"And the bee stings on her face?"

"They have not gotten worse since she arrived here, so there is no fear of further swelling. I will apply honey to them as well. They should improve and possibly fade in a few hours, though they may be painful and itchy for a while."

Kellmara suddenly appeared at the open door. "Cree, I need to speak with you—now."

By the man's abrupt and commanding tone, Cree knew it was important. He released his wife's hand and planted his face close to hers. "Do not dare move from here until I return for you."

Dawn nodded.

Cree looked to Kirk as he headed to the door. "Do not let her leave here."

"As you want," Kirk said.

Cree stopped abruptly. "I want a wife who will do what I tell her so that she does not drive me mad with worry of losing her."

"And I believe my daughter is grateful she has a husband who loves her for who she is and not who he wants her to be... even if she can be trying at times," Kirk said with a smile.

Dawn nodded and smiled at her da, pleased that he had voiced what she could not.

Cree turned to his wife and she quickly tapped her chest, crossed her arms over it and pointed at him, telling him she loved him.

He walked over to her in three quick strides, laid his hands on her waist and lifted her off the chair and sat her on the table, planting his hands on either side of her and his face so close that their noses almost touched. "Your love for me is not in doubt, my sanity is, so take pity on me and at least promise me you will obey me while this threat that looms over our clan is settled."

Dawn did not want her husband to worry over her when he had more important matters that concerned him and she quickly gestured, promising him while hoping she would be able to keep her promise.

Cree kissed her lightly. "Here. Stay right here," he reminded and left her staring after him as he hurried out the door.

It was barely a few moments later that Cree stuck his head in the door and looked to Kirk. "Once Elsa is finished with Dawn, take her to the keep and see that she stays there."

Dawn wondered what news Kellmara had told Cree that appeared to not only had upset him, but had anger smoldering in his dark eyes.

Her da was quiet when he walked her to the keep after Elsa had finished with them. She sensed he was anxious to be off, no doubt to see what Kellmara had found out. She was as well, but that would have to wait. She was feeling much too tired to do anything but rest.

When they reached the keep's steps, Dawn stopped and gestured to her da, letting him know that she intended to go to her bedchamber and take a much needed rest.

"Your word on that, Dawn?" Kirk asked.

She nodded and smiled, though a yawn quickly stole it from her.

Her father waited while she climbed the steps and she waved to him before disappearing inside. She went straight to her bedchamber. She was bone tired and the bee stings itched. She needed to let them heal and get some sleep if she was going to be presentable for supper this evening. She striped off her garments and crawled into bed, stretching out on her back, not wanting to get the honey on her pillow.

Later she would find out everything that was going on, but for now she wanted nothing more than to sleep.

~~~

Dawn woke to the flames crackling in the fireplace. She stretched her arms out and almost sighed, her aches and pains having all but vanished. Her rest did her good and now she would have the strength to face the night ahead with Obern.

She gently felt at her cheek and though it was sticky to the touch, the welt had disappeared and there was no pain or itch. She would wash her face, dress, and go see how long before supper.

Throwing the soft blanket off her, she hurried to the bucket of water near the hearth and stopped abruptly in front of the chair when she saw her husband slouched in it fast asleep.

It must have been later than she thought. Could she have slept through supper? If Cree had seen her sleeping soundly, he would not have disturbed her. He had mentioned sleeping elsewhere tonight, though perhaps with her asleep in the bed he felt safe sleeping in the chair.

She smiled and ran her eyes over him. He wore only his plaid and the flames' light, mixed with shadows, danced across his muscled arms and chest. A few strands of his long hair rested over his cheek and her heart thumped a little faster when she saw how handsome her husband was in sleep.

The sleep they had gotten last night was not enough for either of them. He needed rest just as she had needed it. A good reason to let him be, but the more she glanced over him, the more she wanted to touch him. And the more she thought of touching him, the more aroused she grew.

She placed her finger to her cheek in thought, forgetting the honey was there. Her finger came away sticky and as she held it in front of her a sinful thought entered her head. She told herself not to do it; he needed his sleep. But once the thought was there, she could not chase it away. Besides, his legs were spread apart invitingly and she could not help but think how wonderfully the honey would taste on him.

Heat rushed to her cheeks at the wicked notion and her tiny nub pulsated with such passion that she thought she would come there and then.

She rolled her eyes, shook her head, and prayed for forgiveness for her wickedness as she dropped down on her knees in front of her husband.

Chapter Eleven

She eased his plaid aside carefully, exposing his soft manhood, not wanting to wake him—yet. Even in rest he was a good size and soon he would be even bigger.

She wiped the honey off her cheek with her fingers and slipped them around his manhood to gently stroke him. It took only a few strokes for him to harden and Dawn quickly swiped more honey off her face to coat his growing arousal.

Between how thick and hard he grew and the sweet scent of the honey, she found herself more eager than ever to taste him. And when she slipped him into her mouth, she knew she would be going to hell, for this would not be the last time she spread honey over him.

She licked and sucked, thinking no sweet could taste better than her husband's manhood covered with honey. She felt as if she had just discovered a treat that she would never be able to get enough of and naturally her hunger for him grew. And the more it grew, the closer she grew to climaxing.

"Dammit, wife!" Cree shouted. He had thought himself in the middle of a dream. When he had found his wife naked in bed, all he wanted was to climb in with her. The welts on her face and the bandage around her neck had reminded him that he needed to keep his hands off her and with her naked that would have been impossible. He had gone down to sup with Obern, her lying naked in their bed never leaving his thoughts. And when he returned to find her still sleeping, still naked, he sat in the chair, thinking if he relieved this ache for her himself then perhaps he could sleep beside her.

He must have fallen asleep before he could, and then the dream came, but it was no dream. He discovered that as soon as he opened his eyes and saw his wife between his legs. And now her eyes were smiling at him, for she had not let go of him when he had shouted at her. And truth be told, he did not want her to. But this would do her wound no good. He had to stop her.

Before he could say a word, she took him deeper into her mouth and he dropped his head back and groaned loudly. He was fast losing control and if he did not stop her he would...

Her mouth left him and when he looked to see why, she was climbing on top of him and slipping him into her and when she was settled firmly around him, she dropped her head down to capture his mouth in a deeply erotic kiss.

Honey!

Good lord, she had coated him with honey and damn if she did not taste delicious.

He cupped her backside and helped her to ride him, though she did not need his help. She rode him good and hard, as if she was breaking in a fine stallion. While it felt fantastic, the thought irritated him and he tore his mouth away from hers, wrapped his arms around her waist, and stood.

Dawn quickly wrapped her legs around him.

He carried her over to the bed and kept her firm against him as he lowered them both down on it. He ran his tongue slowly along her cheek, licking off what honey was left. Then he eased out of her as he moved down along her body and with a sweet tongue he licked her tiny nub until she frantically tapped him on the shoulder, letting him know she was near to climaxing.

He entered her quickly and with his climax as near as hers, he set a fast, hard rhythm that had them both exploding in seconds. Her continuous tapping on his arm begged him not to stop and he knew another climax was quickly following her first one, so he quickened the pace even more.

They were left breathing laboriously as their climaxes trickled off and faded away. Cree slipped out of her and collapsed on the bed beside her, his hand reaching out to entwine his fingers with hers.

When his breathing turned somewhat normal, he turned on his side and gave a quick lick at the honey on her cheek. "I think we may have to steal some of Turbett's honey now and again."

Dawn smiled and tapped her husband's arm repeatedly, agreeing with him.

"Your face has healed well," he said and she smiled and nodded. "But taking me so strenuously in your mouth could not have helped your wound."

She gestured, tapping her chest, shaking her head, and slipping her hand out of his to tap his manhood gently.

"Are you telling me that you could not resist me?" Cree asked his smile growing.

She nodded.

He kissed her gently. "I do so love you, wife."

She patted her chest, then his, then hers again, letting him know she felt the same. She then gestured, asking if she missed supper.

"Aye, you slept right through, but then you needed the rest. Are you hungry?"

Dawn's grumbling stomach answered for her, but she stopped Cree from leaving the bed and waking Flanna to fetch her something to eat. She could wait until morning. Besides, she was more interested in hearing about his talk with Obern and with Kellmara. She also wanted to know what happened to the Minnoch warrior who had attacked her and that is what she explained to her husband.

Cree detailed what Obern had said to him and how he had no choice but to give his word to the King not to harm Minnoch.

Dawn gestured, asking if Minnoch will be made to do the same... not harm Cree.

"We will see tomorrow when he arrives, though from what Kellmara heard in the woods, Minnoch wants my head and the person Minnoch's warrior was talking with was one of the King's guards."

Dawn's eyes widened and she felt a catch to her heart.

226

Cree rested his hand on her stomach. "Do not worry. Minnoch's warrior who attacked you was quick to surrender all information. It seems that Obern sent word to Minnoch, letting him know he approached Dowell and would arrive here before him. He was making it clear to Minnoch that there better not be an attack on Dowell with an advisor of the King in attendance."

Dawn sighed relieved and rested her hand over her husband's, relieved that a battle had been avoided, for now.

"That was why Minnoch's warrior was here in Dowell along with two others who never bothered to make themselves known. Only the one drank too much and when he saw you and remembered..." Cree could not finish. The reminder that the man had striped his wife naked and he had not been able to do anything to stop it sent a fiery rage racing through him.

Dawn felt her husband's anger in his tense muscles and she was afraid to ask what he did to the man.

"The warrior was returned to Minnoch. Unfortunately, he met with accident on the way. He tripped and fell and broke his neck."

Dawn knew it had been no accident. Cree had seen that the man paid for his foul deed, and somehow he would see that Minnoch paid as well. And that worried her, for that meant he would go against the King.

Cree yawned. "I will rest my eyes for a moment after which I will wake Flanna and see that you are fed, since your stomach continues to protest."

She had hoped he had not noticed her grumbling stomach, but then she was hungry. He, however, was tired and needed to sleep. She cuddled against him, softly stroking his arm and in minutes her husband was sound asleep, a faint snore confirming just how soundly.

Dawn slipped carefully out of the bed and quietly pulled on a robe and just as quietly went to see if the twins needed feeding. They were just stirring as she entered the room. She was happy to see Lila there and they hurried to hug each other.

"I was not sure if you would be feeding the twins their sunrise feeding, so I came just in case."

Dawn smiled and gestured that she was glad she did. She also thanked Lila for looking after them while she was gone.

"I must admit, I did not think you would be able to free Cree and feared that you would be taken prisoner along with him for attempting such a daring feat. And that you let your throat be cut..." Lila shook her head slowly. "You are truly courageous." Lila shook her head harder as Dawn gestured. "You are not foolish." A sudden smile lit her face. "Well, maybe sometimes."

The two women laughed, and Lila sat and talked with Dawn as she fed her restless son. They talked of pleasant things, about having a picnic with the children before the weather turned too cold, about how abundant the last harvest would be and how more plaids and blankets needed to be stitched before the winter set in.

It was only when Lila needed to go see to baby Thomas' feeding that she remarked on the present circumstances. "All will go well with Minnoch's arrival?"

Dawn smiled and gestured with Lizbeth's tiny hands, the baby smiling wide.

Lila broke out in a grin. "Since you have such confidence, Lizbeth, that your da will see that all goes well, I shall not worry."

Dawn nodded, agreeing with her. She spent some time with the twins after they finished feeding, tapping their tiny chests, then hers, and hugging them to let them know she loved them. She instructed the morning servants who looked after the babes that they were to remain here away from the visitors. After everyone left, Dawn would once again return to spend time outdoors with the twins. They loved when she and Cree would sit under a tree with them and their da would tell exciting tales. They would smile, coo, laugh, and eventually fall asleep in their parents' loving arms and Dawn missed that time they spent together.

She kissed them both and returned to her bedchamber to find Sloan there and her husband dressed.

"I was just going to look for you," Cree said, slipping his dagger into the sheath at his waist. "The sun is up and Minnoch will crest the hill shortly and be here soon after." Cree shot her a glare after she gestured. "You ask me what I want you to do, but

the true question is... will you obey my orders?"
Cree watched her gesture quickly. "I know you
promised me, but will you keep that promise?"

She had hoped he would not ask her that and she
responded truthfully.

"You will try?"

Dawn nodded.

Cree looked to Sloan and he hurried from the
room, closing the door behind him. Cree went to
stand in front of his wife, slipping his finger down
along the front of her robe to spread it apart and
partially expose her breasts. He ran his finger
slowly around her one breast until he circled her
nipple, and then he squeezed the hard, little nub.

"This situation is more dangerous than you
know and I need you to give me your word that you
will remain out of sight until I send for you. You
cannot show yourself before then."

She nodded and gestured with a bit frustration.

"So you think it unfair that I leave you
aroused?"

Dawn gave a quick, firm nod.

"Let it be a reminder of what awaits you later
today when you prove how well you can keep your
promise to me," he warned.

Dawn's brow shot up as she gestured.

"That is correct. If you do not keep your
promise I will not finish what I started here."

Dawn smiled and shook her head, knowing he
would never be able to do that.

Cree grabbed her arms and yanked her hard
against his chest. "You think I would threaten to

bring you to the brink of climax and not satisfy you if this was not of the utmost importance? I will have your word on this and you will keep it."

His anger was touched by a hint of fear and she knew that fear was for her. She nodded.

"You will do as I say?" he asked, needing her to confirm it again.

She nodded, then rested her hand gently on his arm as she scrunched her brow and shrugged in question.

He ran the back of his hand slowly along her cheek. "I do not want Minnoch to know it was you—my wife—he gave to me in the dungeon rather than a peasant lass. Only you, me, and Old Mary will ever know what happened there. And I have no worry that Old Mary will breathe a word of it.

Dawn tapped his chest, then his mouth, then her chest, and lastly tugged at her ear.

"All I had to do was tell you this and you would have listened... and obeyed?"

She nodded.

He smiled. "As you have listened to me how many times when I ordered you to do something?" His smile vanished. "I needed you to see the importance of this and I must know you will do as I say and keep out of sight of Minnoch and his men."

Dawn tilted her head and scrunched her brow, this time in thought, and then her eyes turned wide and her hands flew.

"Yes, I have a plan and no, I will not tell you about it and for a good reason."

Voices outside the door caught their attention and Cree went to the door and swung it open.

Sloan spoke as soon as he did. "Minnoch's messenger waits for you in the Great Hall."

Cree looked to Dawn. "You will do as I say?"

She gave him a vigorous nod and followed him out the door to watch him walk away. She wondered over his plan and his words.

Only you, me, and Old Mary will ever know.

He planned on killing Minnoch. But how, when he gave his word to the King not to harm the man?

Chapter Twelve

Obern was in the Great Hall and spoke up as soon as Cree entered. "You killed Minnoch's warrior?" He did not let Cree answer. "Minnoch now believes himself in danger and after I sent word that he was welcome here and had nothing to fear."

Cree remained silent, letting the man have his tirade.

"Do you wish to ruin everything for the King? I do not know how many times I must tell you how important Minnoch is to the King at the moment. You will do everything you can to make the man feel welcomed. You will do what the King instructed you to do or one word from me and you will find yourself in a far worse dungeon than Minnoch's."

Cree stepped in front of the man, towering over him. "*Never. Ever. Threaten me.* I have done what the King has instructed me to do. I have found out that the King cannot now or ever trust Minnoch, but the King wants what he wants and will trust a fool to get it for him."

Obern sputtered and blustered as he struggled to find the words to speak.

"Do not dare say a word," Cree shouted in the man's face, and Obern drew his head back. "I am a loyal servant of the King and I gave my word to him and I will keep it. I will not harm Minnoch."

Obern finally found his voice. "Nor will your warriors do him harm."

"Nor my warriors," Cree repeated. "Now let us be done with this farce so that I may rid myself of you and Minnoch."

"The King will hear of this," Obern warned with a quiver to his voice.

"Aye, he will, for I intend to make sure he knows what went on here." Cree leaned over Obern and whispered, "You have no idea what I have done for the King, little man. The title, the land, does not begin to repay me and the King knows it. So be very careful how you talk to me, for if the King had to choose between you and me... he would choose me and order me to kill you—and I would."

Obern took several quick steps away from Cree and made sure he kept distance between them.

"Flanna," Cree yelled and the woman stepped up beside him.

"All is ready to receive our guest, my lord," Flanna said.

Cree nodded and whispered, "My wife will be keeping to herself today. See that you keep her abreast of what goes on here."

She nodded and Cree walked over to Sloan, leaving Obern to pout near the dais. The little fool had no idea how important Cree had been to the King and continued to be, though Cree was not foolish enough to think that that could change at any time, especially if a new king was crowned. But at the moment the King required his help and he would see that he got it.

"All is ready?" Cree asked when he reached Sloan.

"All has been seen to," Sloan confirmed.

"Then let us wait outside to greet Minnoch."

~~~

Cree watched Minnoch approach with four of his warriors. His large troop of warriors was stopped at the edge of the village and informed they could go no further, which no doubt produced the scowl that Minnoch wore. Cree would have to be a fool to allow him to enter the village with a troop of his warriors.

Minnoch was off his horse as soon as he brought the animal to a stop in front of the keep's steps. He flew up them, nostrils flaring along with his temper. "How dare you keep my men from entering with me and how dare you kill one of my men."

"I may have given the King my word that I would not harm you, but if you dare to threaten me, my family, my clan, it will negate any promise I made to the King, on that you have my word." Cree stepped toward him. "So go ahead, Minnoch, *threaten me.*"

Minnoch tempered his anger, though it remained close to the surface. "Let me speak to the King's advisor. He has an important message for me."

"Afterwards you can leave," Cree said.

That brought a smile to Minnoch's face. "I was told I would be welcomed here."

"You have no idea how pleased I am to have you here."

"That sounds much better, Cree. Now take me to Obern."

As soon as Minnoch and Obern were introduced, Minnoch insisted that Obern and he talk privately. Cree had them taken to his solar and a guard posted outside the door. Cree did not care what the pair discussed. One of his messengers was already on the way to the King with a missive that explained everything that had gone on here and how Minnoch could not be trusted and that it would be to the King's advantage to deal directly with the chieftains of the Western Isles and the King of Norway himself then through Minnoch. He knew his word held sway with the King, for Cree had been nothing but truthful with the monarch since first meeting him.

It was near an hour later that Cree was summoned into his solar. Minnoch stood by the hearth like a man who believed himself victorious, his chest puffed out and a smug grin on his face.

"It is done," Obern said. "Minnoch will help the King, he forgives you for stealing from him, and you will not harm him. Now let us feast and celebrate that the deed is done."

~~~

Cree made sure that Minnoch, his warriors, and Obern not only got plenty of food to eat, but that they also had plenty to drink.

"Where is your wife? Will she not grace us with her presence?" Minnoch asked, holding his tankard high for a servant lass passing by to fill.

"She is not feeling well," Cree said his tankard still full from when it was first poured over an hour ago.

Minnoch downed some ale, then said, "Such a shame. I was looking forward to meeting her. A voiceless wife no doubt can make a husband's lot much easier, though at other times..." Minnoch grinned. "I was eager to inform your wife how you entertained yourself while in my dungeon. But no doubt she will learn soon enough when you pass on to her what my little gift gave to you." He laughed and finished what ale was in his tankard, then raised it high to be filled again.

Cree did not respond, though it took a tremendous amount of will to sit in silence and wait.

The hour grew late with many of Minnoch's warriors falling asleep at the tables where they sat while others laid passed out on the floor. Obern retired over an hour ago, having eaten and drank himself so full that he could barely walk from the room.

"A lass," Minnoch said and belched loudly, "I need a lass to give a good plowing to tonight. There was a blonde servant with large breasts. She kept filling my tankard. Now I want to fill her." He scratched his head. "Dorrie! I heard her called Dorrie and that she lives secluded from the village."

"Better to entertain the men who thirst after her," Cree said.

"Good, then she will enjoy a hard plowing and know how to please me. You will show me to her cottage," Minnoch ordered, stumbling to his feet.

It was late, the village asleep, and not a soul stirred as they made their way through the village. They entered the woods and after a short time, Minnoch started laughing, and Cree stopped to stare at the man.

"I would never have been so foolish as to follow you in the woods if you had not given your word to the King not to harm me."

"And of course you thought to remind me of that."

He laughed again. "Aye, and I do it with great pleasure."

"Tell me something, Minnoch, why did you falsely accuse me of stealing from you, imprison me, and plan to behead me?"

Minnoch grinned, stood tall, and gave a shout. Four of his warriors suddenly rushed out of the woods surrounding them, their swords drawn.

"I do not forgive and I do not forget," he said with anger. "I once served the chieftain of the Clan Kellmara. He had told me that he wished he had a son like me rather than the son who disappointed him and fell in love with a peasant woman. I followed his orders and saw that his son was sent away and kept away until his father commanded his return. The chieftain sent me to make sure the woman never bothered with his son again. Your mother was more woman than I expected. She fought back and fired my loins until I was so hungry for her that I did not take heed and she..." He growled with anger. "She gave me this." He pointed to the scar on his face. "When I returned to the chieftain wounded badly, he told me that if a woman could best me, then I was worthless to him. So, he cast me out. I had plans to eventually be Chieftain of the Clan Kellmara. It would have been easy to get rid of the son and convince the childless chieftain to pass the title and his lands on to me. I will not bore you with the hell I lived through after that. Or what I had to do to gain the pittance of what I have now to what I would have had if I had become Laird of the Clan Kellmara. It was a promise I made to myself that I would have my revenge one day that kept me going. I am going to take everything from you as your mother took from me, and you can do nothing to stop me."

"I thought I killed the man who had attacked my mother," Cree said more calmly than he felt.

Minnoch snorted as he laughed again. "You as well as Kellmara's fool of a son. Now you know that you never revenged your mother and you never will. Once the King hears that you did not keep your word and that I killed you defending myself, he will give me your lands as compensation and victory will taste sweet. As for your wife and bairns, I will see they serve me."

Cree stood with his hands clenched at his sides, an image of his mum bruised and bloody and struggling against the pain so that her son would not see her suffering hit him hard. He had to keep tight rein on his anger or he would lunge forward and snap the man's neck, though not before beating him much worse than what he had done to his mum.

"I do not forgive or forget either, Minnoch," Cree said his fury on the verge of erupting.

"Perhaps," he grinned, "but you stand without a weapon before me and with a promise to the King not to harm me. You can do nothing about it."

"You are right. I can do nothing... but he can," Cree said with a nod toward the dark woods.

There was a rustling of leaves in the dense line of trees and a shadow slowly emerged, the full moon giving light to the man who stood sword in hand, rage burning in his eyes...Kellmara. His warriors poured out of the woods from behind him and to his sides, surrounding Minnoch and his men."

"This was a trap. You lured me here!" Minnoch shouted.

This time Cree laughed, though there was no humor in it. "Is that not what you did to me? Lure me here with intentions of killing me? Did you really believe me such a fool that I would walk alone in the dark woods with you," —Cree took a quick step toward the man— "especially when I knew what you had done to my mother?"

Shock contorted Minnoch's face. "You knew?"

Kellmara explained. "I recognized you, though it took me a moment, when I saw you speaking with one of your guards in the woods. You were gone when I returned home to my family all those years ago and, when I inquired about you, I was told you disappointed my father and was sent away. It was not until much later that I learned the truth. By then I heard you had died and I thought it done. My only regret was that I did not get to kill you myself. I am pleased that shortly, I will no longer have that regret."

"My men here will see that the truth is known," Minnoch warned his eyes shifting nervously.

"They die with you," Cree said not a hint of regret in his voice. "That woman you so callously had these guards give to me while imprisoned was my wife... and no one treats my wife that way and lives."

Minnoch stared at him speechless.

Cree looked to Kellmara. "Make him suffer."

"With pleasure, but you should go. Return to the keep and make sure Minnoch's drunken men see you," Kellmara said. "I will send word when it is done."

Cree looked to Minnoch. "Now you know why I was so pleased to have you here. I knew you would take your last breath on my land."

"You cannot do this, Cree. You gave your word," Minnoch shouted as Cree turned his back and walked off.

"And I am keeping it," Cree called out and disappeared into the dark woods.

He came upon Elwin and Dorrie at the edge of the woods. Her garments were ripped, her hair strewn with dirt, and her nose and mouth dripping blood.

"Are you certain you are comfortable with this, Dorrie?" Cree asked.

"Aye, my lord, anything to help my lady," Dorrie said.

Cree thought about Dawn's throat and he looked to Elwin. "The blood?"

"Flanna gave it to us."

Cree nodded, approvingly. "I will see you soon, Dorrie."

"Aye, my lord, and I will not fail you."

"Of that I have no doubt," Cree said and hurried to the keep.

Minnoch's men were passed out, some snoring so loudly that he wondered how it did not wake the others. He gave a shove to a few who had their hands grasped on their tankards. "Another drink?"

"Aye," they shouted, though it was garbled.

Cree made sure they saw him take a seat at the dais and raise a tankard to his lips, and then he waited. He was pleased that his wife had kept her word and not shown herself. He would explain it all later to her. It would not be long now. The sun was just rising and the servants entered to clean the hall and ready it for the morning meal, and that was when he had Flanna send for his wife.

He was not surprised that she joined him in only a matter of minutes. He imagined she was sitting in their bedchamber the whole evening, dressed and waiting for him to summon her.

"Good morning, wife, feeling better?" he asked his strong voice carrying across the hall and stirring some of the drunken warriors awake.

Dawn smiled and nodded and rubbed her stomach, following her husband's lead that all was well, though eager to know what went on here last night.

Obern entered the Great Hall a few minutes later, delighted to see the table being made ready and he took a seat next to Cree, while looking over the hall. "A good feast last night, but where is Minnoch?"

"He requested a woman and I saw that he got one," Cree said.

"That was good of you," Obern said. "I am going to let the King know how cooperative you were once the pact was agreed upon."

The terrifying screams rang through the Great Hall like a bell that refused to stop tolling. Minnoch's warriors rushed to their feet, as did his wife, and when Dorrie came barreling into the Great Hall screaming, crying, and begging for help, Dawn hurried to her side, wrapping her arms around Dorrie who all but collapsed in them.

"They killed him! They killed him!" Dorrie screeched.

Cree had gotten to his feet when the screaming had begun and he rushed around the table, Obern following him.

"They killed him!" Dorrie screamed again, turning horrified eyes on Cree.

"Calm down, Dorrie," he ordered. "Who killed who?"

"His warriors," she gasped. "Minnoch's warriors killed him."

"Good lord," Obern shouted and Minnoch's warriors quickly gathered closer.

"What happened?" Cree demanded.

"Minnoch did not want to share me, not until he was done. His warriors were drunk and thought differently. They tried to—" Dorrie shook her head and pulled her torn garments tighter over her chest. "Minnoch lashed out with his sword and the next thing I knew they were all fighting, and then they..." Tears poured from her eyes. "They all lay dead."

Obern turned angry eyes on Cree. "Where were you last night? And do not tell me with your wife since she was ill."

Dawn shook her head, pointed at her husband and patted her chest, letting Obern know that her husband had not been with her. She prayed that was what Cree wanted her to admit to since Obern mentioned she had been ill.

"He was here with us," one of Minnoch's men called out.

"Aye, I saw him," another said.

"He had a drink with me," another chimed in.

"This cannot be happening," Obern said, patting his chest, attempting to calm himself, "not after all my hard work."

"Where are they?" Cree asked Dorrie.

"Near my cottage," she said through heavy gasps.

Cree looked to his wife. "See to Dorrie."

She nodded and hurried the woman off to Cree's solar, wanting to know the truth.

Obern followed after Cree. "I am going with you."

"Are you sure you want to see this?" Cree asked.

"I must report back to the King," Obern insisted.

A short time later Obern was being helped away from the scene, his stomach roiling from the horrible sight. He sat on a stump, pale and shaken. "Whatever will the King do now?"

Hearing Obern lamenting, Cree approached. "The King will do whatever he must; he always does, and you shall be there to help him."

Obern raised his head high, as if suddenly gaining new purpose. "You are right, Cree. I will be there to help the King and I must take my leave immediately so I may do just that." He wrinkled his nose. "Minnoch was crude and vulgar. It is no wonder that he met such an appropriate death."

"You are right, Obern, he met a most fitting death."

Chapter Thirteen

That evening.

"Are you trying to kill me, wife," Cree said, grabbing hold of her backside to slow her down. "You are riding me harder than a stallion does a mare." He watched a tear trickle down her cheek and he let lose an oath, grabbed her around the waist and yanked her off him to roll on his side and place her flat on her back.

"What is wrong?" he asked tenderly wiping her tear away.

Dawn shook her head. Though she could not speak, there were times she actually did not wish to speak and this was one of those times.

"Nothing disturbs you?"

She shook her head again and fought the other tears that threatened to spill.

"You might as well let loose those tears you are struggling to hold back before they gush from your beautiful eyes like a rainstorm."

His voice was tender and his words so loving that she could not contain her tears any longer and she let them fall.

Cree hated to see her cry. He would do anything not to see her cry, but this time he understood that she needed to cry. And every one of her tears that fell pierced his heart like a mighty arrow.

He pressed his brow to hers and whispered, "I love you, Dawn, and there is nothing that can ever change that love. It is rooted deep in my heart and in my soul that I had thought I had long ago lost, though thanks to you, I found."

She went to gesture, but he took hold of her hand.

"I am here safe with you... because of you." He scowled, though a hint of a smile slipped through. "And though it pains me to admit it, it is one time I am glad you disobeyed me."

Dawn's eyes turned wide, her tears subsiding.

"That does not mean you are to disobey me again," he said quickly.

Dawn smiled and gestured.

He shook his head. "No, not only when necessary. Now, from this moment on, you will be a dutiful wife and obey my every word." He shook his head again or maybe he never stopped shaking it, he was not sure, though he was sure about one thing. "You will never be an obedient wife."

Dawn gestured slowly.

"Did I hear you correctly? Are you asking me if I truly want you to be obedient?" Cree said and was about to argue with her when she pressed her finger to his lips, stopping him.

She smiled softly, pointed to him, then to her ear and mouth, then to herself.

"Of course I hear you, but what does that have to do with you being obedient?"

She gestured again.

"I let you be you?" He laughed. "There is no stopping you."

She shook her head and gestured again.

"Are you telling me that I freed you to be you and that you never want to feel imprisoned again?

She nodded and continued her gestures.

To him, his wife had a distinct voice and he loved hearing it. It was in the way she gestured with her hands, the expression on her face, and the movement of her body, and he heard her every word.

I am safe with you. I can say what I feel to you and whether you grow angry or not I know you will never harm me and never stop loving me. Because of you, I faced my fears and conquered them. You freed me to make what I thought impossible... possible. I do so love you, husband.

Her words stirred his heart and he kissed her softly after whispering, "And I you, wife."

Cree rolled to hover over her, his hands braced on either side of her head. "However, there will be times when it will be prudent of you to obey me."

She scrunched her brow and shrugged.

He ordered with a commanding tone, "You will be a good, obedient wife and spread your legs for me."

Dawn grinned and moved her legs as if she was about to obey him, then suddenly shoved him off her onto his back and climbed on top of him, slipping herself over him and taking him deep inside her before he could protest.

Cree gave a groan and grinned. "Ahh, wife, this time I have you right where I want you."

The End... not yet!

An interesting side note... honey has been used since 50 A.D. to treat wounds. Of course the honey today is different from the honey way back when (ex. no pesticides).

Highlander's Winter Tale
A Cree & Dawn Short Story

by

Donna Fletcher

Highlander's Winter Tale
A Cree & Dawn Short Story

Cover art by Kim Killion
The Killion Group, Inc.

Visit Donna's Web site
www.donnafletcher.com
Visit Donna on Facebook
www.facebook.com/donna.fletcher.author

Chapter One

The winter wind whipped around the keep howling like a banshee as the snow fell. It had started with a handful of flurries at mid-day and now near to nightfall, Dawn could not believe how much snow covered the ground. She threw the hood of her blue wool cloak up over her head and went to step off the top stair of the keep.

"Where do you think you are going?" Cree demanded, stepping in front of her, his broad shoulders blocking not only her path but the snow that had been whipping at her face. He hated to see her upset, not that she displayed it for all to see, but he could easily tell when she was troubled. Her smile was not as bright and her gestures were less enthusiastic when she spoke, though he understood them more easily.

She may have lacked a voice since birth, but she made herself heard in every gesture and expression and he was proud to have her as his wife, not to mention that he loved her beyond measure. She and their five month old twins Valan and Lizbeth were his whole world and he could not envision life without them.

Dawn hunched her shoulders and gnarled her hands, then pointed in the distance.

"You are going to collect Old Mary. I thought the same myself. There is no telling how long this sudden snowstorm will last and I would not want her stuck in her cottage alone."

Dawn raised her hand as if catching the falling snow and shrugged.

"We have not had a late autumn snowstorm in some time, and I am glad it arrived before we departed on our journey to visit my sister. It would have been difficult and dangerous enough, though even more so with the twins and Old Mary joining us."

Dawn nodded, aware that her husband was right. Traveling in such a storm could prove deadly, especially for the young and old. Still, she could not help but feel that she was letting Wintra down. She had promised her that she would be there for the birth of her first babe. Even if the snow stopped soon, which did not seem likely, the roads would be too difficult to travel, some barely passable, and Wintra's time was drawing ever closer.

Cree slipped his hand past her cloak to rest at her waist as his other hand took hold of her chin that had drooped along with her shoulders and raised it slowly. "I know you promised Wintra that you would be there for the birth and it upsets you that you cannot keep your promise, but she will understand that it was the snow that kept you away."

Again her husband was right, but that did not make her feel any better. When she had given birth to the twins, she had had family and friends around her, including Wintra, and Dawn had been grateful to have them all there, especially when it seemed that one twin would not survive.

She did not want to see Wintra without family there to help her when her time came. She knew Wintra felt the same, since she had reminded Dawn many times before taking her leave from her brother's home that she was to come help deliver the babe. Dawn had promised her again and again and now...

Dawn turned tearful eyes on her husband.

Cree felt a punch to his gut. Dawn did not cry easily. She was a resilient and courageous woman who more often than not found a way to get what she wanted, though truthfully, more often than not; it was to see the right thing done. She had promised his sister and now she could not keep that promise and it tore at her heart, and seeing her like this tore at his. He yanked her against him and hugged her tight as he said, "If there was anything I could do to get you to my sister, I would."

Dawn's arms went around her husband and she rested her head against his chest as she tapped it and then hers repeatedly.

"I love you more," he said gently before his tone turned to a command. "Besides, you belong to me and always will." Cree was glad to see a smile spread across her face at his familiar remark when she raised her head to look at him.

She gave his chest one hard tap, and then did the same to her own.

He grinned and lowered his head and before his lips claimed hers, he said, "Aye, I do belong to you. We are one you and I, and we will never part."

His kiss was strong and possessive, as if it

sealed his words, and if Dawn had not shivered, the kiss would not yet have ended.

"You are cold," Cree said, easing her away from him. "Go inside by the fire and I will go and fetch Old Mary."

She smiled again, though there was a hint of wickedness to it. She took his hand and shook her head slowly as she stepped closer to him and placed it in the folds of her dress between her legs, making it clear that the shiver had not been from the cold.

He rested his cheek against her flushed one and whispered in her ear, "Tempt me, wife, and I will have you flat on your back in the snow."

She tapped his arm over and over. One tap signified yes, two taps no, so several...aroused him.

"Go now," he ordered with a snarl, stepping away from her. "Or we both will soon be buried in snow."

Dawn hesitated a moment before turning and heading toward the door. She wished her husband had taken her in the snow, at least then—for a brief time—she would not think on how badly she had failed his sister.

Her arm was suddenly yanked and she was once again plastered against her husband's hard chest.

"Later tonight I will make you forget your worries." Cree kissed her quick as he propelled her toward the door, opened it, and shoved her inside. "Do as I say and go warm yourself." He shut the door and hurried off into the snow before Dawn could protest. He would see that his wife had a good night and later when they retired to their bedchamber, he would make certain that she fell into an exhausted slumber.

~~~

The Great Hall was filled with those villagers who felt their meager cottages would not do well against the raging snowstorm. Sleeping pallets were arranged and warm wool blankets supplied for anyone who felt the need to spend the night in the keep. No one was turned away.

There were more villagers than expected, but then many believed that the mighty Cree could protect them against anything, even a fierce snowstorm. Flanna, the woman in charge of running the keep, and good friend to Dawn, made sure food was plentiful. Ale, wine, and cider flowed freely as did conversation.

Dawn watched the comradery with little joy. Try as she might she could not get Wintra off her mind. What would it be like for her to birth a babe without family at hand? Who was there for her that she could trust without question? Wintra's husband's mum had passed as did his one and only sister. So who would be there at this special time? Who would hold her hand, mop her brow, encourage her when needed, and share in the joy of her first birth?

Cree watched his wife with concern, wishing there was something he could do to help her.

"Dawn is troubled that she cannot be with Wintra in her time of need," Sloan whispered, leaning over to Cree from where he sat beside him at the dais.

Cree turned and kept his voice low. "It has grown that obvious?"

"To those who know her well."

"I wish I could distract her thoughts if only for a while," Cree said and when he saw Sloan's grin turn sly and his brow shoot up, he shook his head. "I will be distracting her thoughts far more than a while later this evening. At the moment, she needs nourishment. She has barely eaten today."

"I have an idea that may keep her so engaged that any morsel of food you hand her, she will eat without giving thought to it."

"Tell me of this magic," Cree ordered skeptically.

Sloan grinned, stood, and walked around the dais and over to Old Mary who sat near the heat of the huge stone fireplace. He leaned down and whispered in her ear and the old woman seemed hesitant to his suggestion. Sloan whispered to her again and gave a nod toward the dais. Old Mary smiled and nodded. He fetched a chair and placed it by the front of the dais, then called out, "Time for a tale!"

Cheers echoed off the walls of the Great Hall as Sloan extended his arm to Old Mary and escorted her to the chair. After sitting, she rubbed her gnarled hands while slowly nodding her head, as if gathering her thoughts.

For an old woman, her voice was strong and commanding when finally she began. "The tale I tell is an old one, handed down through time. Some believe it is more truth than tale," —she paused, her eyes looking as though they settled on each and every person there—"I will leave that for you to judge."

Cree saw interest spark on his wife's face and he handed her a small piece of cheese. He was pleased to see her take it and nibble at it. He gave Sloan a nod of thanks when he returned to his seat and settled in to listen.

"What tale is it, Old Mary?" a woman shouted out.

Old Mary waited a moment before calling out for all to hear, "A Winter Tale!"

A handful of gasps circled the room while others looked puzzled.

"You will bring him to life if you tell the tale," another woman warned anxiously.

"Perhaps," Old Mary shrugged and looked around, her eyes settling on Dawn, "or perhaps it is nothing more than a tale to tell when a snowstorm is upon us."

Dawn nodded eager to hear the tale she had not heard about until now and took another piece of cheese her husband handed her.

Old Mary rested back in the chair and began the tale. "It all began over one hundred years ago when a witch cursed a mighty Highland warrior, though some say it is the woman he loved and betrayed who cursed him." She looked around with wide eyes. "His name is not known, though there are those who believe his name is kept a secret, for if spoken during a snowstorm it releases him to walk the earth in search of—" She paused again, her aged eyes glancing over the spellbound faces. All eyes rested intently on her. The only sound heard was the crackling fire. "That is where the tale differs. Some believe he searches for love to correct the mistake he made and others believe he searches for—vengeance."

Dawn leaned forward in her chair enthralled by the story and took the goblet of wine her husband handed her.

"They say the Highlander was a fierce warrior and that no one could best him in battle. It was believed that the old Gods and new God alike watched over him. Men wanted to fight beside him, knowing they would taste victory. Fine features and ample strength had women flocking to him more than willing to please him." Old Mary coughed lightly and someone hurried to hand her a goblet of wine. She took a sip then sent the woman a nod of thanks.

Silence hung heavy, everyone waiting for Old Mary to continue the mysterious tale.

"It is said he was the last one standing in the middle of a battlefield, carnage all around him, his sword thick with blood, when he spotted movement. Someone had survived. He walked toward a stirring of bodies and that was when he saw it, a slim, bloody hand clawing its way out from beneath a pile of dead warriors. He hurried to the spot and what he saw had him lifting lifeless bodies and throwing them aside to reach...the woman who lay beneath.

"Blood had soaked her garments, turned her blonde hair red and was smeared across her face. Her eyes remained closed even when he lifted her into his arms. He wondered what a woman was doing on the battlefield as he walked over the dead warriors away from the carnage. Another troop of his warriors arrived. He was given a horse and with the woman in his arms he rode to the camp not far off." Old Mary paused to take another sip of wine.

Cree refilled Dawn's goblet. He was pleased that he did not need to place anymore food in front of her. She ate by choice or perhaps without thought, since her eyes remained fixed on Old Mary, waiting for her to continue. He had to admit the story did captivate and that was good, since it took worries off the wicked snowstorm.

Old Mary resumed the tale. "Some claim she bewitched him as soon as she opened her violet eyes and looked upon him. Others insist that it was love that struck them both when their eyes met. He tended her and saw to her every need and they became inseparable. Her kind nature won the hearts of most of his clan, except for a few. All went well for several months and even the few who had been uncertain about her began to change their minds.

"Summer passed into autumn and no vows were exchanged between the couple and the clans' people began to wonder why. One day, he went off to battle and before he returned home word was received that he had wed and his new wife was returning with him. The lass, he had claimed to love, was moved out of the keep and into a small

260

cottage at the far edge of the village." Old Mary shook her head. "Thinking this union was forced upon the mighty warrior, the woman waited eagerly to see him and hear the truth. The warrior returned with his new wife and days passed into months and he never came to her. She gathered her belongings and moved to a deserted cottage in the woods. Villagers came to her for healing potions and amulets and such. Her only friends were the forest creatures. She was alone, unwanted, and unloved.

"Tongues began to wag. It seemed that the warrior's wife could not get with child and some claimed it was the woman's doing. Many believed she had cursed the wife for taking away the man she loved. The wife, learning of the gossip, insisted that the evil woman had to die if she was ever to give the mighty warrior a son." Old Mary wiped a tear from her eye.

Cree saw the sorrow on his wife's face and he covered her hand that rested on the table with his, giving it a squeeze. She turned to him and pressed her free hand to his chest and then to hers.

He leaned down and whispered in her ear, "I love you as well and I will show you just how much later tonight." He was pleased to see her smile, though it faded as she quickly turned her head away from him as soon as Old Mary continued the tale. His ire stirred, a scowl beginning to form, when Dawn moved her hand away from his. It dissipated quickly when she entwined her fingers with his and held on tight.

"The mighty warrior's soldiers came for her that

winter and imprisoned her in the keep's dungeon, a dank, dark, and dreadful place. She was ordered to remove the curse from the warrior's wife or she would be hanged and her body burned a fitting end for a witch. She insisted repeatedly that she had not put a curse on the woman nor had she ever bewitched the warrior as many had claimed. Her only mistake was falling in love with the mighty warrior and believing him to be an honorable man.

"Snow began to fall the night before the hanging. All night the woman waited in her small cell, wondering if the man she had once believed loved her would come to see her. But he never came. Snow was falling heavily the next morning, but it did not stop the execution. The woman was taken to a tree, placed on a horse, and a noose slipped around her neck. The only one in attendance was the warrior chosen to carry out the execution, though it was not the falling snow that kept others away. It was the fear of being cursed by the witch that kept them locked away in their cottages.

"The woman sat on the horse waiting for death when out of the falling snow walked the man who had once claimed to love her. He was even more handsome than she remembered and her heart soared, thinking that perhaps he had a change of heart and had come to spare her life. His words were not what she had expected and they cut much deeper than any dagger could."

"You bewitched me the moment your eyes met mine. Now I will finally be free of you."

"The woman thought her heart could not break

any more than it already had, but at that moment her heart felt as though it shattered into millions of pieces. She had been a fool to believe he had ever loved her. Devastated, she lashed out at him, condemning him with her last words. "When death claims you, I curse you to walk the earth only when the snow falls heavily upon the ground and your name is called forth. You will know no peace, no rest until the power of love seals your fate." The woman then shouted out his name and it drifted along on the snowy wind as the execution was carried out with a nod from the mighty warrior."

Old Mary paused for a moment before resuming, her tone full of sadness. "The warrior's wife met an early death that winter from a fever as did many of the villagers and the mighty warrior himself. But when they went to bury his body—it was gone. The following winter when the first heavy snow covered the ground and his name was evoked in remembrance, the mighty warrior appeared. He had not known where he had been and many thought that perhaps he had not died and the fever had him wander off and now he had finally returned and the clan celebrated. After a few days, fear replaced joy, many believing the devil had returned with him. Women he touched turned ill as did animals he laid his hand upon. Men were too frightened to go near him and food stored for the winter began to rot. When the snow was gone, so was the mighty warrior. The warrior who had carried out the execution told everyone about the curse the woman had placed upon the mighty warrior, and all began to wonder. Next winter, fearful that the curse could be true and he would once again bring the devil with him, it was agreed that the warrior's name would not be evoked. However, when a second snow fell a drunken warrior uttered his name with a laugh. The door to the keep flew open and in walked the mighty warrior, snow swirling around him. This time the people did their best to avoid him, but he was laird and his word ruled. Several women in the clan died as did animals, but not the mighty warrior. When the snow was gone, so was he. The next year his name never passed anyone's lips and the warrior was not seen. His clan never spoke his name again. All portraits of him were removed, tapestries of his battles were burned and his name struck from documents and stones—where it had been carved— destroyed, until no remembrance of him existed. The tale, however, spread across the land and through time. Some foolishly evoked names, tempting fate, and the warrior would appear having been woken from his never-ending slumber, bringing the devil and death with him."

The women shivered and some of the men shook their heads while other men laughed and began calling out names.

"James come forth!"

"William you are welcome here!"

"Stop it," one woman shouted. "You will bring the devil down upon us."

The men paid no heed to the warning and continued calling out names.

264

"Ranald!"

"John!"

A woman slapped the one man, who shouted out a name, in the shoulder to get him to stop.

"Charles!"

"Stop!" another woman warned anxiously.

"Alexander!"

"Boyce!"

The wind suddenly screeched like a horde of banshees around the keep and Dawn turned to Cree with fear in her eyes, pointing to the men and shaking her head.

Cree nodded, agreeing that the nonsense must stop, but before he could stand and order the men to cease their nonsense, the Great Hall doors burst open and in with a rush of swirling wind and snow entered a hooded, black-cloaked figure.

Chapter Two

Not a sound was uttered, not a soul stirred.
Everyone sat frozen, staring at the cloaked figure as
he drew closer to the tables.

Cree stood and felt his wife's grip on his hand
tighten and with the sea of anxious faces staring at
the stranger, he needed to end this foolishness
before they all believed that a ghost walked among
them.

"Make yourself known, stranger!" Cree
commanded with a shout.

The cloaked figure halted and as he raised his
head, he threw back the hood of his cloak.

Women gasped, men shook their heads, and
Dawn gripped her husband's hand harder. Cree was
a handsome man and never would she think another
more handsome, but this man's sculpted features
could not be denied. They stole the breath and
captivated attention. His eyes were as blue as a
warm summer day and dark brows arched over
them in perfect symmetry. High cheekbones defined
slender cheeks, a narrow nose, and a square chin.
And his lips were...luscious. Some women would
think him irresistible, not so Dawn. Cree was and
always would be the only irresistible man to her.

Cree understood why the men shook their heads
and watched as every woman scrutinized the man
with more than simple curiosity. Cree snapped his
head to the side to glance at his wife and he did not

266

like the way she stared at the stranger.

"I seek shelter from the storm," the man said his voice so strong and intoxicating, that it brought smiles to all the women's faces.

"Your name!" Cree demanded his voice full of annoyance.

Without pause, the stranger offered his name, slipping off his cloak a he did. "Alexander."

Gasps stung the air again, though Cree was not sure if it was because his name matched one that had been called out or it was the lean, hard, stranger's confident stance that caused the startled responses.

Alexander ran his fingers through his dark hair, pulling the damp strands away from his face to tuck behind his ears and fall to rest at his wide shoulders. The casual movement brought sighs from some of the women.

Cree looked to his wife again and he was pleased she did not appear affected by it.

"May I trouble you for shelter and food until this storm passes?" Alexander asked.

One of the women stood, a goblet in her hand, ready to take it too him when she caught sight of Cree. The scowl he settled on her had her sitting down abruptly and pushing the goblet away.

Cree turned to Sloan and whispered, "See that she is reprimanded for her actions." Cree returned his attention to Alexander. "You are welcome to seek shelter here."

"I am most appreciative of your generosity," Alexander said with a graceful bow of his head.

Cree had many questions for the stranger, but he would not ask them in front of everyone, for he was not sure if the answers would unsettle many. He would wait and speak to the man alone. For now, he said, "Take a seat by the fire and share in our food."

Alexander bowed his head once more before going to a table where women scurried to make room for him and the men refused to budge. The three women at the table fussed over the man as did a couple of servant lasses.

As soon as Cree sat, Sloan whispered to him, "Old or young alike, he has them mesmerized. We should keep a sharp eye on him."

Cree nodded and kept his voice low. "At all times."

Sloan understood and would assign warriors to follow the warrior while he was here.

Cree turned to his wife, raising their joined hands to give hers a kiss. She smiled at him and it warmed his heart, or was it relief to see the love she had for him shining so bright in her dark eyes?

He leaned down and whispered in her ear, "I cannot wait to get you into bed tonight."

Her smile grew and she tapped her chest, letting him know she was just as eager.

While Cree refilled her goblet with wine, he saw that she glanced over at the stranger. He wondered what she thought of him. Did she find him as attractive as the other women did?

Dawn looked to her husband, then to the stranger, then back at her husband and scrunched her brow and shrugged.

"You wonder about him?"

She nodded.

"Aye, I do as well. How did he make his way here in an intense snowstorm in the middle of the night?"

Dawn nodded, agreeing with him.

"I will speak with him privately before we retire."

Dawn frowned and gestured that that would bring him late to their bed.

"Eager to bed me?' he said with a gentle laugh.

She smiled and nodded vigorously.

Cree leaned in close to whisper, "As hungry as I am for you, I need to make certain he poses no threat to our clan."

Her eyes widened with worry and she pressed her hand to his chest.

He rested his hand over hers. "There is no reason for you to worry." She went to gesture and he caught her hands in his. "Please do not even suggest that he may be the warrior of the tale Old Mary spun."

Dawn turned her head to look out over everyone gathered in the Great Hall, then glanced back at her husband and once again over the room.

Cree followed where his wife had glanced to see heads huddled in conversation while stealing looks at the stranger. Tongues were busy wagging. "Now I will have to prove the stranger is no more than a man seeking shelter from the storm before gossiping tongues create another tale."

After Old Mary finished speaking with a few of

the women who had hurried to speak with her, she walked over to the dais. "These old bones are tired. Will you walk with me to my room, Dawn?"

Dawn smiled and nodded only too pleased to help her. Cree went to stand when she did, but she placed a firm hand on his shoulder and shook her head. She tilted her head toward the stranger, tapped her lips, then her husband's and tapped her own chest, as her smile turned inviting.

"I will keep my conversation with the stranger brief since you will be eagerly waiting in our bedchamber for me."

Dawn leaned down and gave him a loving kiss on the cheek. What no one saw was how her hand slipped under his plaid and stroked him teasingly, arousing him.

"That hungry for me?"

She casually placed the tip of her finger in her mouth and sucked on it innocently, nipping at the tip as she withdrew it and Cree turned hard.

"*Enough*!" Cree snapped. "Take Old Mary and settle her in, then wait for me in our bedchamber. I will not be long."

Sloan chuckled as she walked past him smiling and she gave him a nod good-night.

Cree watched his wife take hold of Old Mary's arm and leave the Great Hall, keeping a firm hold on the woman. Then he turned his attention to Alexander and saw how easily he seemed to engage those around him, even the men who at first ignored him. The whole table appeared to be livelier since the stranger had joined them. Smiles and frequent

270

laughter circled the table and those who looked on did so with envy.

Seeing enough, Cree stood, looked at Sloan and ordered, "Bring the stranger to my solar."

Sloan nodded and after downing the last of his ale, walked over to Alexander. "Cree wishes to speak with you."

"As you wish," Alexander said with a pleasant smile and followed Sloan. As soon as he entered the solar he once again thanked Cree for his generosity. "Again, my lord, I am most grateful for your kindness."

"Kind, I am not," Cree said not a hint of a smile breaking his scowl, "though I am curious." He pointed to a chair not far from where he stood by the fireplace. "Sit and tell me where you are from and how you managed to make it here in this blinding snowstorm."

Alexander took the offered seat and had to tilt his head back slightly to look up at Cree. "I call no particular place home and I feel fortunate to have stumbled upon your home in this awful snowstorm that came on so suddenly."

"Family?"

"They all left me too soon."

Cree heard no sorrow in his voice.

"I hope one day to have a home again and a wife to love."

"You had a wife?" Cree asked.

Alexander bobbed his head. "I did and I loved her dearly."

"What happened to her?"

"She took ill."

With Alexander's brief responses, Cree was learning nothing about the man and he got the distinct feeling it was on purpose. "Where were you going when you got caught in the storm?"

"I go where the wind takes me and it seems to have delivered me to your door."

"You wish to remain here?" Cree asked, knowing that was not going to happen.

"Until the snow—"

"Stops," Cree finished for him.

"Could I impose on you at least until the roads are somewhat passable?"

"As long as you present no problem," Cree warned.

Alexander stretched his arms out to the sides. "I carry no weapons and mean harm to none."

Cree stared at him a moment. How had he not seen that? That should have been the first thing he looked for and yet he had not taken notice. He shot Sloan a quick glance and he shook his head, letting Cree know that he had failed to notice himself.

"What kind of man carries no weapon?" Cree challenged.

Alexander's smile grew wider. "A confident one."

"Confidence is nothing without courage. Do you have courage, Alexander?"

His smile faded for the first time since he stepped into the keep. "Courage is discovered when the time comes that one must be courageous."

"When your time came were you courageous?"

Cree asked.

Alexander's silence answered for him, though after the awkward pause, he did speak. "There was a time..." He could not finish. He shook his head as he said, "It haunts me to this day." His smile returned suddenly. "But I hope to rectify that one day. Who knows, perhaps I will find a strong, loving woman here among your clan who will look upon me kindly."

"And see you for who you truly are?"

Alexander laughed. "That would take more courage than most women have."

Dawn. He thought of his wife immediately. How could he not? She was the most courageous woman he had ever met. When he had been taken prisoner and locked in the dungeon of someone seeking revenge against him, she had not hesitated to rescue him. She had succeeded when others could not, though at great cost to herself, and she bore a scar to prove it. He did not believe there was any woman as courageous as Dawn, and she belonged to him.

"I protect what is mine," Cree warned.

"As you should, but as I said, I mean harm to none."

"Make sure of it," Cree ordered, "for if you stir any trouble here, I will see you suffer for it."

~~~

Old Mary sat in the lone chair by the hearth in the small bedchamber to chase the chill from her tired bones. "Sit and talk with me, Dawn."

She grabbed a soft wool shawl hanging on one of three pegs near the door and draped it around Old Mary's shoulder before taking the small footstool from under the chair where Old Mary sat and placed it in front of her, always eager to talk with the woman who was much more than a friend. The old woman had been a good friend to her mum and her when others scorned them because Dawn had no voice, and her way of knowing things had helped Dawn through some troubling times.

"My age is beginning to wear on me," Old Mary said.

Dawn shook her head and gripped her arms and pretended to shiver.

"It is not only the cold. My age has—"

Dawn took her gnarled hands in hers, shaking her head forcefully, refusing to let her finish. She could not bear to think of life without Old Mary.

Old Mary chuckled. "I am not going anywhere just yet, my dear. These old bones of mine may protest, but they still have life in them. It is my knowing that I fear my age is intruding upon."

Dawn smiled, relieved to hear it and shrugged, asking what troubled her.

"It is this stranger who suddenly appeared tonight. I usually get a sense of a person when I first see them. Kind. Strong. Untrustworthy. It helped when Cree took over the village. I knew he was an honorable man and would be a great clan leader and keep everyone safe. I also could see how much he cared for you and how those feelings grew so rapidly into love. You two were fated to be together." She rested her head back against the chair and sighed.

Dawn waited, anxious to hear what Old Mary had to say about the stranger, since she wondered about him herself.

Old Mary glanced down at Dawn. "I felt nothing."

Dawn was quick to respond with a gesture.

"You are right. I am tired and I suppose that might have had something to do with it."

Dawn pointed to her face, produced a lovely smile and fluttered her lashes.

Old Mary laughed. "You think his handsome features got in the way of me sensing something?"

Dawn nodded and smiled as if she was laughing.

"I am too old to respond foolishly to such fine features. What of you? Did you find him appealing?"

Dawn appeared to laugh as she shook her head. She tapped her chest and raised her hand high and looked up with loved-filled eyes.

"You care only for Cree."

She threw her arms wide.

"More and more," Old Mary said and smiled along with her, so happy Dawn had found a good, strong man to love her.

Dawn's smile faded and she gestured again.

Having helped Dawn's mum teach her how to speak with her hands, Old Mary understood Dawn well. "You want to know if the Winter Tale is true, so do many. Some refuse to tell the tale, fearing it will release the undead upon them. Others think it is nothing more than nonsense contrived by a storyteller to capture his audience." She shrugged. "Who is to say whether it be truth or tale? It could be either, though I have always found that there is some truth to any tale."

A shiver settled over Dawn and she held her hands out to the fire to warm them.

"Perhaps the tale did not happen as told. Sometimes when a tale is repeated often, the story grows and grows until it no longer is anything like the original tale."

Dawn frowned.

"Aye, it is a sad tale either way for someone had treated love badly."

Dawn held two crossed fingers in front of her face.

"The curse," Old Mary said, nodding. "It takes power to curse someone and there are only two things powerful enough to produce a curse...hate and love. Who knows which one it could be or if there was a curse at all?" Old Mary shivered.

Dawn stood and pulled the shawl more snugly around the old woman's shoulders.

Old Mary grabbed her arm. "You must be careful. I do not know why, I only know that you must."

It was Dawn's turn to shiver. She trusted Old Mary's knowing and always paid heed to it.

"Things are not what they seem and there is more yet to come," Old Mary said with concern.

Dawn did not like the worried look in Old

Mary's eyes or the way she reached out desperately to Dawn, as if trying to take hold of her and keep her safe. Dawn eased her arms around the old woman and helped her out of the chair and into bed. She was exhausted. It had been a busy day and there was the added concern about the snowstorm, and then she had kept everyone occupied with the telling of the Winter Tale.

With a tuck of the covers around Old Mary, Dawn was ready to leave the woman to sleep and get much needed rest.

Old Mary slipped her hand out from beneath the blanket and grabbed Dawn's wrist before she could turn away. "I fear the devil is upon us, for I have unleashed the cursed undead spirit of Winter Tale."

Chapter Three

Dawn jumped frightened out of her wits when the door to her bedchamber swung open just as she was about to place her hand on the latch.

Cree was headed out the door to find his wife, annoyed she had not been there waiting for him when he had entered their bedchamber. He was about to snap at her and demand to know what had taken her so long when he caught the frightened look on her face.

He reached out, snagged her around the waist, and yanked her up against him, then gave the door a kick shut. "What is wrong?" he more demanded than asked. His wife did not frighten easily, so something had to have disturbed her for her to have been so startled when he opened the door.

Dawn laid her head on her husband's hard chest and wrapped her arms around his waist, hugging him as tight as she could.

That did it for Cree. Something was wrong and he intended to find out.

With a quick lift, Dawn found herself up in her husband's strong arms, a place she always felt safe in. He carried her to their large bed, a place she always enjoyed sharing with him and a smile crept over her.

"First you will tell me what has frightened you and then I will make that small smile of yours grow." He grew more concerned when her smile faded instead of growing. He eased her head off his shoulder and slipped his finger beneath her chin to raise her head, about to ask her again what was wrong. Instead, his finger drifted down along the scar across her throat. It was fading, more slowly than he would have liked, but it was fading and Elsa, the clan's healer, felt in time it would fade completely. He was relieved, for the scar reminded him how much she had given to save his life.

He ran a gentle finger across the scar again. "You are the bravest woman I know, so it concerns me when I see fear in your beautiful eyes." Her sigh might be silent to others, but to Cree it was as though she spoke aloud when he saw her chest expand and her shoulders slump. "Tell me what has frightened you?" he said and kissed her lips gently.

Dawn was ever so grateful for her husband. He might scowl much too often and be overly demanding, but he loved her and that would never change. She began to gesture.

Cree interrupted as soon as she gnarled her fingers. "There is something wrong with Old Mary?"

Dawn shook her head and pointed to her mouth.

Cree nodded. "She has told you something that has upset you."

Dawn bobbed her head and continued.

Cree understood her every gesture and shook his head when she finished. "You have nothing to worry about. Alexander is a man not a ghost. He will bring harm to no one. I will make certain of it. Old Mary worries for naught."

Dawn scrunched her brow, displaying her doubt.

"You would have thought nothing of his presence if Old Mary had not told the tale." She went to gesture and Cree caught her hands in his. "Do not tell me that he would not be here if Old Mary had not told the tale."

Dawn slipped her fingers out of her husband's grasp and pressed her hands to each side of her head, sticking a finger up on each and shrugged.

Cree laughed. "Listen well, wife, if he is a ghost and has brought the devil with him, the devil will soon realize he has met his match in me, for he will face a far worse hell than what he is used to if he harms what is mine."

Dawn frowned, made the gesture for the devil once again, and then poked her husband in the chest while shaking her head.

Cree laughed again. "Are you forbidding me from taking on the devil?"

She tapped his arm once and gave a firm nod at the same time.

His laughter faded and he pressed his brow to hers. "I met the devil a long time ago and he wanted no part of me."

Dawn felt a catch in her chest, recalling her husband's infamous reputation, though that was before he had met her. She liked to believe her love for him had tamed him some...or so she tried to convince herself. He was still the fierce and mighty warrior everyone feared, though not her, she loved him.

She did what came natural when in his

arms...she kissed him. It was a soft brush of the lips to start, a gentle prelude and he returned it in kind. She loved these moments with him when there was no want to rush, no overwhelming urge, just the simple pleasure of a simple kiss. He touched her then, a light brush of his hand across her breast and a warm tingle settled over her.

It was at times like this that she wished she had a voice, wished that he could hear her tell him how much she loved him. But then perhaps silent words said far more. She moved her lips away from his and took his face in her hands so that he would have to look directly at her. She saw worry in his eyes, but then perhaps it was her own reflection of concern she saw there. With her heart beating madly, she slowly mouthed each word, *I. Love. You.*

Cree's dark eyes widened along with his smile. "I think the whole keep heard that."

Dawn laughed and a tear trickled down the corner of her one eye as she threw her arms around her husband's neck and hugged him tight.

He tugged her away from him and kissed the cheek the tear had touched. "I love hearing you say that, but I hear you just as loudly when you tell me as you have always done." He kissed her lips, and then whispered, "Besides, I love having your hands touch me when you speak."

She smiled and ran her hand over his chest and down along his waist and just as it appeared as though she would slip her hand further down between them, she took hold of his hand and pressed it against her breast.

His smile turned to that wicked grin he wore just before...

"Let us see whose touch makes the other surrender first."

She shifted on his lap, so she could reach down to touch him when he quickly stood and placed her on her feet.

"No, no, wife, we will make this a fair battle. We do not start until we are both naked and on the bed."

Her hands went to her garments, eager to be the victor in this little skirmish of passion when a knock sounded at the door.

Cree muttered several oaths as did Dawn. She shook her head and admonished herself for speaking so unfittingly, even though it could not be heard, it was not proper for her to do so. But damn just did not seem strong enough to quell her anger at being interrupted.

Cree swung the door open to find Sloan there.

Sloan held up his hands. "Before you kill me, I thought it important you know that two of the women who served the stranger have suddenly taken ill and the food being cleared off the tables have soured so badly it is turning the stomachs of all in the Great Hall." He scrunched his nose and shivered, as if demonstrating just how bad the odor was.

Before Dawn could approach her husband, he turned and ordered, with his finger pointed at her, "You stay here and I mean it. Do not dare leave this room. Wait for my return." He shut the door on her startled face before she could say a word.

Sloan chuckled as they walked to the stairs.

"Do not say it," Cree warned.

Sloan chuckled again. "You think you would have learned by now that she does not pay heed to your words."

"She will pay heed this time," Cree snapped.

"And why is that?"

"She fears the devil and she fears the devil has been unleashed on us. She will keep her distance this time."

Sloan shuddered from the sudden chill that ran threw him. "What if the devil is here?"

"Then I will send him back to hell where he belongs."

The stink hit Cree when he was a few steps from the bottom of the stairs and his anger sparked. When he stepped into the Great Hall, he was once again glad that he had Flanna to oversee the servants and running of the keep. She had the servants scrubbing the tables and benches with fresh snow while two servants began tossing pine cones into the flames of the large fireplace. He wondered what was in the tankards that everyone in the hall was holding close to their noses. It did not take long to find out. Flanna approached with two tankards.

"It will help quell the odor."

Cree sniffed at one of the tankards she held. It was a pleasant apple scent, but he refused it. The room might stink, but he had smelled far worse in his life, especially after battle. Besides, it would be a sign of weakness to take the tankard and he did not have to look to see that Sloan refused it as well.

"You have done well, Flanna," Cree said.

She bobbed her head. "The pine cones, greedily being consumed by the flames, will soon chase the odor and all will be able to sleep comfortably tonight."

"The women who took ill?"

"I had them moved to the far corner of the hall," she said, pointing in the direction. "I thought to send for the healer and two warriors volunteered to fetch Elsa, but the storm has worsened and between the darkness and the snow a hand in front of your face cannot even be seen. It will have to wait until daylight. Even then it may not be possible, if the snow continues to fall so heavily and rapidly."

"Does anyone tend them?"

"They all fear going near them, the fever having come upon the two so suddenly."

"Where is the stranger?" Cree asked.

"The last he was seen was in the kitchen," Flanna said.

A servant yelled out for Flanna, and Cree shot a warning look to who had dared to interrupt him when he was engaged in conversation with someone. But when he saw that a servant had collapsed in another servant's arms, he and Sloan, along with Flanna, hurried over to them.

Sloan lifted the slumped woman into his arms and looked to Cree.

One look at the servant spoke louder than words. She was the one of the servants who had served the stranger.

"Bring her over to the others," Flanna said and Sloan followed her.

Cree watched them carry the young lass off, his thoughts on protecting his clan. He went to turn to go to the kitchen when his glance caught the look in the eyes of many of the men and women huddled together in fright in the room. They all looked to him to protect them, keep them from harm even from the devil himself.

~~~

Dawn left the room shortly after her husband. She had to go speak with Old Mary, had to let her know what was going on...unless she already knew.

As she went to grab the latch to Old Mary's room, it was yanked from her hand as before with Cree and once again she startled.

"I have been waiting for you," Old Mary said and hurried her in with an anxious wave. "It has begun, has it not?"

Dawn nodded.

Old Mary paced the room. "I do not know how to undo what I have done. I have brought evil down upon the clan."

Dawn had never seen her so upset. She stepped in front of Old Mary, stopping the woman's pacing and rested a hand on her shoulder. She shook her head, not agreeing with her.

Old Mary reached her hand up to take hold of Dawn's hand and winced from the quick movement.

Dawn took Old Mary's hand, shook her head, and pointed to the bed.

285

"You do not understand. This stranger is nothing like what Cree has faced before. He is neither alive nor dead, which means he cannot be destroyed. There is no way for Cree to defeat him."

Her warning words sent a shiver rippling through Dawn, especially since Old Mary trembled herself.

"Keep your distance from the stranger and pray that the melting snow swallows him whole once more."

Dawn tucked the old woman into bed once again and bid her good-night with a gentle kiss to her forehead. She closed the door quietly behind her, her hand lingering on the latch as thoughts churned in her head, much of which did not make sense.

Old Mary was the one who she went to when troubled and needing help. Not so this time. Old Mary was as upset as everyone else, perhaps more so, since she felt she was the cause of the problem. Dawn hated to see her distressed, especially after having placed her own life in danger to help Dawn free Cree when he had been held captive in a dungeon that many believed he would never escape. But she and Old Mary had gotten him out, and if it had not been for her dear old friend she would have never succeeded.

Now it was her turn to help Old Mary and ease her worrisome burden. Tomorrow, she would see what there was to learn about the stranger. She let go of the latch and turned to walk to her bedchamber, hoping Cree had not returned yet to find her gone. She did not want to listen to a lecture from her husband...she wanted him to make love to her.

The thought brought a slight smile to her face and she hurried her steps even more when she saw her husband standing in the shadows at the end of the narrow hallway. She slowed her steps considerably as she got closer.

It was not her husband standing outside the door of their bedchamber...it was the stranger.

Chapter Four

"Forgive the intrusion, my lady, but I seem to have lost my way."

Dawn stopped a distance away from him aware he was not being truthful with her. He should have remained in the Great Hall where he had been offered food and a pallet to sleep upon. There was no reason, no reason at all that he should be here standing in front of the door to her and Cree's private chambers.

She pointed to the stairs, keeping her arm extended to let him know he was to leave immediately.

"I can tell my presence has upset you and I am sorry for having disturbed you, but I would be most appreciative if before I took my leave I could see a forgiving smile on your lovely face."

Dawn was far too apprehensive about the stranger for his charming tongue to have any effect on her. She gave him no smile when she wagged her finger at the stairs.

Her frown did not stop him from turning a compelling smile on her. "At least let me know your name."

He would learn soon enough, if he had not already, that she had no voice, but for the moment she thought it more prudent that she did not make him aware of it.

Dawn gave a scowl that could best her

288

husband's and shook her whole arm as she once again pointed to the stairs.

He was about to speak when voices coming up the staircase had Dawn turning her head. She was relieved to hear the sound of her husband's strong voice and that of Sloan's. Soon, she would no longer be alone with the stranger.

She turned, intending to turn a smile on the man and stared wide-eyed—he was gone.

"Dawn, I told you to stay—" Cree stopped as soon as he caught the look of fright on her face. "What is wrong? Tell me," he demanded, slipping his arms around her.

Dawn shook her head.

"You will tell me," he insisted.

She tapped his arm twice for no and pointed to her shaking head.

"If you do not shake your head at me, then who?"

Dawn gestured, as if pulling the hood of a cloak over her head and shivered.

"Are you telling me Alexander was here?" Cree asked.

Dawn was troubled by the doubt she heard in her husband's voice and nodded.

"Where did you see him?"

Dawn pointed to where Alexander had stood.

Sloan went to the spot near the bedchamber door. "Are you sure it was not a shadow you saw?"

Dawn shook her head forcefully and pointed to her lips.

"He spoke to you?" Sloan asked surprised.

Something was wrong and she looked from Sloan to her husband and shrugged as she wrinkled her brow in question.

"I have had Alexander watched since his arrival. He has been in the kitchen storeroom with one of the servants for the last hour or more. The warrior watching him has confirmed it."

Dawn felt a chill run through her as she shook her head once again.

Cree gave a nod to Sloan and he hurried past them and down the stairs.

Dawn rubbed her head. She had seen the stranger. It had not been her imagination.

Cree rested his hand to her lower back and eased her toward their bedchamber door. Once inside, he took her in his arms. "You are tired and the stranger arriving after Old Mary's tale did not help matters, as did a few people falling ill."

Dawn stared at him a moment before asking a question she never thought she would ask of him. She tapped her chest, pointed to him and shook her head.

"Do not ask me such nonsense," he scolded. "Of course I believe you saw him, but I also know from experience that our minds play tricks on us when we are overly tired or upset. When I was held prisoner in the dark cell, I thought I saw you there with me more than one night."

Dawn tapped her mouth and pointed to him.

"No, you did not speak to me, but then I would not have expected you to."

She frowned at her own foolish question. How

290

would she have spoken to him without a voice? She gave thought a moment, and then gestured once again.

"Are you asking me why I do not ask what Alexander said to you?"

She nodded.

"Tell me," he said. Cree grabbed hold of his wife's hands before she finished gesturing. "Do not dare ask me again if I would believe you, I believe your every word and always will."

Dawn dropped her brow to rest on her husband's chest. Why had she asked him that? She had never doubted him before.

He cupped her chin in his hand and raised her head. "I love you."

She tapped her chest and then his to let him know she felt the same.

"You need sleep," Cree said and he was surprised when she nodded and stepped away from him to reach for a nightdress she seldom wore. He had expected her to gesture that it was not sleep she needed, but him to make love to her.

He was shocked when after she slipped her nightdress on that she crawled into bed without even kissing him good-night. It was a rare night that they did not make love. Some nights it was a quick joining, other nights they took their time and the nights they simply went to sleep was because they had made love during the day. Today had not been one of those days.

Cree disrobed and slipped beneath the blanket, curling himself around her and hugging her close.

She made no move to touch him nor did she cuddle up against him. She lay unresponsive, something she had never done before when in his arms and it angered him.

He was about to say something when he felt the familiar movement of her body...she was crying. He turned her around in his arms, annoyed that he had failed to see how upset she truly was and held her close and let her shed her tears.

When they finally subsided, he kissed her wet cheeks and whispered, "All is well, wife, sleep and know you are always safe in my arms."

He felt her heavy sigh and was pleased when she snuggled against him and a moment later fell asleep.

Cree lay thinking. Had Dawn imagined the stranger in the shadows and had she also imagined he spoke to her? She was a strong and brave woman, having faced more than her share of burdens and hardships. Never once had he known her mind to play tricks on her. But if he accepted what she told him as truth, then how could Alexander have been in two places at once? The guard had not only confirmed that Alexander never left the storeroom, but the servant lass he had been with also had confirmed he had been with her the whole time.

Still, he had a difficult time believing his wife had imagined seeing and speaking with Alexander. He had to learn more about Alexander and he had to learn more about this Winter Tale. On the morrow he would speak with Old Mary and see what she could tell him, and he would also order his wife to keep her distance from the stranger.

For a moment, he thought he heard laughter, a reminder from Sloan that Dawn was not likely to obey. The laughter came again, as if confirming his thought, but for some reason the sound disturbed this time.

Cree eased his head up to cast a glance around the room. The fire's flickering flames caused shadows to dance in the dark corners of the room, making it seem as if someone moved among them. While he never paid heed to nonsense, the Highlands were filled with myths and superstitions that were hard to ignore. Besides, a wise leader never discounted the improbable, for it could be his undoing.

Cree gently eased himself away from his wife, glad that she was in a deep sleep and did not protest his absence, and tucked the blanket around her after he got out of the bed. He stood in the middle of the room naked, the muscles in his body growing taut as he allowed the warrior in him to take over and a deep scowl took hold of his face that in the fire's light made him appear more demon than man. But then at that moment, Cree was ready to fight whoever had dared to enter his private bedchamber whether he was ghost, demon, or man.

He walked slowly from corner to corner and the dancing shadows stilled, some dissipating as if in fright of the fearless warrior. It was the last corner, the one not far from the bed, that sent a chill through him from the cold, but then it was nearest to the lone window in the room. Still, he could find nothing and so he returned to the bed, ready to slip beneath the blankets and take his wife in his arms once again.

You did not believe her.

Cree's instincts had him reaching for his sword, but when he looked there was no one there to turn it on.

You disappointed her.

Laughter echoed in the room.

She keeps her distance the only way she knows how.

Laughter came again, then drifted off.

Cree wanted to roar with rage, but held back, not wanting to wake his wife and alarm her. Where had the voice and laughter come from or was his mind now playing tricks on him? He placed his sword close enough to the bed where he could reach it if necessary, then he joined his wife, taking her in his arms once again and holding her close.

She snuggled against him, her body at ease in his arms. She did not keep her distance. She wanted to be there close to him, entwined with him, loving him.

Still the words resonated over and over in his head.

She keeps her distance the only way she knows how.

He felt it then like a punch to his stomach. The nightdress. Suddenly the soft wool felt like an impenetrable shield that separated them. Why had she chosen to wear it tonight? Earlier she had been eager for him to make love to her. She had always been eager for them to join together. His touch fired her passion just as much as her touch fired his.

What had happened to change that tonight?

He had told her that he believed her, but his words and actions had spoken otherwise.

They had always believed and trusted one another. He would not have it any other way. Tomorrow they would talk and settle this and she would never again wear a nightdress to bed.

Chapter Five

Dawn woke, stretching her arms above her head and arching her back. She startled when she opened her eyes and saw her husband standing beside the bed fully dressed and his fur-lined cloak draped over his shoulders.

"The snow has stopped and I must see to the well-being of the villagers. You and I will talk as soon as I am done. Until then you will not go near Alexander."

He sounded angry with her and she was about to gesture her concern when he reached down, his arm wrapping around her to lift her up against him. His mouth captured hers in a kiss that was more a hungry demand and it quickly fired her blood. But before she had a chance to wrap her arms around his neck and let him know that one kiss would not appease her, he released her and took a step away from the bed, then turned to look at her.

Dawn stared at him bewildered.

"I do not trust him."

He worried for her that was why there was anger in his voice, it was for the stranger, not her.

She tapped her chest and nodded her head, letting him know she felt the same.

"Then you will obey me on this?"

Dawn nodded. She would keep her distance, though she would find out from others what she could about him.

"One other thing, wife," —anger sparked in his eyes— "never ever wear a nightdress to bed again."

Dawn smiled ever so softly as she rose up on her knees and pulled the nightdress up and over her head and threw it to the floor.

Cree stared at her. He loved her body from the first time he saw her naked, but even more so now after giving birth to the twins. Her curves were a bit more rounded, especially her hips. He loved taking hold of them as he entered her from behind and squeezing them as he drove into her over and over. He grew hard just thinking about it.

Dawn saw the hunger in his eyes and she stretched her arms out to him. When he did not make a move toward her, simply remained there staring, she cupped her one breast and squeezed the nipple until it turned hard, then beckoned him with her other hand as her body heaved as if with a heavy sigh or moan.

"Damn it, wife, I have no time—"

She quickly turned, falling on her hands and knees and presented a wiggling backside to him, inviting him to quickly take her from behind.

Cree let loose with several oaths as he flung off his cloak and went to her. He slipped his finger inside her and was not surprised to feel how ready she was for him or how she pushed against him wanting more.

He shoved his plaid aside, grabbed her hips, and entered her with a forceful thrust. She pushed back against him, taking him deeper. He did not hesitate, he slammed into her again and again, the feel of her and his relentless need firing his blood. He would not last long, but he was not supposed to. This was a wild joining born out of need and love that would have them both soon bursting in climaxes.

He felt her then, arching her back, pushing harder against him and he knew she was near to coming and so was he. He slipped one hand around her to tease the small nub that would send her reeling over the edge, and it took only a light playful touch for her body to slam against him in a shuddering climax that sent him into a never-ending one.

When the last of the climax trickled away, he dropped down over her back, his arm winding around the front of her. He pushed her hair off her neck and placed gentle kisses along it and felt another shudder ripple through her. He nibbled along her shoulder until finally and reluctantly, he tore himself away from her and when he did, she got to her knees and turned to face him.

Dawn smiled, threw her arms around his neck, and hugged him tight, then let him go and fussed with his garments so that no one would know what their laird had been up to.

"It will matter not, all will know, for I will be wearing a smile instead of my usual scowl," he teased and her cheeks flushed red. He gave her bare backside a tender slap. "Later, wife, we will take our time."

Her grin grew as she nodded.

He turned and picked up her nightdress and threw it into the fire for the flames to greedily devour. "You will not be needing that—ever. I will burn the other one you have later." Then he walked out the door, though took a moment to glance back at her. "Remember—"

She waited for him to remind her to stay away from the stranger. Instead his words warmed her heart.

"You belong to me and always will."

~~~

Dawn dropped back on the bed as soon as the door closed and pulled the covers up over herself. Her silent sigh could not be heard, but she felt it ripple through her body. She loved her husband beyond words and he loved her with equal measure and that was something that would never change. Their love was forever.

She did not know what had gotten into her last night that she had worn her nightdress to bed or that she was overcome with tears. But worse, she had not felt like making love with Cree. It was almost as if she had not trusted him and that disturbed her. She trusted him beyond measure, so why had she felt that way?

The blanket was off her in an instant and she donned her warm winter garments, a soft blue wool tunic over an equally soft green wool shift, almost as quickly. She fashioned her long red hair in a braid and after slipping on her shoes, she rushed out of the room eager to feed her son and daughter, then she would go see how Old Mary was doing.

The twins were just waking when she arrived in

their bedchamber, the servants who saw to their care were fussing over them. Dawn had recently started taking the twins, after their morning feeding, down to the Great Hall so that Cree and she could spend more time with them. But this morning she felt it was wiser they remain in their room and the servants as well. The servants agreed, having learned of those who had taken ill in the Great Hall.

Valan, however, got fussy when she returned him to the arms of one of the servants after feeding him. He made it clear he wanted to go with his mum and Lizbeth did as well once her feeding was done, but the servants diverted their attention and Dawn left the room feeling guilty and annoyed. This stranger had disrupted their lives and it had to stop.

She stopped in her bedchamber for a shawl before she went to see Old Mary. Though fires burned in all the fireplaces in the keep, it was difficult to keep the cold completely out. She entered Old Mary's room with a smile, eager to see how she was and eager to speak with her.

Her smile faded as soon as she stepped into the room and was met with bitter cold. The fire had died to near embers and Old Mary was buried beneath the blankets. Dawn hurried to the fireplace and quickly got a roaring fire going. Then she rushed to Old Mary's side and grew frightened when she saw how the covers trembled. She eased them back and was shocked to see how pale the old woman was and how badly she trembled. Her hand went to the old woman's brow and she grew more upset to feel her burning with fever.

It did not take long to see what was causing her to tremble. The fever had caused her to sweat, soaking her nightdress. How long had she lain like this with no one to help her? Old Mary had always been there for her, yet she had failed to be there when the woman needed her.

She quickly gestured to Old Mary, though Dawn was not sure if she understood. She seemed unaware and that frightened Dawn even more. She rushed out of the room and down the stairs to the Great Hall and hurried to Flanna, explaining what had happened and what she needed, then she ordered one of the warriors to go fetch Elsa. Once finished, she raced back up the stairs to Old Mary.

Flanna was not far behind her after issuing orders to two servants.

"Good lord, how long has she been like this?" Flanna asked upon seeing the pale woman.

Dawn shook her head, tears pooling in her eyes.

"Do not worry, we will have her warm and feeling better soon," Flanna encouraged.

Dawn hurried from the room after gesturing to Flanna that she would be right back. She grabbed the last nightdress Cree intended to burn and returned to the room, relieved he never got a chance to feed it to the flames. The servants arrived shortly after her with fresh bedding and Dawn and Flanna got busy tending Old Mary.

With the old woman barely responsive, it took time to get her out of her wet garment and the bedding removed and replaced. Dawn had moved the lone chair closer to the fire and draped the nightdress over it, so when they slipped Old Marry into it, it was toasty warm.

By the time they had her settled snugly and warmly in bed, she was beginning to respond to them. She tried to talk, but Dawn put a finger to her lips and shook her head. She then placed the chair beside the bed and took the tankard with the healing brew in it and began to spoon it into the old woman's mouth.

"Drink as much as you can, then rest. Someone will be with you at all times," Flanna said, reassuringly.

Dawn nodded vigorously, intending to be the one who remained by her side.

Old Mary managed to slip her hand out from under the blanket and point to Dawn.

Dawn patted her chest and with firm gestures, assuring the woman she would not leave her.

Old Mary seemed to calm and took the brew eagerly from Dawn until her eyes drifted closed and she fell asleep.

Flanna approached Dawn after speaking with a servant who had appeared at the door and from her solemn expression Dawn knew something was terribly wrong.

"One of the cows is sick, some food in the storehouse has turned bad and...Elsa has fallen ill."

Dawn started praying then. She prayed as hard as she did when her mum had taken ill. She only hoped this time her prayers would be answered.

Chapter Six

Cree watched his warriors as they worked hard along with the horses and long logs to plow through the huge amount of snow that had fallen throughout the night. Everyone helped to dig paths through the village and dig out those the snow had nearly buried in their cottages. Animals were seen to and the storehouse unlocked so that food could be distributed amongst the villagers and more brought to the keep's kitchen for fear the snowstorm would return. The sky was a heavy gray and the air so bitter it felt like sharp teeth nipping at the skin.

His men needed little direction or encouragement. They had fought too long and hard not to take care of the place they finally called home. They were ready to settle, get themselves wives, have a bunch of *bairns* and war only when necessary.

He wanted the same after far too many years of fighting endless battles for the highest bidder. Now he fought for his home, his clan, and surprisingly for his wife and twins. He had never thought he would fall in love. He had expected to secure a profitable marriage bargain, nothing more. He was glad it had not worked out that way and he was lucky that Dawn had entered his life.

A smile tugged at his lips. He had wanted to talk with her this morning, but when he had been informed of all the snowfall that had trapped some of the villagers in their homes, there had been no time.

Gratefully, Dawn had answered his misgivings when she had stripped bare in front of him and wiggled her bare backside at him. She wanted him with the same eagerness, or more, that she always did. He was a blessed man to have such a loving wife and he would do anything to keep her safe and never lose her.

A shout from Sloan drew his thoughts away from Dawn and he focused on the present situation.

"Unsettling news and more unsettling news," Sloan said, stopping in front of Cree.

Cree scowled. "Tell me and be done with it."

"One of the cows has taken ill and she is being isolated in hopes that she has not affected the others. Some of the food in the storehouse has rotted, though no one can understand why," Sloan paused and it was obvious he did not want to deliver the last of the bad news.

"Tell me," Cree ordered.

"Elsa has fallen ill."

"Where is she and how bad is she?" Cree demanded.

"She is at her healing cottage and I do not know anything beyond that."

"See to the men," Cree ordered and went immediately to the healer's cottage. He did not announce his arrival. He simply walked into the cottage that had been added on to her cottage for Elsa to tend the sick.

Neil, the man Elsa had come to love, was sitting

beside her, worry on his aging face as he laid a cool cloth upon Elsa's hot brow. He shook his head when Cree entered. "I do not understand it. She was fine and all of a sudden she was struck by fever and now she is barely responsive. And I do not know what to do for her. As soon as the large snow drift was dug away from the door and she heard that many had taken ill, she prepared several baskets with her healing potions to take to the keep. The fever struck before she left."

Cree stared at Elsa looking so lifeless on the bed. He had rescued her from dire circumstances years ago and she had been with him ever since. She had helped many of his warriors and those in the village, including Dawn. They could not lose their healer and he could not lose his friend.

"What of the two women who help her tend those in need?" Cree asked.

"Lara came here as soon as she could and Elsa sent her with one of the healing baskets to the keep. Ann I have yet to see, but she may be stuck in her cottage since she lives nearer to the woods and I have heard that the men have yet to dig their way there."

"And Elsa saw no one before she turned ill?"

Neil shook his head, then stopped. "Someone came to the door, but did not come in. Elsa stepped outside to treat him, a minor wound I believe." Neil shrugged. "Probably one of the warriors who was anxious to get back to the task of digging out the village. That is another thing. I have never seen so much snow fall in one night. And with those falling ill in the keep," —he shook his head again— "it is as if someone has cursed us."

It was not what Cree wanted to hear, but it was something he could not ignore.

"I will have the men work to dig Ann free and have her sent here immediately," Cree said. "For now do what you think is best."

"I do what I have seen Elsa do in such a situation. I only pray I am doing the right thing," Neil said, choking back a tear.

It was not until Dawn had come along that Cree had allowed himself to begin to feel again. Having a cold heart and barely a soul was the only way he had been able to be victorious in battle and do the many things demanded of him.

Only a year ago, he would not have wasted his time to see how Elsa fared. He would have had Sloan keep him informed and as for Neil, he would have ordered Neil to return to his duties and not been concerned with how worried the man felt for the woman he loved.

But now, since Dawn...Cree walked over to Neil and rested a strong hand on the man's shoulder. "Elsa is strong. She will be fine."

Neil looked up at Cree. "I pray it will be so, for I do not know what I would do without her."

Cree gave the man's shoulder a reassuring squeeze and then left the cottage. He knew exactly how Neil felt, for he could not think of life without Dawn.

Once outside the cottage, Cree looked around for Sloan. He did not spot him, but he did see Lila,

Dawn's closest and dearest friend, and Dorrie, a friend to Dawn now, but not always, heading toward the keep.

He shouted out to Lila and the two women halted and respectfully bobbed their heads at him when a few feet away and together they said, "My lord."

"Where are you off to?" he asked.

Lila answered. "We go to the keep to help those taken ill and see how Dawn fares."

"Dawn is well," Cree said, "but I do not want either of you at the keep and spread the word to others that they are to remain away from the keep. Also there is a stranger among us. He arrived last night and no one is to go near him."

"Do you believe he has brought an illness upon us?" Lila asked with concern.

"I am not sure, but I intend to take no chances. Keep to your cottages until you are informed otherwise," Cree ordered and seeing Sloan called out to him.

The two women bobbed their heads again and turned and hurried off, huddled together talking as they went.

"Have you seen Alexander today?" Cree asked when Sloan approached.

"Not that I recall, though one of our warriors discreetly follows him," Sloan said and lowered his voice. "When the villagers who were not at the keep last night heard about the tale being told and a stranger suddenly appearing, tongues started wagging and fear now can be seen in far too many eyes."

"Time to lock Alexander away until this matter can be settled," Cree said.

"My thought as well," Sloan said and walked with Cree to the keep.

~~~

"Is there anything I can do to help?"

Dawn jumped, dropping the cloth she had been bathing Old Mary's brow with, upon hearing Alexander. She snatched the wet cloth off the bed where it had fallen and wondered how she had not heard him enter the room. The door always gave a soft creak when opening or closing, yet she had heard nothing.

She shook her head and waved him away. She did not want him there. She was not comfortable with his presence and she wanted nothing to do with him. Besides Cree had ordered her to stay clear of him and this was one time she agreed with his demand.

"You dismiss me again and all I want to do is help you," he said and took a step closer.

Dawn glared at him. So she had seen him outside her bedchamber last night, but how was that possible when a servant had insisted he had been with her the whole time and a guard had confirmed it?

Ghost? Demon? What was he?

"I am merely a man who offers his help."

A cold shiver ran through her. He answered as if he had heard her clearly, as if she had spoken aloud.

Dawn stood and pointed to the door as her brow furrowed in anger and, to see if what she believed was true, she spoke in her mind. *Leave at once!*

"Do not be so hasty to chase me away yet again. I only wish to return the kindness shown to me."

Dawn felt a tingle of fear creep over her. That he could hear her thoughts so clearly disturbed her. She would have to be careful around him, but then she did not plan on being in his presence often, if at all. But how did she get him to leave.

His smile vanished for a moment, his head tilting to the side as if he heard something, and then his smile returned. "I do not wish to make you feel uncomfortable. I will take my leave." He sent her a nod. "Until next time, my lovely lady." He went to the door, opened it, and walked out.

Dawn heard the creak as he opened the door and again when he closed it. She wondered again why she had not heard it when he had entered before. Her husband may believe Alexander was nothing more than a man like any other man, but she did not agree. Though what he was, she was not sure, and how did one combat something that was possibly already dead or could not die?

She shook her head and lowered herself to the chair. This was far worse than any nightmare. One could wake from a nightmare, but this...was all too tangible. She gave past nightmares a thought. How had she escaped them?

Her mum had always been there to comfort and counsel her. She missed her dearly and she was pleased that her wise words would always find a way to her when needed, as it did now.

Chase the nonsense away and see what remains and then fight it, refuse to let it conquer you, and you will always be the victor.

How did she chase away the nonsense of the present situation when that was all there seemed to be?

Winter Tale.

The tale was like a nightmare. She had to push away the nonsense and see what she could find out. But she did not know the tale well enough after hearing it only once and Old Mary—she turned to look at her sleeping peacefully—was not well enough to speak with her. She felt the old woman's head and was pleased to find the fever had lessened, though remained. She wondered if there was anyone else in the village familiar with the tale.

The door creaked open and Cree entered.

Dawn smiled and hurried to him and as always he caught her in a strong embrace. She was never happier than when she was in his arms. Problems and worries seemed to melt away and all that was left was the love that embraced them as powerfully as his arms.

"I was sorry to hear that Old Mary took ill. Does she fare any better?"

Dawn nodded, patted her brow, and raised her hand up and down slowly.

"Her fever goes up and down?"

Dawn nodded again.

"I wish I could say the same for Elsa. She remains the same."

Dawn patted her chest and pointed to her ear, letting him know she had heard about Elsa falling ill and shrugged, her brow going up and her eyes full of concern, asking how Elsa was doing.

"Neil is with her and more fearful than I have ever seen him. He is doing what he can until the men can reach Ann's cottage and dig her out. Lara is seeing to those in the keep who have yet to improve." His brow knitted. "The illness strikes so fast, fever coming on without warning and without Elsa it will be difficult to combat it."

Dawn agreed, telling Cree how she had found Old Mary, the fire dwindled to embers, unable to call out for help and her nightdress soaked through from the fever.

Cree followed her gestures. "You should have given her your only nightdress since you will never be using it."

Dawn tapped her chest and nodded.

"You did?" And when Dawn nodded, Cree said, "Wise woman. I wish we knew what causes this illness so that we can stop it from spreading. I have ordered all those who have not been to the keep to remain a distance from it, though it concerns me that Elsa took ill without being in contact with either. Whether the stranger has something to do with this sudden illness or not, I can take no chances. I have ordered him locked in the tower room with guards posted outside the door until a path has been cleared from the village and he can be sent on his way."

Dawn gestured, letting Cree know that the

311

stranger had been here, speaking with her. She was eager to tell him how Alexander had seemed to hear the thoughts in her head.

"When was he here and what did he say?"

She held up two fingers, keeping them only a short distance apart.

"Not long ago? That is not possible. He was in the Great Hall when I entered, half asleep on his pallet, and I had him locked away immediately."

Dawn shook her head and pointed her finger down at the floor, insisting he had been there. When Cree went to speak, she pressed her finger to his lips, then tapped her temple as she shook her head again.

Cree scowled. "I was not going to say you imagined him. I am trying to understand how he can be in two places at the same time."

Dawn stuck a finger up from each side of her head.

"For the last time, he is not the devil—"

"I tend to agree with Dawn," Sloan said, stepping in through the open door. "The two warriors guarding Alexander heard a loud noise coming from inside his room. They unlocked the door to see what was wrong—the room was empty."

Chapter Seven

"I have had enough of this nonsense. Find him now!" Cree ordered with a shout.

"I have men searching, but many are questioning the stranger's sudden arrival so close on the tail of Old Mary's telling of Winter Tale and they have begun to grumble among themselves, especially now that Elsa has fallen ill. Without her to keep them well, they fear what may happen and," —Sloan hesitated a moment—"it has started snowing again and the men have yet to dig the whole village out. There is no way for anyone to leave here."

"And no reason for anyone to," Cree was quick to say, then ordered, "Have another bed brought to this room and have Elsa moved here before the snow traps her and Neil again. Also have someone brought here to watch over Old Mary. Dawn will be coming with me."

Sloan nodded and went to do Cree's bidding.

Dawn looked to her husband with a scrunch of her brow and tilt of her head.

Cree's strong hand wrapped around Dawn's, gripping it possessively. "For some reason this stranger has appeared to you twice and I intend to be there the next time he does."

Dawn smiled, slipped her hand from his and gave her husband a tight hug, then stepped away from him to gesture.

Cree interrupted her, asking, "Why the hug?"

Dawn rested a gentle hand to his warm cheek for a moment, then mouthed slowly as she gestured. *You believe me.*

He brought his lips close to hers and whispered, "Always."

After he gave her a quick kiss, she gestured anxiously.

Cree nodded. "I thought the same myself. We should have a look at the room where he was being held."

A servant entered then and after Dawn showed her how to tend Old Mary, she grabbed her husband's hand and hurried out of the room with him to the tower room. The higher they climbed the colder it got. The cold winter wind was striking the keep so hard that it was creeping through the cold stone wall.

Dawn rubbed her arms, wishing she had thought to bring her shawl with her, though her wool cloak would have served her better.

Seeing that a chill had seeped into his wife, Cree took a moment to step behind her and rub some heat into her shoulders and arms. Then he leaned down to nibble along her neck and instead of a chilled shiver running through her, a warm shiver took hold.

Dawn sighed silently, though she knew Cree would feel it being so close to her. He always looked after her, always thought of her well-being, always loved her and that thought not only warmed her heart, but her body as well.

314

"Let us be done with this task and get you where you will be warm."

Dawn leaned back against him and took hold of his arms and wrapped them around her, letting him know she would always be warm in his arms.

With an arm lingering around her waist, Cree opened the door, having to give it a hard push with his shoulder. It groaned as if annoyed at being disturbed, but then this room had sat abandoned until today when Cree finally made use of it.

A sudden chill whipped out at them and Cree quickly moved in front of Dawn to block the mighty blast from hitting her. The only light in the confined quarters was from the fire that barely burned in the small fireplace. Shadows congregated in the dark corners, as if huddling in whispers.

The shiver that ran through Dawn this time was not from the cold, but from a small tingle of fear that hurried through her and settled in the pit of her stomach. The sooner they finished here the better.

Cree went to the fireplace, taking his wife with him, though he doubted he could dislodge her, she clung to his arm so tightly. He threw the few remaining logs into the dwindling flames and they were greedily attacked and set ablaze.

"How kind of you to visit."

Dawn jumped, startled by the unexpected voice, though her husband did not budge.

They both turned to see Alexander stepping out of the shadows that the bright flames were beginning to chase away and that also revealed a sleeping pallet on the floor.

"I was sleeping and did not hear you enter."

Dawn stared at him. How could he not have heard them enter when the door had groaned? And he certainly did not appear as if he had just woken from sleep. Actually, he appeared much too well-groomed for one locked away in this cold, damp room.

"I can only assume that this lovely woman on your arm is your beautiful wife." Alexander bowed graciously. "I am honored to finally meet you, Lady Dawn. Your clan speaks highly of you."

Dawn wanted to step forward and demand he speak the truth. That he had already met and spoken with her, but part of her was too frightened to do so. A man, one of flesh and blood, could be subdued and conquered, but not so a man neither alive nor dead.

Cree stepped forward, keeping Dawn slightly behind him. "A loud sound was heard from this room a short time ago and the guards entered and did not see you here."

A smile caught at the corners of Alexander's mouth and grew as he spoke. "I must have been sleeping the sleep of the dead, for I heard nothing."

He plays with words, she thought and when he turned a subtle grin on her, she realized he had heard her.

"I mean no harm to anyone and I would help if you would let me."

"You are helping, by staying here away from others who believe you evil and just may attempt to take your life," Cree said.

Alexander gave an abrupt laugh. "Evil is not easy to destroy, but then you are well aware of that since evil has reared its ugly head in you in the past."

Cree took a step forward with a nudge to his wife to remain where she was. "Many times and no doubt it will again. Let me demonstrate."

Alexander held up his hands and took a step back. "I meant no disrespect."

"A wise choice, though true evil would never apologize, which leads me to believe you would not be a difficult man to conquer."

A flash of anger crossed Alexander's face before it was replaced with a smile. "I have no wish to battle with you. All I ask is shelter and comfort from the storm."

"And so you shall have it," Cree said and took a step back, never taking his eyes off Alexander and with a hand to his wife's arm urged her toward the door.

Dawn did as her husband bid and stepped toward the door.

"It was a pleasure meeting you, my lady."

Dawn turned and looked at him and purposely thought. *I cannot say the same about you.*

Alexander laughed and bobbed his head at her silent acknowledgement.

"Bring the guards," Cree ordered.

Dawn hesitated a moment, then nodded at her husband and left the room. She hurried down the stairs to fetch the guards as fast as she could. Her first thought had been to argue with Cree, but she had forced the thought from her head. It would not do to let Alexander know what she was thinking. The second thought she quashed was that she did not want to leave him alone with this—creature. There was no telling what he would do to Cree, but she would not disrespect her husband in front of the stranger and so she had taken her leave without protest. It did help that he had told her to 'bring the guards', his way of ordering her to return.

She rushed over to Sloan when she spotted him in the Great Hall and her hands gestured so fast that he summoned Flanna over to interpret. When he found out that Cree was in the tower room alone with Alexander, Sloan gave a shout and four warriors rushed out of the room with him. Dawn was quick to follow them.

Her name was called just as she was following the guards up to the tower room. She looked down behind her to see the servant, Bessa, she had left to care for Old Mary, standing there anxiously waving to her.

"Please, my lady, Old Mary is awake and says she must see you right away."

Dawn did not hesitate to turn around and hurry along with Bessa down the stairs to the room. Dawn gave the few furnishings that had been moved around to make room for Elsa, who had yet to be brought there, a cursory glance and went directly to Old Mary.

Old Mary gripped her hand as soon as Dawn was in reach. "Go see Elwin. I do not know why. I only know you must speak with him." She shook her head. "My mind is jumbled. I cannot make sense of things. You must go. You must go now."

Dawn felt her brow. The fever had risen, but it was not as high as it first had been and she related that news to Old Mary.

"Like a poison to the mind," Old Mary mumbled, "must fight it." Her eyes closed and she was soon asleep.

Dawn felt as confused as Old Mary sounded. Why the old woman urged her to go see Elwin made no sense. He had not even been in the Great Hall the night Old Mary had told the tale.

A poison to the mind. Could the fever be poisoning her mind, robbing her of her senses? Dawn turned, shaking her head to find Bessa standing directly behind her, her face pale and wringing her hands.

"He is poisoning us one by one," she said tears gathering in her eyes.

Dawn shook her head and eased Bessa down on the chair beside the bed. The servants she came in contact with often understood her gestures and the ones she only saw occasionally did not. Dawn was not familiar with Bessa. She did her best to comfort her and ease her worries and was relieved when Flanna entered the room followed by several male servants who got busy assembling a bed in the spot that had been cleared.

Dawn gestured to Flanna that she had to hurry off and left Bessa to explain her tears to Flanna. She stopped in her bedchamber to change from her shoes to her boots and to grab her fur-lined cloak.

Then she made her way through the keep, taking note of how upset and worried people appeared. Fear was brewing and it would soon bubble over if something was not done.

~~~

"He was not here, my lord, I swear by all that is holy," the one warrior said after being questioned by Cree.

"That is nonsense," Alexander said with his usual laugh. "How could I have left here when the door was bolted? Besides, it is a tower room, I would not survive such a fall, if foolish enough to jump if there was a window, and I certainly could not have gotten passed you and the other large warrior." He gave a nod to the warrior, standing beside the one who had spoken.

"Evil cannot always be seen," the large warrior said, glaring at Alexander.

Alexander threw his arms out from his sides. "Do I look like I am evil?"

The same warrior responded. "Evil has many faces and more often it is the most unlikely face of all that evil wears."

"Does evil bleed?" Alexander challenged, stretching his hand out, his one finger bandaged and stained with his blood that had seeped through the cloth.

"Who tended your wound?" Cree demanded.

"Your healer," Alexander said, "and her touch was most tender."

Cree caught the smug look that flashed across
320

his face.

"You have no worries from me. I am but a wanderer seeking shelter from the snowstorm. When the snow is gone," —Alexander looked to each one of them— "I shall be gone as well."

Alexander sounded as if he recited part of the tale and the one warrior shouted, "And what will you leave in your wake?"

Alexander's smile grew. "Nothing!"

Cree's hand went up, stopping the warrior from responding. "Man, demon, ghost, evil or not, I do not care. If one more of my clan falls ill or anyone dies, I will see you sent where you belong."

"And where is that?"

"Hell!"

Cree had four warriors guard the bolted door and though none refused or protested the chore, he knew his men well enough to know that not one of them wanted to be there. There were some things that struck fear even in the bravest of warriors and a man cursed by an evil witch was one of them.

"Where does Dawn wait for me?" Cree asked as he and Sloan descended the stairs. When Sloan failed to answer him immediately, Cree stopped abruptly. "Do not tell me you do not know where she is?"

"The last I saw her, she was trailing behind the warriors on our way to you."

Cree took the stairs faster. "My message was clear for her to return with the guards."

"It is not for lack of hearing or understanding that Dawn sometimes fails to obey you," Sloan said.

Cree stopped abruptly again and nearly shouted, "Sometimes?"

Sloan shrugged. "Most of the time, but you must admit that her disobedience often proves helpful in certain situations."

"Like when she rescued me from that prison when no one else could?"

"You have proved my point."

Cree shook his head and hurried down the stairs. "Then we best find her, for no doubt she has gone off on her own to try and solve this problem."

Chapter Eight

Snow was falling, not as heavily as yesterday, but steadily and without the accompanying vicious wind. If it continued, it could add to the already burdensome snow on the ground. Dawn kept a brisk pace. Having failed to return to her husband's side, he would be searching for her soon enough and demanding an explanation. She hoped to return to the keep before he became too irritated and hoped her visit with Elwin would prove beneficial so that she had something to share with her husband that would soothe his annoyance. She smiled, thinking that there were others ways she could find to soothe him that were much more enjoyable—for them both.

Dawn moved aside, along the only clear path through the snow to the keep, when she saw a large warrior carrying Elsa in his arms. Neil walked behind him and another warrior followed behind him. She tapped her chest and pointed to Neil when he glanced her way, letting him know her heart went out to him. He acknowledged her with a nod, looking more worried than she had ever seen him. Neither Neil nor Elsa had ever married or had any intentions of falling in love. Elsa had always been too busy with her love of healing and Neil too busy warring alongside Cree. But since settling here in Dowell, the two found each other and were now inseparable.

Dawn hurried on once they passed by, knowing Elsa would be urging her to find out what was causing so many to fall ill instead of worrying over her.

Not all snowdrifts had been cleared away from doors, especially the further away from the keep she got. She nearly panicked when she saw that up ahead the path stopped abruptly. How would she ever get to Elwin? She smiled with relief when she saw a clear path had been dug off the major path, and she took it straight to Elwin's cottage.

Elwin opened the door to her knock. He was impressive in size, but not in features. He was a plain man, soft-spoken, and considerate, and the opposite when it came to battle. He was one of Cree's most seasoned warriors and one her husband greatly respected.

"My lady?" he said, wondering what she was doing at his door.

Dawn hugged herself and pretended to shiver.

"Forgive me, my lady, come in, come in," he said, stepping back and waving her in. "I was so surprised to see you here that my manners failed me."

Dawn stepped into the one room cottage and smiled at the delicious scent that wafted off the cauldron bubbling over the flames in the fireplace. Seeing that Dorrie was not there, Dawn gestured to Elwin who surprisingly understood Dawn much easier than most.

"Dorrie took some fresh baked bread to some of the older clan's people stuck in their cottages."

At one time that would have surprised Dawn, but not now. Dorrie had changed and for the better. She smiled and nodded and pointed to the chair at the table.

"Sit, please sit," Elwin said, shaking his head at himself. "My manners elude me again." He grew concerned when he saw Dawn's smile fade as she sat. "What is wrong, my lady?"

She shrugged and shook her head slowly and gestured, explaining why she had come to see him.

Elwin scratched his head and appeared as confused as Dawn. "I cannot think why Old Mary would send you to me. I do not know how I can help."

Dawn sighed, her hope of finding something that would help calm, settle, and end this strange situation slowly fading away. She gestured with little hope of it helping, though needing to try, asking how and where he had heard of the tale.

"It has been many years since I first heard of the tale and once I did, I wanted nothing to do with it," Elwin admitted. "Many in the Highlands carry a talisman to protect them against witches. It is a shame the man of the Winter Tale did not follow that custom."

It troubled Dawn that Old Mary could be wrong, sending her to Elwin. She had never known the old woman to be mistaken. Though, there had been occasions she wished Old Mary had been wrong. This was not one of them.

Dawn thanked Elwin and took her leave. She almost bumped into Dorrie coming up the path, the snow falling so heavily they could barely see each other.

"My lady, whatever are you doing out in this snow, it worsens by the minute. I barely found my way back here. I will go fetch Elwin and have him see you safely to the keep."

Dawn shook her head and indicated that she would follow the path and hurried off before Dorrie could summon Elwin. She did not wish to take the chance of having Elwin stuck at the keep, leaving Dorrie isolated in their cottage.

She paid heed to her steps, making certain she remained on the path, but it seemed that the snow fell more heavily with every step she took. She could barely see in front of her. A strong wind suddenly joined the snow, swirling the snowflakes around her like a whirlwind and blinding her steps. She stumbled a few times and one final stumble had her falling to her knees. She fumbled, trying to get up and when she did, she could not tell if she was facing the path to the keep or away from it.

A chill ran through her and she pulled her fur-lined cloak more tightly around her. She had to get to the safety of the keep or at least find a cottage that would help her determine what direction to go in.

It took only a few steps for her to realize that the snow would not let her see anything, not a cottage, not the keep, not the next step in front of her. She could not, however, simply stay where she was, she had to keep moving. The bitter cold whipped at her as she trudged along, praying she was headed in the right direction.

Dawn stopped suddenly, thinking she heard a voice. Was someone calling her? It was difficult to tell with the wind whistling around her. She remained still for a moment and heard it again. Was that her name she heard? She could not be sure since the sound was caught on the wind and rushed off before she could hear it clearly.

"Dawn!"

Her name was clear, but not who called it.

A voice rose on the wind again, but failed to reach her

"Dawn!"

The voice seemed to come from one direction. Had Cree sent his men out searching for her? Were they calling out her name? Were they expecting her to follow their shouts? And if so, why was she reluctant to do so?

"Dawn!"

Her name sounded like a quiver on the wind, making it impossible to tell who called out to her. Who was it who waited out there in the blinding snow for her?

Could it be Alexander?

He was locked away or so everyone thought. Dawn did not believe there was a lock or chains that could hold the strange man. He went where he pleased and no one could stop him, and he would not leave them in peace until the snow was gone.

"Damn it, Dawn, I am going to shackle you to me."

Cree! That was Cree. His strong voice tore

through the vicious wind and snow and landed clearly around her. Please! Please call out again so I can follow your voice.

Dawn!

Her hand pressed at her stomach that roiled at hearing her name so clearly spoken in her head. Alexander was here.

"Dawn, follow the sound of my voice the best you can. I will keep speaking until you are standing in front of me, and then I will give you a good scolding for disobeying me, something you do daily."

Dawn listened to her husband continue to talk, following the sound of his voice more powerful than the winter wind.

"I am growing impatient, wife. There is much I have to say to you and much explaining you have to do."

Dawn listened to his voice grow closer and closer as he went on and on until finally she saw a shadow ahead in the whirling snow. She hurried toward it, wishing she could call out and let him know she was there.

She almost fell to her knees, she stopped so abruptly when she realized the shadow was not her husband—it was Alexander. His body seemed to sway with the wind for a moment before turning more solid like a specter taking form.

He held his hand out to her, smiling, confident that she would take it.

"Dawn!"

Her husband's voice broke through her fright

and she wanted to run to him, but how did she get passed the ghostly Alexander? Dawn was not sure if it was the bitter cold or fear that had her body trembling or kept her legs from moving. Obstacles were not strangers to her and she had faced the largest obstacle of them all the day she was born without a voice. Strength was something she had found out of necessity and courage she had gained along the way. Yet at this moment both failed her.

She had met with some harsh situations, one of them being the day she first met Cree and, though fear had held her captive, she had survived. But Cree was a man of flesh and blood while Alexander was a cursed man neither living nor dead. How did one deal with such an ungodly creature?

In the next instant, her husband's action answered her concern.

Like a mighty warrior eager to enter a battle, Cree stepped right through Alexander, dissipating his ghostly form like nothing more than a puff of smoke.

Cree was ready to give his wife a good tongue lashing as his arm slipped past her cloak to circle her waist. The words on his tongue died before they reached his lips when he felt how icy cold she was and how violently she trembled. He scooped her up in his arms, shouted for Sloan that he had found her so that he could alert his warriors who searched for her, and hurried her into the keep, up the stairs, and straight to their bedchamber.

He disposed of his cloak and hers after setting her on her feet, then sat her in the chair by the fire.

329

He grabbed a blanket from the bed, tucked it snugly around her, and knelt in front of her to quickly remove her wet boots. He took one ice cold foot in his hand and began to rub warmth back into it, alternating between both.

A knock sounded at the door and after Cree gave permission, Flanna entered with a steaming pitcher and two tankards. She filled one and handed it to Dawn and looked to Cree. He shook his head.

Dawn's hands trembled when she reached out from beneath the blanket to take hold of it and Cree reached up and closed his hand around her two to help steady the tankard so she could take a drink.

Flanna closed the door on the couple as she left the room.

Dawn rested the tankard on her lap after taking several sips of the hot brew, cupping her hands around the heated vessel and letting it warm them.

Cree returned to rubbing her chilled feet that had yet to warm, looking up at her as he did. "Did I not command you to return with the guards?"

Dawn nodded and went to gesture with one hand, but Cree stopped her.

"I am not finished," he snapped. "If the servant had not told me that Old Mary insisted you go speak with Elwin, I would not have known where to look for you." He settled an angry scowl on her that would have silenced her if she had a voice. "You not only put yourself at unnecessary risk, but also my men who went in search of you. You rush headlong into things without thought or consequences."

Dawn nodded, agreeing.

"You placate me by agreeing with me?" he snapped again, though gave her no chance to respond. "I should keep you tethered to me, but somehow I think you would feel that more a reward than a punishment."

Dawn could not stop from smiling.

"You smile when you drive me mad with worry?" he said, trying to temper his voice and anger.

Dawn's smile quickly vanished and she gestured an apology.

"Sorry does me little good when I suffer the tortures of hell, thinking something has happened to you and I cannot reach you. I want to roar to the heavens in anger and give my soul to the devil himself to see you safe."

A small smile crept up to tickle her lips as she gestured.

While his scowl remained strong, his words held less anger. "You are right. The devil would fear me and give me what I wanted just to be rid of me." He tapped the tip of her nose. "Listen to me well, wife, for I will not—" He shook his head. "There is no point in telling you I will not repeat myself, since it is something I find myself constantly doing with you. What might actually have you listening to me is the severity of this situation. This problem is different from others. This stranger seems capable of odd and unexplainable things. It will take more than a mere weapon to defeat him." He gave his chest a hard tap as he issued a forceful command. "I forbid you," — he poked her chest—"to leave the keep without my permission. And I will make everyone aware of my command, so that you are stopped from leaving, if you should try."

Dawn cherished the freedom her marriage to Cree had given her and though he demanded obedience more often than not, she failed to obey him more often than not and without barely any consequences. But in this instance, she thought it wise to follow his dictate.

Cree watched as she gestured her response, ready to do whatever was necessary to protect her from her foolish actions. His scowl slowly lessened and when she finished, he said, "You are telling me that you will let each person you speak with know where you go next, letting me easily keep track of your whereabouts?"

Dawn nodded and pressed her hand to her chest, giving her solemn word.

"And you will not leave the keep?"

She nodded, smiled softly, and reached out to give his hand a squeeze.

He gripped her hand tight, stood, leaned over her, and brought his lips to rest close to hers. "An obedient wife at last." Then he kissed her.

It was a kiss that claimed her, demanded from her, and loved her. His hand went around her neck to take hold and he kissed her with all the strength of a mighty Highland warrior and with all the love of a husband who cherished his wife.

The kiss aroused Dawn and sent a shiver of passion racing through her and relief that she was in her husband's arms. Between the raging snow and Alexander's ghostly apparition appearing, she had feared she might never feel Cree's touch or his kiss again.

"You are still chilled," Cree said and went to reach for the blanket. Her hand took hold of his arm and stopped him. One look in her eyes told him what she wanted. She wanted him to warm her.

His manhood had stirred when taking her in his arms and carrying her to their bedchamber. Rubbing warmth into her cold feet had stirred him even more. But what had aroused him the most was that she was safe, here with him, and not lost to him. The one way to reaffirm that was to join with her and become one as they so often did. The hungry kiss and the desire in her dark eyes let him know that she felt the same.

Though he was certain of it, he wanted to hear her say it since her gestures were like words to his ears. His grip on the back of her neck tightened as he asked, "You want me?"

She mouthed her response, since their lips were so close. *Always.*

If she could speak, it would be soft but strong, for that was how her response drifted around him, hugging with the strength of her love.

His mouth claimed hers once again, only this time with an unrelenting passion.

This would be no tender joining, their need was too great.

Dawn reached out and hurried her hand beneath his plaid to feel him hard and ready. She grew more excited as her hand stroked the length of his silky, smooth manhood.

Cree tore his mouth away from hers and rested his brow to hers, his breathing labored as he said, "Keep touching me like that and I will spill in your hand."

Dawn pulled her hand away and smiled when he groaned in regret.

Cree yanked her out of the chair, his hands going to her waist, lifting her so that her feet barely touched the floor and rushed her to the bed, tossing her down on it. He pushed her garments up, spread her legs, pushed his plaid aside and fell into her.

Dawn's chest heaved with a gasp and her arms hurried around her husband. This was what she needed—him inside her. There were many times she felt close to him and loved, but when they joined it was as if they truly became one.

She let herself drift in the passion that consumed every part of her. There was only here and now and the exquisite feel of him making love to her and try as she might to linger in it, she found herself too close to the edge. She let him know it, squeezing his arms and pushing ever harder against him.

"I can feel you are ready. We will come together," he commanded.

This was one order Dawn did not mind obeying.

Cree quickened his thrusts and the next moment they both burst in a blinding climax that had Cree tossing his head back with a hardy groan and Dawn squeezing his arms so tightly that he feared her fingers would snap against his rock-hard muscles.

They lingered in the aftermath, neither wanting to move until Cree rolled off her and took her in his arms. "Good God, but I love you."

Dawn smiled and patted his chest, letting him know that she loved him just as much.

They lay there, enjoying the satisfying pleasure that making love could only bring.

Cree eased Dawn on her back as he rolled on his side and pushed a loose strand of her hair behind her ear. "There was a moment there in the blinding snow that I thought I saw you approaching me, but you stopped. I worried that you did not see me and feared that you would turn in the wrong direction."

Cree listened as his wife explained what had happened, a scowl surfacing on his face after a few moments. "Are you saying Alexander was there in the snow?"

Dawn nodded and pointed to Cree, then herself and rolled on her side to wave her hand in the space between them.

"He stood between us?"

Dawn nodded, tapped at her eye, pointed to him, and shook her head, then moved her fingers as if walking and tossed her hand up, her fingers spreading apart.

"No, I did not see him, and are you saying I walked through him, chasing him away?"

Dawn nodded. There were times, her husband seemed more the mighty warrior to her than the loving man she knew him to be. This was one of those times. The heated anger in his dark eyes, the way the muscles in his jaw tightened, and the way his arm muscles grew taut as he fisted his hands...he was ready to do battle.

"Did he speak with you?" Cree demanded.

She took no offense to his commanding tone. She knew it was out of concern for her safety. She demonstrated how Alexander had stretched his hand out for her to take.

"He wanted you to come to him?" Cree asked, the words fueling his anger.

Dawn nodded and moved her fingers as if walking away, then quickly grabbed herself by the arms and pretended to struggle.

"You feared he would take hold of you and not let go?" When she responded with a nod, he snapped as if issuing a command. "You will not go near him if he approaches you again."

She wanted to share with him what had been even more frightening to her. That he could hear her thoughts, but a knock at the door interrupted her.

"Who goes there?" Cree shouted.

A quivering voice answered, "Forgive me for disturbing, my lord, but Old Mary insists that she must see, Lady Dawn."

"A moment," Cree called out and helped his wife off the bed and after seeing to adjusting their garments, he opened the door to find Sloan standing behind the servant lass, Bessa.

His concerned glance fell on Cree. "You are needed immediately in the tower room."

Fear gave courage to Bessa to speak, though did not keep her tears from falling. "Many say that evil dwells among us and will see us all dead."

"Hush your foolish words," Sloan scolded and silenced the lass' tongue, though not her tears.

"Return to Old Mary and let her know that Dawn will be there shortly," Cree ordered the lass and she hurried off. He then bid Sloan to enter.

As soon as the door was closed, Sloan said, "Alexander toys with us. He escaped again and reappeared again, and the guards grow concerned and rightfully so. If a bolted door with warriors standing guard cannot stop him, what can? And Bessa is right. Fear runs rampant in the keep. Many want to go to their homes. They no longer feel safe here."

Dawn stood and went to her husband's side. She tapped his chest, then his lips, and shrugged.

"Dawn has a point, perhaps you should speak to those in the keep," Sloan said. "Calm them. Reassure them. They trust you."

"Not for long if I cannot end this madness. I will speak to them when the time is right." He turned to his wife. "You will do as you promised."

Dawn nodded with a smile.

He kissed her quick. "Shoes and a shawl," he ordered, "I will not have you catching another chill." His wife's broad smile told him that she was thinking how she enjoyed the way he warmed her. He leaned down to whisper, "You will wish for a chill after I get finished heating your body later tonight."

Dawn kissed him quick, as if sealing his words with a promise and she hurried to do as he said.

Moments later, he saw her to Old Mary's door

and reminded her of her promise before closing it behind her.

"I would be a fool if I did not admit that this man's unnatural abilities concern me," Sloan said as they took the stairs to the tower. "There is no proof that he is responsible for the illness that has befallen the keep and he is cordial and mannerly to all, leaving us no reason to harm him."

"I do not need a reason," Cree said and took the stone steps two at a time.

~~~

Dawn sat on the edge of Old Mary's bed, the old woman appearing more lucid than she had in days.

"Before you tell me what Elwin had to say, tell me how you fare. I worry about you," Old Mary said with concern.

Dawn had brought her joys, hopes, and sorrows to Old Mary, since she had been young. The old woman always had time for her and had always listened when Dawn needed to talk. And presently, Dawn needed to talk with her desperately. Once her hands began moving, they did not stop. Everything poured out of her right down to how she heard the stranger in her head.

Old Mary gripped Dawn's wrist and tugged her close, whispering so no one else would hear. "Tell no one that you can hear him. *No one.* Especially Cree, or soon you will be accused of being possessed by the evil man and accused of possessing Cree."

338

Dawn felt a grip to her chest. She had never given that possibility thought, but Old Mary was right. And never would she take a chance of placing her husband in harm's way.

"Be diligent of your thoughts," Old Mary warned. "Now hurry and tell me what Elwin had to say so I can try and make sense of this madness, while I have my wits about me, and hopefully put a stop to it."

Dawn could not agree more. The snowstorm had turned into a nightmare that she wanted desperately to see end. She gestured slowly, feeling as she went that she had failed the old woman, not having learned anything of importance.

"A talisman can keep a witch at a distance, but we do not deal with a witch here," Old Mary said after listening to Dawn and turned silent for a few moments. Her voice was a whisper when she spoke again, her strength waning. "What am I failing to see?" She rubbed her head, hoping it would help clear her thoughts and after only a moment stopped and reached out to take Dawn's hand. "You must think on this and see what we are missing or more will suffer." She squeezed Dawn's hand. "And some may die."

Dawn shook her head, tapped Old Mary's arm, and tapped her own chest repeatedly.

"You cannot stop death." Old Mary squeezed Dawn's hand when she once again protested with a strong shake of her head. "Listen to me while I can make some sense of my words. I am usually the one helping others, but not this time. This time I am one of many who need help. The fever confuses my thoughts and I cannot think clearly and I fight, without success, against the sleep that constantly claims me. It is in your hands now. You must find a way to stop this madness."

Chapter Nine

Dawn bathed Old Mary's feverish brow with a cool, wet cloth as she drifted off to sleep once again. Old Mary was counting on her help as Dawn had counted on hers through the years. She could not fail her, though she worried she would.

Myths, tales, beliefs, grew as wild as the plentiful heather that covered the Highland hills. There was not a Highland child that did not hear a tale or two that left them with nightmares and worries that some evil creature would get them. According to tales Dawn was familiar with, there was no way of getting rid of such a creature. You simply stayed clear of it and prayed that one never came for you.

So how did she rid her clan of this cursed man? *Cursed!*

What if there was a way to remove the curse? Who would know how to do that? Dawn frowned. Old Mary would likely know, but she did not remain lucid long and the fever kept her thoughts confused. Dawn turned and looked at Elsa. She might know as well, being a healer, but there was no way of waking her from her deep sleep.

Who else would possibly know? *Flanna.*

There was a chance she might know. Flanna, more than anyone, knew the most about things that went on here in the keep and with the clan. She would speak to her and find out.

Dawn refreshed the wet cloth and rested it on Old Mary's brow, then stood to go find Flanna and stopped when she turned and saw Neil. Worry weighed heavily on his slumped shoulders and in the deep wrinkles around his eyes. She walked over to him and pointed to Elsa, pale and lifeless in sleep.

"She will not wake up," he said, choking back his tears.

Dawn offered encouragement with her heartfelt gestures.

A hint of a smile touched his lips. "Elsa would say the same and admonish me for not staying strong and having faith."

Dawn smiled as well and nodded, agreeing. She cast another glance at Elsa and was about to take her leave when she recalled that Elsa had once been accused of being a witch. Cree had saved her from a horrible fate and at first his men had feared her. It was not until she began to heal many of their battle wounds and illnesses that their fear faded and they accepted her.

Dawn hoped that Elsa had mentioned something of that time that might be of some help. She gestured slowly to Neil so that he would understand her.

"Elsa has spoken of that troubling time," Neil said with a nod. "She was accused of cursing several women in the village who had fallen ill. She was ordered to remove the curse or die. She tried to explain to the villagers that the women were ill not cursed, but they would not listen. If Cree had not come along when he did, they would have hung her and—" he could not finish.

Dawn's heart ached for the man and made her all the more determined to get rid of the blight that had befallen the clan. She gestured slowly once again, hoping Elsa had spoken more on curses with Neil.

Neil nodded, understanding her question. "Elsa did mention that there was some who had come to her, hoping she could remove a curse." He looked at the woman he loved with a heart-warming smile. "She would give some potions to rid them of the curse, though in truth, she told me, there was never a curse on them to begin with. It was the ones who were truly cursed who she could not help."

Elsa stirred, drawing Neil's attention and he was quick to bathe her brow with a wet cloth and speak reassuringly to her. "It is all right, Elsa. We will make you well again."

Dawn left him to look after and comfort Elsa and for Bessa to do the same for Old Mary. She would not expect Dawn to look after her. Old Mary would expect her to do as she said and find out what she had missed, concerning Alexander.

The solemn and frightened faces that greeted her when she entered the Great Hall in search of Flanna had her stopping and offering comfort to those there. She took trembling hands in hers, and gave them reassuring squeezes while smiling. She gave generous hugs to those with tears in their eyes and helped bathe the brows of those who had fallen ill. She shared a brew with an old woman who wanted desperately to return to her cottage. And when two women spit at a warrior walking past them, claiming he was one of the few who were responsible for bringing the devil down upon them, foolishly having called out names, she shook her head and made them understand that only by protecting one another could they stop evil from touching them.

When she finally spotted Flanna, she asked if there was any bread and honey for the people to enjoy.

"Turbett just made fresh loaves," Flanna informed her and in no time had them brought out to the people who were soon smiling and chatting about how lucky they were to have such a generous lady of the keep.

Dawn motioned to Flanna that she needed to speak with her and they made their way to a secluded spot just off the Great Hall. She did not waste a moment in asking her what she knew of curses.

~~~

Cree and Sloan entered the tower room to find Alexander poking at the burning logs in the fireplace with a long stick. Cree ordered the two warriors guarding the prisoner to leave and they did so with haste, though the door remained open behind them.

Alexander tossed the stick into the fire and watched a moment as it was devoured by the flames, then he turned to Cree. "It is time for the truth."

Cree crossed his arms over his chest, glared at the man, and demanded, "Who are you?"

"I am Alexander once laird of a clan whose name is no longer mentioned out of fear. I am the man, ghost, creature of Winter Tale."

Cree did not stir and his scowl remained firm on Alexander.

"You are braver than most," Alexander said. "The man behind you stirs nervously as do your warriors outside the door, but I sense not an ounce of fear in you."

"I do not fear you," Cree said

"Your courage gives your men courage, though you are foolish not to fear me, for I am not of flesh and blood and therefore cannot be harmed."

"Yet you bled. Cree pointed to his bandaged finger.

"Another's blood," Alexander said, yanking the bandage off to reveal his unmarred finger.

"Elsa would have noticed that you had no wound."

"A bit of diversion saw to that. As I said, I am not of flesh and blood and cannot be injured."

"Anyone or thing can be wounded in some way, but let us see if you speak the truth." Cree took several quick steps toward the man and landed such a hard blow to his jaw that it sent Alexander to his knees.

After a moment, Alexander got to his feet laughing. "It is one time that I am relieved I cannot be harmed, for that blow surely would have bloodied my mouth." His laughter faded replaced by a wicked sneer. "You see now that you cannot harm me and there are no walls, no chains that can keep me prisoner." Alexander approached Cree, getting close enough so that their bodies almost touched. "I will take what I want from you and you are helpless to stop me."

"I would not count on that," Cree said and grabbed Alexander by the throat, lifting him off his feet and slamming him against the stone wall. "I will see you sent to hell where you belong."

Alexander laughed again. "Hell would welcome me."

Cree released Alexander, realizing that no matter how hard he squeezed the man's neck, he suffered nothing. He turned away from him to see the sheer look of terror on Sloan's face, and that terror would soon spread throughout the keep.

"You are right, Cree," Alexander said. "Once the people learn there is nothing you can do to stop me, the terror your friend exudes will spread, and your clan will bargain with me for their lives."

Cree wanted to wrap his hands around the man's neck and snap it.

"Watch your thoughts, Cree, I can hear them clearly and influence them just as easily as I will do to everyone here. By the time the snow melts, all that is yours will be mine. I may keep your wife and no influence will be necessary. She will surrender to me easily, for I can give her something that you cannot."

"There is nothing you can give her that I have not."

"Not even a voice?"

~~~

"The only thing I know of curses is what I have heard from others," Flanna said. "So this stranger is the cursed man from the Winter Tale?"

Dawn shrugged.

"I suppose it is difficult to be certain of such a thing, for who knows how much of the tales and myths are true. My mum used to warn me to believe or one day the banshee would come for me." She shivered. "I suppose I should have listened to her, though she would be pleased that I have kept the two talismans that she had given me all those years ago. She made me give her my word to always keep them near. She insisted one would let no banshee near me and the other would repel witches. There is also a talisman that can capture a witch's power and destroy it or so my mum claimed." She shook her head. "I thought it just a tale, but with what is happening here, it makes me wonder if my mum was wiser than I thought. I will be searching for that other talisman when this is done. It is near impossible to find and only the one who finds it can use it against a witch. In anyone else's hands, it is useless. But try I will."

Dawn drew her shawl snugly around her, a chill drifting off the stone wall, then gestured, letting Flanna know she was more interested in curses.

"I know little of curses. I have heard the most

common of tales and—" Flanna bit back her words.

Dawn tapped her lips and pointed to Flanna, urging her to finish.

She reluctantly did so. "Many believed you were cursed when you first arrived here with your mum. It was the reason most everyone kept their distance from you. They feared if they bothered with you in any way that they too would be cursed and lose their voice." Flanna seemed hesitant to say more, but Dawn urged her to continue, and she did. "Have you not wondered if you were cursed at birth? You are not like others who have no voice. They can at least grunt, make some type of sound, but you? You cannot even make the barest of sounds. And why would a *bairn* newly born not have a voice?" She lowered her own voice. "Some would say a witch stole it, cursing you to live your life voiceless."

"What nonsense do you speak?"

All color drained from Flanna's face upon hearing Cree's irate voice and her body trembled as she turned to face him. Her voice quivered as she went to explain, but Cree's sharp words prevented her from speaking.

"Watch your tongue, woman, or I will see it—" Cree stopped himself from saying what he knew would disturb his wife and tried to temper his anger.

Flanna remained silent and fearful.

Dawn stepped beside her husband and laid a gentle hand on his arm and when she had his attention, she gestured.

Cree listened, watching his wife's hands speak

and said nothing until she finished. "You may have asked Flanna what she knew of curses, but I will not tolerate anyone believing you were cursed."

Dawn turned to Flanna and took her hand, then looked to her husband and shook her head.

Cree glared at Flanna. "My wife defends you. What have you to say?"

"I beg your forgiveness, my lord. I never meant to offend, only to help. I do not believe Lady Dawn is cursed, but many once did."

"Be grateful my wife calls you friend or I would see you punished. Now go and do not let me see your face for the rest of the day," Cree ordered sharply.

Dawn took hold of Flanna's arm when she went to hurry off and gestured for her to remain where she was.

"I gave an order," Cree commanded.

Dawn could tell that her husband was angry, but being angry in return at his harsh command would do no good. Besides, it was obvious to her that his potent anger had been brewing over something else and had finally bubbled over with Flanna.

Dawn kept her gestures gentle and watched the scowl on her husband's face begin to soften.

"You do not need to remind me of what a great help she was to you when I first arrived here and how she continues to be of help to you. But I will not tolerate anyone even suggesting such nonsense that a witch robbed you of your voice."

"I am truly sorry, my lord, I meant no harm," Flanna apologized again.

"Then mind your tongue and suffer the minor punishment without complaint."

"As you say, my lord," Flanna said and bobbed her head and went to take her leave once again and once again Dawn stopped her.

"She will do as I say, Dawn, now let her go," Cree warned then turned to Flanna. "Remain out of my sight before I inflict a harsher punishment on you."

Flanna bobbed her head and hurried off.

Cree glared at his wife. "Never use my own orders against me, wife. If she is the one you must tell where you go to next, then you will instruct her to have someone else deliver the message to me. Do not fail to obey me on this or Flanna will suffer for it."

Dawn nodded and gave her word, then laid her hand on his arm and gave it a gentle squeeze as she shrugged and raised her brow, wanting to know what troubled him.

It took a moment before he grudgingly said, "You are much too astute."

She tapped two crossed fingers to his chest, after tapping them to hers.

He ran a tender hand down her cheek and along her chin. "Aye, it is like you and I are one, hearing what the other one thinks or will say before words are spoken. We need to talk."

Dawn nodded, agreeing with him and listened closely. She did not like the worry she heard in his tone or the way the lines that fanned out from the corner of his eyes deepened. Something was wrong and she knew without him saying that it had something to do with Alexander.

"We will talk in my solar."

Dawn followed along beside him, passing through the Great Hall to reach his solar. Everyone appeared terrified, tears filled many eyes and all of them followed Cree, as if begging him to save them. Terror had replaced fear and it frightened her, for it could mean only one thing.

Evil was about to strike again.

Chapter Ten

Cree turned after closing the door to find his wife right there in front of him, a questioning look on her face. "We will sit and I will tell you everything."

That he suggested they sit frightened her all the more, for it meant the news would leave her limbs too weak to stand.

Cree placed his hand to her back and eased her over to the chairs in front of the hearth. He saw the fear in her dark eyes and he worried that it would grow once he told her all. Terror was already growing amongst those in the keep, the warriors who had kept a keen ear outside the door of the tower room as Cree and Alexander spoke had been quick to spread the word...there was no stopping the evil man of Winter Tale.

Dawn urged him to speak, anxious to hear what he had to say, yet frightened at what she would hear.

Cree explained it all and Dawn asked a question she feared her husband could not answer.

"How do we defend against him is the question I keep asking myself and one I intend to find an answer to. Though time is of the essence, for he will continue to toy, frighten, and influence us and take great pleasure in doing so." He reached out and took hold of her hand, lacing his fingers with hers, feeling their warmth, their softness, and their strength. "There is something I have not told you."

Dawn titled her head in question, worried over what he would say.

"Alexander says you will surrender to him, for he can give you something that I could never give you."

Dawn shook her head and gestured.

Though her gestures were quick, they were clear to Cree. "I have given you everything you have ever wanted."

She nodded and smiled.

Cree waited a moment before he spoke again. "He says he will give you a voice." He felt his heart swell when without hesitation he spoke her response aloud. "You already have a voice. I helped you find it and allowed it to grow strong. Alexander has nothing to offer you that you would want."

She nodded vigorously, then frowned, pointed at him, and tapped her temple.

"Of course I already knew that, but I wanted to hear you say it."

Dawn got up from her seat and moved to sit on her husband's lap, her arms going around his neck and her lips settling gently on his in a kiss. She loved him so very much, for he truly had helped her to find her voice and have it heard, and she was grateful every day for him and the love they so generously shared.

After a tender exchange, Cree tightened his arm that rested at her waist. "I will see this done. I will destroy him."

A sudden burst of laughter filled the room,

sending a shiver through Dawn and rushing anger through Cree.

"You heard that?" Cree asked.

Dawn nodded and patted his chest.

"Aye, I heard it as well and I believe I heard him once before in our bedchamber."

Though, Old Mary had warned her against telling Cree how Alexander could hear her thoughts, she felt now was the time for him to know. She explained it all to him, even Old Mary's warning of telling him for fear the clan would think their chieftain possessed by evil.

"I am glad you told me. We will need to be vigilant of our thoughts and though it is not something I would have ever thought to say to you...you must not think before you speak."

Dawn nodded with a smile.

Cree kissed her softly, then whispered, "I am going to make that bastard suffer for what he has done."

A heavy pounding at the door startled them both.

"Cree, hurry you are needed in the Great Hall," Sloan shouted.

Dawn hurried off her husband's lap and followed him to the door.

Cree threw it open to find Sloan pacing in front of it. He stopped and shook his head. "Madness has struck the Great Hall."

Dawn hurried along after her husband and was shocked to see all those in the Great Hall arguing with each other. Not one of them stopped or acknowledged Cree's entrance. They continued to squabble among themselves, some even shoving one another.

Cree stepped up on the dais, behind the table, and his strong voice thundered throughout the room when he shouted, "Silence!"

The Great Hall turned silent instantly and wide, frightened eyes turned on Cree.

His angry, strong voice boomed throughout the hall. "I will not tolerate foolishness. Behave properly or I will see every one of you punished." His fist came down on the table with a mighty blow and it sounded as if the wood cracked. "I rule here and you will obey me or suffer a far worse fate than the one you believe has been delivered upon you."

Dawn watched their frightened yet hopeful faces. They wanted to believe that Cree would keep them safe and rid them of the evil that had descended upon them, but they also feared the evil too strong for Cree to defeat.

"You will all busy yourselves in tending the ill and helping the servants who have tended to your needs since this has begun." His fist came down on the table again. "Do not make me return here again or you all will regret it." Cree turned to Sloan. "Have Flanna see this done, and then meet me in my solar."

Sloan bobbed his head and Cree walked out of the hall, talking his wife's hand as he went. They returned to his solar and once he entered, he went and poured himself a tankard of ale. He raised it to his lips, though it never touched them. He slammed the tankard down hard on the sideboard, the ale spilling over the sides.

"What am I failing to see?" he said angrily.

Old Mary had said the same. What were they all failing to see? Something in the curse or the tale itself? And why had Alexander said that when the snow melts all that was Cree's would belong to him when he would once again disappear...or would he?

Dawn did as her mum's words had reminded. She stripped away the nonsense and was left with one burning question. Why did evil follow Alexander? No evil-doing was mentioned in the curse. On the contrary, love was to seal his fate. He would find no peace or rest until then.

A knock sounded before Sloan entered and Dawn took her leave, letting Cree know that she was going to see how Old Mary fared.

"Keep me apprised of your whereabouts," he reminded.

She sent him a nod as she walked out the door, and then hurried up the stairs and prayed that Old Mary was awake. She was disappointed to find the old woman still slept.

"She had not stirred since you left," Bessa said.

Dawn walked over to Neil and pointed to Elsa.

"She rests comfortably, though I worry she will not wake."

Dawn shook her head and wagged her finger, reminding him that he should not think that way.

"It took me a long time to find a woman I could love and I do so love Elsa."

Dawn gestured slowly to Neil, urging him to

have faith.

Neil nodded. "She is a strong woman. Even when they accused her of being a witch she had remained strong and tried to make them see reason. But fear has no room for reason. Not even when she held a talisman in her hand that repels witches did they believe her."

Elsa stirred and Neil was right there to assure her all would be well, though he was not sure of his own words.

Dawn left them alone after telling Neil if Cree came looking for her that she went to speak with Flanna and hurried down the stairs to the Great Hall. It was calmer than before and everyone was busy. No doubt due to Flanna who stood in the middle of the room issuing orders as sharply as Cree. Dawn waved her over and Flanna directed one of the warriors to take her place. His voice boomed as strongly as hers had.

"You need something?" Flanna asked.

Dawn nodded and gestured.

"Aye, I have both talismans with me," Flanna said, patting the pouch hanging from the belt at her waist. "After speaking with you, I fetched the pouch from the kitchen where I kept it."

Dawn patted her chest and held up one finger.

"You need one?"

Dawn nodded, holding up one finger to confirm, then gestured again.

"You want the one for a witch?" Flanna asked surprised.

Dawn bobbed her head.

Flanna opened her pouch and withdrew a bunch of small oak sticks held together by a worn strip of wool and handed it to Dawn.

Dawn took it and pressed a finger to her lips, letting Flanna know she was not to tell anyone about this.

Flanna nodded.

Dawn's hands spoke once more.

Flanna easily understood. "The talisman that captures a witch's power is a stone that has a hole going through it. When the stone is held in front of a witch, the hole draws the power out of the witch and into the stone. The stone then must be broken, breaking the witch's power forever." Flanna shook her head. "It is not only difficult to find such a stone, but even more difficult to break it and both must be done by the person who found the stone."

Dawn tapped her head, pointed to Flanna, then shrugged.

Flanna shook her head. "I do not know of anyone who has found such a stone." She paused a moment, a look of fright in her eyes. "Do you think—"

Dawn once again pressed a finger to her own lips, warning Flanna to remain silent, then hurriedly gestured that she was going to join Cree in his solar.

Flanna nodded. "Be careful."

Dawn gave her a hasty hug and hurried off.

"Lady Dawn!" Bessa called out, stopping Dawn before she reached the solar. "Old Mary is crazy with fever."

Dawn flew past the lass and up the stairs to Old

Mary's room. She paused a moment upon entering, staring at the scene before her. Neil, his face wrinkled with fear, stood with his eyes fixed on Old Mary thrashing around in the bed, her arms swinging wildly and though she talked, she made no sense.

Dawn hurried over to her, hearing prayers on Neil's lips as she passed him that Elsa would not suffer a similar fate. With some difficulty, she got hold of Old Mary's thrashing hands.

Old Mary glared at her. "No sense. Nothing."

Dawn tapped her chest gently, letting her know it was all right.

"No! No!" Old Mary insisted her eyes wild with fear. "Evil." She gasped. "Cree must save us!"

Bessa started wailing. "We are doomed. We are all doomed. The devil will get us all."

Dawn looked with pleading eyes at Neil and he hurried over to the lass and slipped his arm around her, comforting her enough that her wailing subsided. Try as she might, Dawn could not calm Old Mary and as she continued her tirade, it grew more senseless.

"You know! You know! Hurry!"

Dawn let go of her arms, afraid her old bones would break if she kept tight hold of them. Instead, she bathed the old woman's head, fighting to get the fever down.

Finally, Old Mary calmed and seemed lucid for a few moments. "No time left. No time."

Dawn stared at Old Mary as she fell into a restful slumber. After seeing that she would remain so, Dawn turned to Bessa.

"That is our fate...to go mad," the young lass cried.

Dawn was grateful that Neil silenced her. "Hush now. That is not our fate. Lord Cree will keep us safe."

Dawn nodded in agreement, then gestured to Neil that she was going to speak with Cree.

He gave her a brief nod and kept his arm wrapped around Bessa, speaking soothingly to her.

Dawn closed the door behind her and was about to hurry to the stairs when she saw Alexander standing in front of them.

"It is time to meet your fate, Dawn," he said with a smile and started walking toward her.

Chapter Eleven

Dawn waited until he was a few feet away from her before she pulled out the talisman she had tucked in the shoulder of her tunic and held it out in front of her.

Alexander stopped abruptly, his smile fading. "You discovered my secret."

You are a witch!

"I am, but how did you know?"

Dawn spoke as she always did...with her hands. She refused to let him into her head, and she purposely gestured rapidly to see if he could follow her.

Alexander's smile returned. "You have a strong mind. You lock me out of your thoughts and you realize what others have failed to see all these years. Some believed it was revenge I was after, but from whom when the woman who cursed me was dead?" He shook his head. "No, it was not revenge I wanted."

Dawn gestured again.

"Aye, you are right, it is power I searched for and gained through the years. You truly do have a wise mind; we could do very well together."

Dawn posed another question to him.

"Of course you would be curious to know the truth of the tale. I will tell you, and then it is finally time for me to create my fate and yours as well."

Dawn did not like the sound of that, but she

361

made sure not to think on it or the fear that was turning her skin to gooseflesh.

"People can be made to believe anything, especially when it comes to love. Glenna is the woman spoken about in the Winter Tale. The one I supposedly loved. Though, it was not a battlefield where I found her, but a small skirmish and it was Glenna who found me beneath those bloodied corpses. What she did not know was that it was me who took those lives. When I learned she was a chieftain's daughter I saw an opportunity and I began to bend her to my will. Her father was not quite as trusting as his daughter and not as easy to influence. He stood in the way of my plans," —he grinned— "As does your husband."

Dawn struggled to keep her fear from surfacing, knowing he would feed off any he sensed. Though, she could not stop the already creeping gooseflesh from continuing to crawl further up her body.

"I planned on wedding Glenna and becoming chieftain, but then I realized that she was growing skeptical of me. She was wiser than I thought and an excellent healer, which made her more aware than most others. Too late, she discovered I was a witch. By then, I had convinced her clan that she was the witch and that she must be banished. But my dear Glenna was so much wiser than I thought. She left her clan only to return years later when I was wed and had her clan well-in-hand. It was my turn to learn too late that she had acquired the skills of a witch and attempted to free her clan of my hold over them. Naturally, she could not match my skills, though I must say she surprised me in the end when I had her hung. She was skilled enough to curse me, though foolishly left my fate to love. Love can never overpower evil. Her weakness in letting me survive year after year allowed my power to grow even stronger, and too wait for such a moment as this. I will finally be able to free myself of endless slumbers and walk the earth once again with far greater power than ever before."

Dawn kept still as he continued.

"It was not in my power to change the wording of the curse through the years, but it was easy to instill enough fear into the telling of the tale to help me gain the power I craved and that power will allow me to break the curse in a way that will benefit me." He laughed a most unpleasant laugh. "No one, not one soul ever questioned the curse—until you. You understand what Glenna meant for the curse to do."

Dawn nodded and gestured.

"You are right. She meant for the curse to contain and punish me throughout time. And as far as love sealing my fate, that baffled me. She knew all too well that love mattered not at all to me. Soon I will be free and have a clan to rule, to bend to my will, to do my bidding." He pretended to shiver with pleasure. "I can just feel the fear nourishing me." He pointed at her hand. "Now put that thing away and come with me."

Dawn shook her head.

"Do not be troublesome. One way or the other you will submit to me. It would benefit you and your children if you comply. Your husband's fate is already sealed. He will die either way. In exchange, I will give you a voice and let your children live. If not, I will cast a spell on you and you will serve only me and not care what I do to your children. Either way, you will be my companion and lover. If you think to delay the inevitable, know that once Cree arrives all it takes is one touch and he will fall ill. I will take great joy in letting him linger and suffer unless, of course, you plead for mercy with a clear distinct voice for all to hear. The choice is yours."

Silence filled the narrow hall for a few moments, Dawn keeping her thoughts silent.

"My lady—"

Dawn, startled by the unexpected voice, turned to see Bessa standing behind her, her face turning pale. Dawn's thought quickly went to Old Mary.

"Lady Dawn wonders if Old Mary has worsened." When the lass remained quiet, staring wide-eyed at him, Alexander commanded, "Speak up."

Bessa jumped in fright and her voice quivered as she spoke, "There is no more brew left and Old Mary stirs restlessly."

Dawn let him hear what she wanted him to hear as she reached out to Bessa and took her hand. Fear held the lass captive and Dawn understood why. It was obvious Alexander was speaking Dawn's thoughts and only evil could do that.

"Lady Dawn says to go to Flanna and she will know what to do," Alexander said.

Dawn nodded, confirming his words and stepped in front of Alexander so the young servant could hurry past him without him laying a hand on her. And she could give Bessa's hand a reassuring squeeze.

The talisman forced him to take several steps away from her. "To your bedchamber to toss that horrid thing into the flames so no else will be tempted to use it, then you will tell me your decision. If I am pleased with it, I may let Old Mary remain lucid long enough for you to bid her farewell."

Dawn hurried down the hall, prayers clear in her head.

"They will not help you," Alexander said with a laugh and followed behind her at a safe distance from the talisman.

~~~

Bessa rushed into the Great Hall and ran to Flanna, grabbing her hand. "He is no longer in the tower room. He roams free and will see us all dead."

Those people close enough to hear her gasped and began spreading the word.

"Where did you get this?" Flanna demanded, seeing the talisman sticking from her clenched hand and pulling it free.

"Lady Dawn shoved it in my hand after the devil spoke for her. He can hear her. The devil has possessed Lady Dawn."

"Nonsense! Now tell me what he said," Flanna

demanded anxiously.

The lass repeated it. "Lady Dawn says to go to Flanna and she will know what to do."

Before the lass could say anymore, Flanna ran out of the room, straight to Cree's solar. She did not knock, she threw open the door, and rushed in.

Cree was about to reprimand Flanna for disobeying him when he saw the horrified look on her face. "Dawn?"

Flanna nodded and hurried over to him, her hand opened wide with the talisman in it.

~~~

Dawn went to the hearth and pretended to toss the talisman, she had slipped to Bessa, into the flames. She poked at a spot in the fire with a stick, wanting Alexander to believe she did as he had ordered.

Alexander entered the room cautiously and once he reached the middle, he said, "You comply nicely, Dawn, which has me believing that you will submit to me willingly to protect your family and clan from harm and endless suffering."

Dawn had no doubt Cree would come for her. She only needed to bide time until he did and the only way she could do that was to keep him talking.

Alexander stepped closer to her. "Do not think to play games with me. I know it is only a matter of time before Cree appears—to late—to save his wife."

Dawn took cautious steps back away from him.

"Why delay what you know is inevitable? There

366

is nothing—nothing—that can stop me. I will take what I want and you can do nothing. Now give me your hand and at least prevent those you love from suffering."

Cree!

Alexander laughed. "He cannot hear you, my dear."

The door suddenly flew off its pins and before it came crashing down on the floor, Alexander and Dawn rushed out of its path.

Cree stood in the doorway, fury swirling in his dark eyes and the thick muscles in his body taut and ready for battle. His glance went to his wife and he held his hand out to her.

Alexander rushed toward her, his hand outstretched and Cree rushed at him, landing a vicious blow to his jaw. Alexander cried out as he went down from the pain. Cree did not wait, his powerful fist landed punch after punch to Alexander's face.

Dawn's hand yanking at his arm was the only thing that stopped him. He was quick to grab Dawn and move them both away from Alexander, crumpled on the floor.

"Another talisman," Alexander said with anger as he rubbed his jaw and sat up.

"The same one," Cree said, holding it up for Alexander to see.

Alexander turned a furious glare on Dawn. "You will pay for this."

"Do not dare threaten my wife," Cree warned.

"What will you do?" Alexander challenged as

he got to his feet. "You think a bunch of sticks will protect you from me. He held his arms out to his sides. Do you see blood on me anywhere? And how many times did you strike me? The talisman may weaken my ability to protect myself, but it cannot do any great harm and it cannot destroy me."

"But I can!"

Cree and Dawn turned to see Sloan standing in the doorway, grinning and holding a stone with a hole in its middle in one hand and a smithy's hammer in the other.

Alexander's eyes turned wide with fright as Sloan ran toward him. He frantically looked about and grabbed a split log from the basket near the hearth. He swung it at Sloan, knocking the stone from his hand.

Cree pushed his wife aside and lunged once again, grabbing Alexander. They fought, Alexander's attempts weak thanks to the talisman.

"Where did that damn stone go?" Sloan said, getting on his hands and knees to search over the floor.

Dawn dropped to her knees and joined Sloan in the search. She found it under the bed out of her reach. She turned and tapped Sloan's arm, pointing under the bed.

Sloan reached for the stone, but it was out of his grasp. He inched himself forward, his fingertips just grazing it, but unable to grab it.

Dawn watched Cree struggle with Alexander. Her husband's strength went far beyond any man's and his struggle to hold Alexander was obvious.

What was more obvious was that Cree held the talisman so tight in his hand that the twigs were beginning to break one by one. If the talisman was destroyed before Sloan could reach the stone, her husband would not stand a chance against Alexander—none of them would.

She tapped on Sloan's leg, letting him know he needed to hurry.

"I am trying," he said and Dawn heard how hard he was trying in his strained voice as he stretched his arm further under the bed.

Dawn hurried to the basket of logs and found a stick used for kindling and hurried to reach under the bed and place it next to Sloan's arm so he would know it was there. Then she returned to the basket of logs, grabbed one, and without hesitation slammed it against the back of Alexander's knees. He went down with an angry growl and turned toward her as he did, his arm outstretched, reaching for her. Dawn had no room to scramble back away from him, the hearth right behind her. She was about to kick his hand away when he suddenly was lifted off the ground by his neck.

"Enough," Cree shouted as he slammed him against the wall and stepped aside.

Alexander's eyes turned wide with fright as Sloan moved in and planted the stone with the hole in it against his chest and held it there.

Cree, Dawn, and Sloan watched and waited but nothing seemed to happen. No dark mist was sucked into the stone, nor did Alexander shrivel up and dissipate. Nothing happened.

Alexander laughed. "It is nothing more than a tall tale. The stone holds no magic over me. My power is too strong, nothing can destroy me." He sneered with sheer wickedness and shoved Sloan's hand with the stone away. "Now it is your turn to suffer, Cree, and since you favor fists let me show you what little effort true power takes."

~~~

Cree grabbed Alexander's fist in his large hand before it reached his face and squeezed tight. The man's eyes turned wide in pain. Cree shoved his hand away and quickly landed a brutal blow to Alexander's nose. The crack of bone resonated off the stone walls and blood poured from his nostrils as he crumpled to the floor.

"Break the stone," Cree ordered before bending down and delivering a vicious blow to Alexander's jaw. That crack of bone was heard as well.

Sloan retrieved the hammer from the floor where he had dropped it and with a broad smile he brought it down on the stone, smashing it to pieces. He did not stop smashing all the pieces until there was nothing left but dust.

Chapter Twelve

Four days later...

"I feel fine. I am going home," Old Mary insisted as she reached for her cloak on the bed.

Dawn quickly snatched it up and draped it around the old woman's shoulders. She knew there was no arguing with her and she truly was doing well. Everyone struck by the strange illness had begun to get better after the stone had broken Alexander's powers.

"Walk me home," Old Mary said, "since I know you will anyway."

Dawn smiled and nodded and took Old Mary's arm as they left the room that Dawn had feared would not only be the old woman's death chamber, but Elsa's as well. Elsa had improved quickly and as soon as she was on her feet, she was helping others to recover. Neil was happy when she did, since it proved to him that she was herself once again.

The Great Hall was empty when they entered it. Those who had taken ill there, having returned home two days ago. Life was returning to normal once again.

"Your cloak," Flanna said, rushing over to Dawn to help her on with it. "It is good the snow has stopped and it is no longer bitter cold, though some insist we will have more snow before this winter ends. At least, there will be no more Winter Tale to tell."

"The tale will be told again," Old Mary said and Flanna and Dawn looked startled. "Tongues have already started speaking about it and merchants that pass through here will hear of it and spread the word how the Winter Tale is no longer to be feared thanks to the mighty Cree and his fearless clan." Old Mary patted Flanna on the shoulder. "Dawn told me all about how you bravely disobeyed Cree's order to keep from his sight to save not only Dawn but the whole clan."

Flanna's cheeks reddened. "It is a small brave act compared to what Lady Dawn has done for all of us here in Dowell."

A crash in the hall had Flanna turning around abruptly and hurrying off, yelling at the poor servant who had dropped something.

Dawn held firmly onto Old Mary once outside, not wanting her to slip and fall. It was obvious after a few steps that the old woman had gotten her strength back and that pleased Dawn.

"A winter cloak, that is what the snow looks like upon the land," Old Mary said. "I hear that Sloan is enjoying the attention from many lasses for being so heroic, but tell me how did he come by the stone with the hole through it?"

Old Mary spoke aloud Dawn's gesture. "He came across it before going into a battle that he did not think he would survive. He believed it was a special stone and kept it close always, though told no one but Cree about it." Old Mary smiled. "He was right about it being special and it not only saved him that day he went into battle, but it saved all of us from Alexander."

Dawn pointed to her eyes, then shaded them as she looked around as if searching.

Old Mary laughed. "He looks for another one now."

Dawn nodded and banged a fisted hand against the palm of her other hand.

"His is that adamant about it?"

Dawn shook her finger and her head and spread her arms.

"I do not blame him for never wanting to be without one again. I am sure Elsa would have gladly used hers if she had been able to and it is probably why Alexander made sure she was struck with the illness."

Dawn stopped and gestured quickly.

"How did he know she possessed one?" Mary continued after Dawn nodded. "Many healers look for such a stone and if lucky enough to find one, keep it a secret. Alexander probably did not want to take a chance that Elsa had one, so he struck her with the fever. He did the same to me, though it was my knowing things that he could not take a chance with. I knew something was not right, so I fought as hard as I could, though I remained much too confused to be of any help."

Dawn disagreed, letting Old Mary know she was of great help, fever or no fever.

Old Mary brushed the compliment off and gave a nod toward the storehouse. "I see Alexander's punishment is going well."

Dawn looked over at Alexander, gagging as he cleaned the rotted food from the storehouse.

"Cree was wise in not simply killing the man. It is better the clan sees that there is no longer any reason to fear him. I hear Alexander is also being made to tend the cow he turned ill."

Dawn pressed her hands together and pressed them to the side of her head.

"He has been made to sleep in the barn with the cow as well?"

Dawn nodded.

"What will Cree eventually do with him?"

"My wife encourages me to set him free and let fate seal his destiny. She feels it is what Glenna, the woman who cursed him, intended," Cree said, joining them and taking Old Mary's arm to help her along as they walked.

"And how do you feel?" Old Mary asked.

"I prefer to hang him, then burn him and be done with it."

"Would he not suffer far more if he was made to live without his powers?" Old Mary asked.

"You think like my wife."

"I take that as a compliment."

Cree scowled when he saw that Lila and Dorrie were waiting at Old Mary's door. He had hoped to have some time alone with his wife, the last few days having kept them too busy to spend barely any time together. Dawn also had little time to spend with friends and he did not want to deprive her of that after all that had happened.

"Stay well," he said to Old Mary and turned to his wife. "I will see you when you finish here," he said gruffly and walked away annoyed. He scowled and mumbled growing more irritated with each step. People hurried out of his way, though he took no notice of them. His thoughts were on his wife.

He turned, deciding to remind her that he was not a patient man and was met with a snowball to his chest. Another one followed catching him in the shoulder. Gasps mingled with chuckles around him as he swatted away a third snowball that nearly caught him in the face.

"You are asking for trouble, wife," he said as he advanced on her slowly.

Dawn grinned and danced around like a child thrilled with her actions as she packed another snowball and threw it at her husband. It caught his leg and she was quick to make another and this time she got him in the face.

Dawn's mouth dropped open in shock as he stopped abruptly and slowly wiped the snow off his face.

"You will pay for that, wife," Cree said.

She did not wait to see exactly what it would cost her, she took off running. She heard his heavy footfalls not that far behind her and she hurried toward the woods, not an easy task with all the snow.

She got only a short distance into the woods when her husband pounced on her, sending them both tumbling into the snow. She soon found herself flat on her back, her husband straddling her.

"Now I have you where I want you," he said, a rare smile surfacing on his handsome face.

She shook her head and gestured.

"You have me where you want me?"

She patted the snow, then slipped her hand beneath his plaid and caressed him.

He groaned and reluctantly grabbed her hand. "It is a romp in the snow you intended?"

She smiled softly as she gestured.

"You want to make memories with me?'

She nodded.

He leaned down, kissed her, and whispered, "We shall make a memory neither of us will ever forget."

And they did.

The End... for now!

Look for more adventures of Cree & Dawn coming your way!

An interesting side note... a hole that is created by nature in a stone is known by some as a Hag stone, warding off witches, and to others a Holey stone that protects. It's rare to find them and luckily I have found not only one but two. So keep an eye out for your very own Holey stone.

If you want to make certain you don't miss any of Donna's books subscribe to her Book Alerts on her website www.donnafletcher.com.

Titles by Donna Fletcher

Series Books

Highlander Trilogy
Highlander Unchained
Forbidden Highlander
Highlander's Captive
Highlander's True Love A Cree & Dawn Short Story #1
Highlander's Promise A Cree & Dawn Short Story #2
Highlander's Winter Tale A Cree & Dawn Short Story #3

Macinnes Sisters Trilogy
The Highlander's Stolen Heart
Highlander's Rebellious Love
Highlander The Dark Dragon

To see a listing of all Donna's available books and purchase links go to her Bookshelf on her website at http://www.donnafletcher.com.

About the Author

Donna Fletcher is a *USA Today* bestselling author of historical and paranormal romances. Her books are sold worldwide. She started her career selling short stories and winning reader contests. She soon expanded her writing to her love of romance novels and sold her first book SAN FRANCISCO SURRENDER the year she became president of New Jersey Romance Writers.

Drop by Donna's website www.donnafletcher.com where you can learn more about her, peruse her bookshelf, sign up for her Book Alerts, and read her blog where she keeps her readers updated on what's next.

Printed in Great Britain
by Amazon